PEOPLES

PEOPLES:
The Ethnic Dimension in Human Relations

Jerry D. Rose

State University College, Fredonia, New York

Rand McNally College Publishing Company / Chicago

Rand McNally Sociology Series/Edgar F. Borgatta, Advisory Editor

For my parents,
white southern Methodists who, like their son,
never knew they were ethnics, and

for my children,
who, like their peers, will have to find out
for themselves.

PREFACE

There are those who feel that, to parapharase the biblical author, the writing of many textbooks is an abomination and a vexation of spirit. I am, nonetheless, going to hazard vexing the spirit of colleagues and students by presenting this book as an instrument for teaching and learning about the ethnic dimension in human relations.

The relevance of such an effort to academic or practical concerns hardly needs to be stated. Manifestations of the new ethnicity—an awakened sense of the relevance of ethnic group membership to the perennial search for personal identity—are superimposed on the all-too-old and all-too-persisting tendency for ethnicity to serve as an excuse for the mistreatment of people of "minority" social status. The search for identity and for solidarity with one's "own people," the struggle for fair treatment of all peoples—these are themes in the human condition that recur everywhere and in all times. They are accordingly dominant themes in the field of sociology, with its presumptuous effort to define generally human dimensions of social existence.

Such vast themes have served to sensitize large numbers of sociological studies of different ethnic peoples and of different systems of ethnic relations. As with all other areas of human social experience, those who would understand more fully the ethnic dimension must let their minds travel widely in this rich area of sociological research. There is something to be said for travel *without* a travel guide, letting one's unprompted impressions establish generalizations about the country of the mind in which one is traveling. Yet there are points—and the wise instructor of sociology presumably knows these points—at which the student-traveler can use some guidance from a somewhat more experienced traveler: "Now, over here we see an example of . . ."

To write a travel guide for any field of sociological study is no easy task. In the field of present concern, ethnicity, the task has apparently seemed impossible, judging by the dearth of efforts. This is not to derogate in any way the several textbooks currently available on race and ethnic relations or on minorities. They have not attempted to do what this book tries to do. In some cases, they provide very useful compendia of information on the ethnic factor in some particular area of the world; or, where written from a more generalizing perspective, are addressed to an audience of professional colleagues or of very advanced students of sociology. In other words, either these textbooks find the students where they are already located, already enmeshed in a society and an ethnic group of their own kind—and these texts commendably satisfy the curiosity of such students to understand more of that social surrounding—or they are written over the heads of neophyte students, leaving them to undertake their own unguided travels. The spirit in which I have written this book is one of saying to the student: Take my hand and *together* we shall go on a learning journey in one of the dimensions of human existence. I say *together* we shall learn because we are all really beginning students of sociology. When the most learned of us understands maybe 1 or 2 percent of what there is to understand about something, it is arrogance indeed to say to one who knows virtually nothing: Follow *me* and *I'll* show you.

Perhaps more of my colleagues have not attempted such travel guides because they, like myself, are impressed with the enormity of what they do *not* know about the territory to be covered. Still, all of us, as sociology teachers, are faced with that feeling of What in the hell do I do? two or three times a week when twenty or thirty intelligent faces are turned toward us with the expectation that we *do something* to further their education. It frees us, I think to do something helpful if we can convey to our students *and* to ourselves some of that fellow traveler spirit referred to above. Among the cardinal sins of teaching and writing cannot be included the sin of being on occasion wrong in our perceptions, because we are all floundering toward accurate perception. The greater sins, as I would define them, are those of obfuscation and intellectual dishonesty, which stem from an egoistic need to feel that, because we have a Ph.D. behind our names and an academic title in front, we must impress our students that we "know it all." Since we do not, in fact, know it all, we either claim to be more certain about a matter than we actually are (intellectual dishonesty), or we phrase our perceptions in such vague or jargonistic terms (obfuscation) that a critic cannot dispute us since we can always claim that the critic did not "understand" our point.

If this is indeed a kind of game that professors (myself included) have played, I would like to urge that a whistle be blown and that we play something else for awhile. In setting rules for this new game, let us assume that the intellectual (as opposed to the social) distance between professional and lay students of sociology is really very slight. Let us use the present book (or some far better book of the same type that may appear) as a guide for venturing together into an essentially uncharted area of intellectual experience. Let us not be afraid to make mistakes as we learn and discuss our learning; only let us remain *open* to correction, and be able to state our views clearly enough that our critics can understand them and give us the benefit of insights we have missed. Together, we may push ourselves collectively toward a little closer understanding of an aspect of our human condition. Even failing this, we shall have enjoyed the comforts of a companionship of coequal strivers in a worthwhile effort. And we have the rest of our lives—whether a few days or many years—to coparticipate as students of the vast mystery of human life.

My acknowledgments for this book are very easy for me to recognize but difficult to put into words. It was written over a period of two or three years, years that were essentially lonely in terms of my communicating its contents to others for purposes of criticism and correction. This, despite the fact that the book is presented as an instrument of intellectual communication. Yet, like another lonely sociologist, Charles H. Cooley, whose life I have studied closely and have tried in some respects to emulate, I am acutely aware of the absolute dependence of my work on that of many other persons. The influence of the writings of such giants in this field as Philip Mason, Michael Banton, and Pierre L. van den Berghe is probably not fully obvious in the book itself. What has to be obvious is that an attempted synthesis of this kind would not have been possible without an enormous number of laborers in the vineyard producing material to be synthesized.

If she does not edit out this paragraph—which I hereby forbid her to do —I acknowledge that Martha Urban is the ideal editor for a book of this sort. Herself a wise person who can spot a faulty generalization at ten paces, she has insisted that with every phrase and sentence of the text I *say* exactly what I *mean*. If the book is the instrument of fuller communication on the subject than it aims to be, it will be the result in no small measure of her loving ruthlessness on this score.

Beyond this, I owe the author's usual full measure of apologies to those persons without whose forbearance a book could never be produced. My editor at Rand McNally, Larry Malley, grew extra gray hairs in his youthful beard as the organization of this book was shaped and re-shaped over a period of some years. During the crucial last stages of the manuscript's completion, he generously allowed me to disrupt the routines of his office for a considerable period of time, and through it all remained my good and staunch friend. Closer to home, my department chairman, Ed Ludwig, and the president of my college, Dallas Beal, acted in their usual humane way to lighten the burden of competing academic obligations. Finally, apologies are owed and joyfully tendered to those who were hurt the most because they are the most loved: my wife and children. The lapses in familial obligation because "Daddy is writing his book" were, in retrospect, enormous ones, and the daddy in question can only hope that his work and its influence will contribute in some way to a fuller life for those who have suffered from these lapses.

Jerry D. Rose

CONTENTS

PEOPLES

INTRODUCTION

PEOPLE AND PEOPLES

Sociology seems to be gaining a reputation—a somewhat unsavory one for some tastes—for viewing people in terms of kinds or categories and attempting thereby to account for differences in their behavior. If John Jones votes differently than Tom Smith or prefers another make of automobile or has a different sort of sex life, it is because John is a lawyer or a southerner or a Catholic while Tom is a teacher or a northerner or a Jew.

Like many other reputations, this one has a basis in fact, although there is undoubtedly some embellishment on the fact by people with only a pedestrian acquaintance with the field of sociology. Let the reader open the pages of any of the leading professional journals in the field, and he will be confronted with table after table of "data" showing the frequencies with which different kinds of people act or feel in a given way: lower-class people "tend to" be more conservative on civil rights issues than middle-class people, women "tend to" seek out psychiatric aid more readily than do men, etc.

The frequent objection to this generalizing is that it ignores the fact that each human being is unique, not reducible to the indignity of being simply a member of a category. Although to all outward appearances Sally Smith is simply the typist in row 4 seat 16 in an office full of typists just like her, she is really the one and only Sally, as will be affirmed by her family, her friends, and the man who will marry and detach her from 4–16 (and perhaps attach her to a house at 416 Elm that, to all outward appearances, is just like the house at 414 Elm).

All of which is true. And all of which is irrelevant in the light of the broader sociological insight that, while everyone is unique in some respects, there are other respects in which everyone is like all others of his or her "kind" and unlike all others of other "kinds." It is the never-quite-resolved problem of the sociologist, or of anyone else who tries to live intelligently with other people, to sort out what is idiosyncratic from what is generally human from what is common or shared among some less-than-universal category of people. It is in this middle range of categorical similarities that the sociologist operates. Just *what* is it, the sociologist wants to know, in Sally's social behavior (and, just as importantly, in the behavior of other people toward *her*) that is attributable to the fact that she is a woman, the daughter of a professor, or the wife of an Italian immigrant?

The study of categories of people is based on the sociologist's perception that the differences people make among different kinds of people *do* make a difference in the way they act and in the way that other people act toward them. In this book we look at one kind of difference: distinctions of ethnic-group membership. To be a black or a Chicano in the United States, a coloured person in Britain, or a Catholic in Northern Ireland is to be something that has predictable consequences for one's social relations with those of one's own kind as well as with those of other ethnic kinds. Exactly what these consequences are under different conditions of social existence is the simply stated but immensely complex problem of this or any book dealing with the role of ethnicity in human society.

ETHNIC GROUPS AND ETHNIC RELATIONS

Sociological writings on ethnicity—an immense body of literature—tend to take one of two different forms. Either we find studies that deal with specific ethnic groups in specific societal or community contexts, such as the "coloured" of South Africa, the Maori in New Zealand, the Polish-Americans of Los Angeles; or we find studies that detail the *interaction* between two or more ethnic groups in a given society or community, such as the relationship between the English-speaking and the French-speaking people of Canada, or between black and Jewish groups in New York City.

While these are obviously related matters—no single ethnic group can be understood in isolation from its relationships with other groups, and no system of ethnic relations can ignore the nature of the groups between which relations exist—it still provides a useful tool in focusing and refocusing on our subject to maintain this distinction between types of approaches. Part 1 of this book focuses on ethnic *groups* and examines several relevant sociological dimensions in the study of *any* group, ethnic or otherwise. Part 2 examines in some detail the varying relationships between ethnic groups that may be observed at different times and places. The introductions to Part 1 and Part 2 will examine more closely the dimensions of ethnicity involved in each such focus.

SOME BIASES IN THE ANALYSIS

Any book on ethnicity will display some of the author's predispositions, and the work will have a personal stamp even if the word *I* is avoided out of respect for the conventions of the literary genre involved. In this section a few of these dispositions or biases are spelled out by way of preparing the reader for the analysis that follows or—if this be the reader's reaction —to save him the trouble of reading something that is not what he expects or wants.

1. The whole tone of the book is intended to be analytic rather than prescriptive in nature. The author has no remedies for the "ails" of contemporary society with reference to the problem of interethnic relations, or at least none to be huckstered from the podium of this forum. Many students of sociology—and some of its professional practitioners—are inclined to downgrade the value of sociological analysis if it is not accompanied by solutions to troubling social problems. Certainly the sociologist of ethnic groups and ethnic relations is subject to this pressure to be "relevant" to the contemporary conflicts between ethnic groups. The author happens to believe that sociology in general and the sociology of ethnicity in particular *are* relevant to such concerns. A prison administrator or the director of an organization devoted to bettering race relations would certainly be well served to have a background in the study of penology, ethnic relations, or, indeed, of sociology in general. But it may well be that this relevance exists precisely *because* professional sociologists have maintained an attitude of value neutrality toward the subject matters of sociological investigation. The person of affairs in the "real" world of politics, business, etc. may find sociological insights valuable because they were developed by people with no ideological axes to grind.

Whether this is a valid reason or a self-serving excuse for the kind of analysis that follows, it remains a fact that the reader must live with, namely, that the author intends to provide the framework for an analysis of ethnic groups and ethnic relations and that he has somewhere mislaid his R_x pad for the ills of the world.

2. The kind of analysis that follows is *nomothetic* rather than *idiographic* in nature. What these terms imply is that the purpose of the analysis is to develop certain generalizations or propositions about those conditions that tend to stimulate certain states or changes of state in the phenomenal world. The specific instances that demonstrate the generalization are simply illustrations of such general principles. The interaction of blacks and whites in a small southern American town is not described in any rich ethnographic or historical detail, but it might be mentioned as an instance, along with a great many other instances that could have been cited, that typifies some general tendency in human social organization.

There are surely some pitfalls that need to be avoided in such an approach. Nomothetic or so-called theoretical sociology is often criticized for its armchair character, its development in splendid isolation from actual cases in the empirical world of reality. When the theoretical sociologist "stoops" to talking about this world, it is merely to illustrate the articulated principles. Certainly some of the founders of sociology were guilty of such practices. Auguste Comte practiced "cerebral hygiene," whereby he resolved never to read anything that disagreed with his views. Herbert Spencer was jokingly accused of authoring a book (which he *might* have written) called *A Beautiful Theory Murdered by a Brutal Gang of Facts.* If this is a caricature of tendencies toward selective perception based on preconceived notions, it still describes in exaggerated form a temptation in much of sociological analysis to look for a "beautiful" idea about human social relations and then to search for various instances that allegedly "prove" the validity of the idea. The fallacy in this, of course, is that just as statistics can be made to "lie" to prove a point, so truth can be muddied when dredging up empirical examples to validate a preconceived theory or principle. Given the great variety of human behavioral tendencies and, even more so, the variety of human perspectives that can be brought to an understanding of that behavior, it may be possible to "illustrate" the most outlandish of propositions with instances that, with a little imagination, can be seen as exemplifying the proposition.

Such observations have led some students to conclude that a more idiographic approach is necessary, one that emphasizes the uniqueness of each human condition that necessitates a full historical analysis of each situation. From this perspective, the "story" of human behavior is essentially narrative or chronological, without any necessary rhyme or reason. With some exaggeration no doubt, history has been described as just "one damned thing after another." In contrast, sociologists tend to take the risk of attempting to generalize about which damned thing *usually* coexists with other things. The enormity of this risk will be demonstrated at many points in this book, where the author is skating on the thin ice of really sparse empirical evidence to back up suggested propositions. The reader is usually given fair warning at these points by expressions like "it may be that . . ."

3. An extension, really, of the last point is another feature of this book: an emphasis on cross-cultural material from outside the boundaries of the United States. Sociological treatises on ethnic groups or ethnic relations have tended to be quite U.S.A.-centered in their approach. The comparative or cross-cultural perspective adopted here is designed to indicate that the social world is not bounded by the Atlantic and Pacific oceans and by Mexico and Canada. For many interesting reasons not to be gone into here, the field of sociology—including the sociology of ethnicity—has been dominated by American practitioners. Perhaps because sociologists, like most other people, are more comfortable in familiar social settings, they have tended to study and record social situations close at hand. Chicago and New Haven are two cities that have been much studied sociologically; not, perhaps, because of the intrinsic sociological interest of these places, but because major departments of sociology were located at the University of Chicago and at Yale University. Whatever the reason, sociological writing and instruction in the United States have tended to concentrate on deviance, the family, politics, etc. as these are found in American society.

Nor is this tendency absent from the present book. The author is a lifetime American and certainly "knows" American practices in ethnic relations far better than those in any other society. Also, in many cases, the primary aim in citing empirical cases of ethnic groups and ethnic relations is pedagogic, to help the student grasp the nature of the general principle being enunciated. For this purpose "familiar" examples are appealed to on the assumption that students, too, will be most familiar with the American social scene. Nevertheless, a generous citation of non-American cases will be found here. This practice not only exemplifies that a viable sociology should be a sociology of *human* (not simply American) social behavior; it also reflects a value bias of the author's that should probably be stated: Americans, myself included, are far too parochial, too wrapped up in our own experiences, with little appreciation of the value to our society that could follow from a wider knowledge of the world beyond our boundaries.

4. One final point can be made in this definition of perspectives and motives for the following analysis. A number of contemporary scholars have complained that, while there is an overdevelopment of sociological analysis in the field of ethnic groups, there has so far been little attention given to the sociological analysis of such nonethnic minorities as women, youth, homosexuals, ex-convicts, etc. Since the author agrees with this criticism, it might be wondered why still another treatise on ethnic groups is being put forth when the crying need today is for sociological investigation of these other minorities. The author is likewise convinced of the need for a reorientation of sociological study toward such nonethnic minorities, and it was with this need fairly constantly in mind that the following pages were written. It is hoped that the set of analytic tools described for the study of ethnic groups and ethnic relations are tools that can be transferred to the study of nonethnic minorities. When we reach that sociological nirvana wherein all of human grouping and intergroup relations can be understood in terms of a single set of explanatory principles, this book may be cited, it can be hoped, as a minor footnote in a history of how we moved from detailed knowledge of quite specific human situations in the direction of those "general ideas," the development of which, after all, must distinguish human beings from any of the "lower" animals.

PART 1
ETHNIC GROUPS

OVERVIEW

GROUPS

Sociology is sometimes characterized as the "study of human groups" and, while this definition is debatable, it points to a fundamental set of sociological problems. This "set"—or at least a major part of it—is represented in the three chapters in this section.

Common to all these aspects of ethnic groups is the general problem of ethnic group *survival*—one version of the age-old question, How is society possible? in the face of all the forces that tend to keep people from associating with one another. Ethnic groups are certainly notable for the fact that their survival is problematic. People complain that Polish-American clubs do not have the strength they once had, that intermarriage between Jews and Gentiles threatens the very survival of a Jewish people, etc.

Chapter 1 takes up the matter of *identity* of the person with the person's ethnic group. Without some we-feeling, some sense of commonality of interest with other members of one's group, it would be difficult to imagine how any human group would survive. If each person were an "island" or a bundle of self-interests, without any sense of shared fate with other members of his or her group, the group existence would be ephemeral at best. As Durkheim put it, if group membership were based on mere coincidence of self-interest of persons—what each person can do for each other person—in the mode of thought that Durkheim attributed to Spencer, then human association would be short-lived indeed, because the "interest" that unites people at one time may divide them at another.[1] On-going society requires more solidarity or cohesion than this, and much of sociological analysis has been concerned with those conditions that promote identification or dis-identification of people with others of their "own kind."

Chapter 2 deals with ethnic group survival from a somewhat different perspective. One of the forces that certainly holds a social group together is the shared culture or way of life that is usually seen, in ethnocentric fashion, as distinguishing "we" who practice this valued way from "they" who practice alien and "inferior" ways. The central problem discussed in Chapter 2 is the phenomenon of acculturation, the adoption of alien ways by members of one ethnic group in contact with other groups. Acculturation is clearly a threat to ethnic group survival, and the nature of this process and of those conditions that encourage or retard the process is the focus of concern in this chapter.

Chapter 3 examines the degree of community that is characteristic of different ethnic groups. Two rather different meanings of *community* are examined here, both being vital conditions for the survival of ethnic groups. The first meaning refers to at least a minimum of harmony and feelings of mutual liking and respect that must exist between group members; group survival is certainly threatened by internal bickering and factionalism. The second concept of community involves the idea of the relative self-sufficiency of a group in providing all the basic needs of its members. Thus ethnic group survival is measured by the degree to which, on the one hand, group members look to their ethnic group for educational, welfare, medical, religious, and other kinds of needs or, on the other hand, the extent to which ethnic group members must resort to special agencies outside the ethnic group to supply these needs.

ETHNIC GROUPS

Most readers of this book—and their reasonably well-educated friends —will have an intuitive understanding of the concept of "ethnic group."

---

[1]Emile Durkheim, *The Division of Labor in Society,* trans. by George Simpson (New York: Macmillan, 1933).

When news commentators, for example, discuss the impact of ethnic groups on the outcome of an election, it is understood that the reference is to the voting behavior of such groups (in the United States) as Jews, blacks, American Indians, or descendants of East European immigrants. When one tries to put this understanding in words for precise definition, as sociologists must do in order to keep the referent for their discussion clear, they may find the words hard to come by.

Ethnic groups are the categories in terms of which we describe the existence of different "peoples." Shibutani and Kwan have provided a useful definition: "An ethnic group consists of those who conceive of themselves as alike by virtue of their common ancestry, real or fictitious, and who are so regarded by others."[2]

This definition emphasizes the role of ancestry in ethnic definition: people are seen as inheriting their ethnic labels by virtue of their birth to parents who themselves were born to parents who had acquired their own ethnicity in the same way. The definition also, in terms of real vs. fictitious, indicates an important fact about ethnic groups: that they are creatures of the system of perception prevailing among a people, and may well incorporate errors of fact about the history of a group of people. Many people in the United States who identify themselves ethnically as "black," and are so identified by others, are in fact the contemporary products of a history of much racial intermixture among their ancestors. But what these ancestors "really" were in ethnic terms is not sociologically relevant. The important thing is that people are *assigned* an ethnic heritage by the conventions of a given society, and this assignment may well have an element of the fictitious about it.

One limitation of the Shibutani and Kwan definition of ethnic groups should be noted. The definition implies that a consciousness of being a part of a group with likenesses derived from common ancestors is restricted to ethnic groups. A little thought on the matter will show that this is not so. People who engage in a particular occupation—whether bricklayer or professor—regard themselves and are regarded by others as similar partly because they ply a trade according to a set of traditions established and handed down by their predecessors in that trade. Yet we do not consider plumbers or prostitutes or priests as peoples or ethnic groups. The crucial

---

[2]Tamotsu Shibutani and Kian M. Kwan, *Ethnic Stratification* (New York: Macmillan, 1965), p. 47.

difference, perhaps, is the *ascribed* quality of membership in the ethnic group. One does not choose one's ethnic ancestors, they are ascribed at birth; whereas one typically does (in most societies) choose an occupation with its set of attached "ancestors." Ethnicity, unlike these other group identifications, is acquired as a kind of birthmark that one may sometimes attempt to conceal but can never quite renounce: "Once a _____, always a _____."

If we want more detail, then, on those likenesses of people that constitute the basis for ethnic classification, we must determine just what social statuses are assigned to a person on the basis of the status of that person's parents. One of the more obvious of these is *social class:* the overall level of prestige or respectability of the person. Although the social-class status of the parents is ascribed to the child in virtually all societies, there is in most societies an opportunity for class status to be altered by the person on the basis of his or her adult accomplishments. Only when social mobility is severely restricted and *castes* are created is it appropriate to think of social classes as peoples or ethnic groups. Most sociological discussions of ethnicity treat social class not as an ethnic group but as another kind of differentiation of people coexisting with ethnic differentiation, often with profound effects on the consequences of ethnicity for social life.

What similarities, then, are more appropriate criteria for defining the membership of ethnic groups? A number of sociologists, including Gordon, have argued that ethnic groups should be seen as involving commonalities of *race, national origin, religion,* or some combination of these three criteria.[3] This suggestion is generally adopted for the present analysis, with the understanding that there is some questionability about each of these criteria. For example, individuals certainly do acquire their physical features (their race) from their biological parents. But the well-known phenomenon of racial "passing" is an indication that racial ancestry, at least as "regarded by others," may vary from the strict facts of the racial makeup of a person's parents. One's national origin, the country of one's birth, is likewise an ascribed and inescapable classification; but, again, by name changing and other concealments, the individual may succeed in falsifying his or her ethnic background.

---

[3]Milton Gordon, *Assimilation in American Life* (New York: Oxford University Press, 1964), p. 27.

Religion would seem, at first glance, the most tenuous of this trilogy of criteria of ethnic status. Certainly children are baptized or otherwise incorporated into the religion of their parents long before they reach the "age of consent," and certainly this ascribed religious status will remain with most persons throughout their lives as they honor the faith of their fathers. However, religious conversion does occur, and while this conversion might be compared to racial passing or the concealment of one's national origin, there is an obvious difference in that conversion is given public sanction, often in an elaborate ceremonial, while passing and concealment are lonely acts of ethnic denial. For all this difficulty in the use of religion as a criterion of ethnic membership, the fact remains that, in many situations, religious affiliation is essentially an act of affirmation of peoplehood. Catholics and Protestants in Northern Ireland and Jews almost everywhere tend to feel and act *as if* their religious affiliation bound them to a people with a common ancestry. On these pragmatic grounds, at least, there is good reason to include religion as an additional basis of ethnic group membership.

CHAPTER 1
ETHNIC IDENTITY

WHO AM I? OR WHO ARE THEY?

One of the more disarmingly simple approaches to studying the way people identify themselves is to ask them to write several answers to the question, Who am I?[1] Given complete freedom to determine their approach to writing such answers, most people will begin by listing various *categories* of people of which they are members: I am a woman, a student, a Catholic, a construction worker. Note that these are all designations that *distinguish* that person from persons of other categories: other occupations, religions, etc. Only occasionally do respondents in this situation think to offer the information that "I am a human being" or a "child of God" or "part of the universe" or some other label that will identify them with all of humanity. Some of these identifications will come under the heading of *ethnic groups,* as when people identify themselves by race, religion, or national origin.

With ethnic identification, as with all other self-identifications, there is always the possibility that individuals may not identify themselves as they

---

[1]Early research using this research instrument was reported in Manford H. Kuhn and Thomas S. McPartland, "An Empirical Investigation of Self-Attitudes," *American Sociological Review,* 19 (February, 1954):68–76. For a more recent summary of such research, see Clark McPhail, "The Classification and Ordering of Responses to the Question 'Who am I?' " *Sociological Quarterly,* 13(1972):329–347.

are identified by others. A man may see himself as young, a Methodist, a doctor; others, observing that in fact he is forty-eight years old, never attends church and is still a medical intern, may question these self-definitions as inaccurate or inflated. Ethnic identification is often a matter of disagreement between the namer and the named.[2]

Sometimes this discrepancy results from individual egocentrism and the tendency to see oneself in the better light. In Brazil, where the *preto,* or black, is a derogated physical appearance, few people consider themselves *preto,* which leads to the observation that it is always the man next door or down the road who is *preto.* This egocentrism of self-definition sometimes takes a collective form, in which a whole group of people deny their membership in an ethnic category to which outsiders attempt to assign them. Berry has described the problems of some of the numerous bands of "triracial isolates" in the United States, people who are an indeterminant mixture of European, African, and American Indian backgrounds.[3] Such people are frequently classified as blacks or "niggers" by their southern neighbors, much to their distress, since they see themselves as basically Indian in origin. Such people are marginal in the fullest sense, being clearly located in neither one social category nor another. The people studied by Berry, for example, were caught in the middle of the dichotomous segregation of schools in the South. Being suspected, at least by whites, of having Negro "blood," they were not allowed to attend white schools. Adamantly rejecting the Negro label for themselves, they refused to send their children to black schools.[4]

Many other examples could be cited of such painful marginality in terms of ethnic identification. We might, for example, consider the "coloured" people of South Africa, people of mixed native and European ancestry who traditionally speak Afrikaans (the language of South Africans of Dutch descent) and who have enjoyed some political rights that set them apart from "natives." In recent years, with an increasingly stringent *apartheid* system in South Africa, the coloureds have in many cases found themselves "reclassified" as natives.[5] In much the same way, the Indian resi-

---

[2]For an analysis that treats social identity largely as a matter of "naming" or applying labels to oneself and others, see Anselm Strauss, *Mirrors and Masks* (New York: Free Press, 1959).

[3]Brewton Berry, *Almost White* (New York: Macmillan, 1963).

[4]Berry, *Amost White,* pp. 112–133.

[5]Pierre L. van den Berghe, *South Africa: A Study in Conflict* (Middletown, Conn.: Wesleyan University Press, 1965), pp. 39–42.

dents of Rhodesia greatly resent being classified by whites in a way that identifies them with the native people of the country.[6]

One other observation about the nature of ethnic identity will be entered as a caveat to the kind of analysis that follows. In much of the sociological writing about variations in ethnic or other group identities, ethnic identity is treated as a variable *between* individuals whose personal sense of ethnic identity is presumed to be persistent and unvarying. Actually, it seems more accurate psychologically to treat ethnic identity as a *latent* tendency of the individual, a tendency that may be activated or minimized according to the situation.[7] In other words, the Who am I? or Who are they? question might realistically be countered with, When—yesterday, today, or tomorrow? What a person is or is thought to be "essentially" will vary with the occasion.[8] On a heterosexual date, the fact that one of the pair is a woman may a fundamental element in her and her date's consciousness in the structuring of the social relationship. The fact that she happens to be a doctor is kept latent by the situation, this identity being defined as situationally irrelevant.[9] In an operating room where she is the surgeon, however, the salience of her sex and occupational identities is

---

[6]Floyd Dotson and Lillian Dotson, "Indians and Coloureds in Rhodesia and Nyasaland," *Race,* 5(July 1963):61–75.

[7]Father Greeley, an Irish Catholic professor at the University of Chicago, illustrates this fact by noting that the sociological question is *not* whether his nationality, religion, occupation, or city of residence is his most important identity, but "under what circumstances" he would "define himself" in terms of one of these identities. Andrew W. Greeley, *Why Can't They Be Like Us?* (New York: Dutton, 1971), p. 86.

[8]This situational character of the human self is strongly emphasized in the self-presentational or impression management mode of analysis associated with the work of Erving Goffman. For a specific application of this approach to the study of ethnic groups, see Stanford M. Lyman and William A. Douglass, "Ethnicity: Strategies of Collective and Individual Impression Management," *Social Research,* 40(Summer, 1973):344–365.

[9]Using games as examples of social encounters in which people typically ignore what is going on outside the narrow confines of the activity at hand, Goffman comments on the "rules of irrelevance" by which encounters are protected from being "inundated" by extrinsic considerations such as the social statuses of the players. Erving Goffman, *Encounters; Two Studies in the Sociology of Interaction* (Indianapolis: Bobbs-Merrill, 1961), pp. 19–26. On the other hand, Hughes notes the frequency with which supposedly irrelevant status characteristics *do* intrude on many situations. Most people *expect* a doctor, for example, to be white, male, and middle-aged. The fact that a doctor turns out to be a woman, a black, or very young or very old is disconcerting at least. Adjustments are made accordingly: an "ethnic" doctor confines his practice to those of his own ethnic group, a woman doctor specializes in gynecology or pediatrics. Everett C. Hughes, "Dilemmas and Contradictions of Status," *American Journal of Sociology,* 50(1945):353–359.

likely to be reversed. In some situations, a person and his interactants may genuinely forget that the person is a Jew, though all parties may be intensely reminded should the conversation turn to the state of Arab-Israeli relations. Implicit in much that follows is the idea that ethnic identity is not constant in any individual or group but is subject to situational variation.

VARIATIONS IN ETHNIC IDENTITY: BETWEEN ETHNIC GROUPS

The sociologist's interest in ethnic identity, as in almost every other subject of sociological investigation, concerns the variation in this phenomenon in different situations. In the remainder of this chapter we examine two dimensions of this variability: (1) the intensity and kind of ethnic identity of different ethnic groups in different social situations, and (2) the degree of ethnic identity of different kinds or categories of people within an ethnic group. It is one thing, for example, to compare the overall ethnic consciousness of blacks and Chicanos in the United States; it is quite a different thing to compare the degree or kind of ethnic consciousness found among the middle classes and the lower classes in these groups. This section takes up the first of these two kinds of variability.

Variations in Ethnic Consciousness between Societies

Ethnicity, like age, sex, social class, or any other categorical difference, can be emphasized or relatively ignored in a given society. The pattern of social relations may be such that it is brought home constantly to the person: you are a white man, or an Englishman, or a Catholic; or a person's ethnic background may be permitted to sit lightly upon his consciousness. Since a fairly high degree of ethnic consciousness seems to be a "normal" feature of human society, we may learn something about conditions encouraging ethnic consciousness by looking at some "deviant" cases of societies in which this aspect of identity seems to be minimized.

First, we can look at the situation of societies with major ideological commitments to the minimization of ethnic differences. The example of the United States of America comes readily to mind. The value system of the country proscribes discrimination on the basis of race, color, or creed. In somewhat more technical terms, American society has been characterized as embodying an *achievement* rather than an *ascriptive* set of values.[10] According to American ideals, it is not "who you are" (in terms of ethnic or other ascribed characteristics) but "what you do" that determines the social estimate of one's worth.

At least since the publication of Myrdal's *An American Dilemma,* it has been widely recognized that there is considerable disparity between the equalitarianism espoused in the Declaration of Independence and the realities of American practice, in which invidious ethnic distinctions are constantly being made.[11] It has been widely assumed, however, that awareness of this discrepancy would lead to efforts to bring the reality into line with the ideal, so that eventually American society would be as ethnically undifferentiated as the value system implies. In fact, we continue to hear a great deal about "unmeltable ethnics" and the rather surprising persistence of ethnic consciousness in America.[12] Nevertheless, it is probably true that the ideology of the inherent equality of all persons has had a corrosive effect on ethnic identity in the United States, and that many "hyphenated" Americans have come to feel more identity with the entity following the hyphen than with that preceding it.

Another possible factor in diminished ethnic consciousness is the situation in which, in a given society, some nonethnic basis of differentiation is emphasized at the expense of ethnic consciousness. Racial identity in Brazil serves as an example. Brazil's so-called racial democracy has allowed blacks and racially mixed persons to assume major social positions in the society.[13] These opportunities for blacks have been facilitated by Brazil's extreme social-class consciousness, in which a derogated racial background may be overlooked if the person has wealth or the other symbols of social esteem.[14] There is even the feeling that racial member-

---

[10]Talcott Parsons, *The Social System* (Glencoe, Ill.: Free Press, 1951), pp. 63–65, 182–191.

[11]Gunnar Myrdal, *An American Dilemma* (New York: Harper, 1944).

[12]Michael Novak, *The Rise of the Unmeltable Ethnics* (New York: Macmillan, 1971); Greeley, *Why Can't They Be Like Us?*

[13]Emilio Willems, "Racial Attitudes in Brazil," *American Journal of Sociology,* 54(March, 1949):402–408.

[14]There are many popular Brazilian expressions to indicate this interrelation of status and racial traits. For example, "a rich Negro is a white and a poor white is a Negro," cited in Charles Wagley, *Amazon Town* (New York: Macmillan, 1953), p. 135. That class and color are interrelated features of ethnic identification elsewhere in Latin America is indicated in Julian Pitt-Rivers, "Race, Color and Class in Central America and the Andes," *Daedalus,* 96 (Spring, 1967):542–559.

ship itself can be altered by the social mobility process: the belief, for example, that "money whitens."[15] An additional factor in Brazilian society is the fact that the substantial interbreeding of the Portuguese colonizers with the indigenous Indians and with imported African slaves has created a great variety of mixed racial types in the country. Thus the many gradations of physical appearance make uncertain the exact racial type of any one person.[16] With race so complex and controversial a basis of differentiation, and with social class such a strongly developed one, the relative weakness of racial identification in Brazil is understandable.[17]

Variations in the Basis of Ethnic Identity

We have noted the view that ethnicity is based on common ancestry deriving from race, religion, or national origin. A closer examination of ethnic identity will show that, in a given society, one or more of these three criteria of ethnicity may be emphasized at the expense of the others. Sometimes, of course, the three reinforce one another and provide a conception of peoplehood that is at once racial, religious, and national: "white Anglo-Saxon Protestant," for example, or "Irish," which, when applied to an American, implies not only his nationality but also his Catholic religion and white race.

More restricted versions of common ancestry emerge when two or more of these criteria of ethnic affiliation work at cross-purposes. The common Roman Catholicism of a group of people may not prevent them from dividing sharply along racial or national lines. In the United States, for instance, Catholics will identify themselves as Irish Catholic, or Italian Catholic, or Polish Catholic. And in Belgium, a largely Catholic country,

---

[15]Carl N. Degler, *Neither Black nor White* (New York: Macmillan, 1971), pp. 105–107.

[16]Harry W. Hutchinson, *Village and Plantation Life in Northeastern Brazil* (Seattle: University of Washington Press, 1957). The same situation may be noted in Mexican history, where colonial administrators charged with the racial classification of Mexicans, among whom interracial breeding was so common, ultimately threw up their hands and allowed people to define their own racial membership. Chester L. Hunt and Lewis Walker, *Ethnic Dynamics* (Homewood, Ill.: Dorsey Press, 1974), p. 139.

[17]It has been suggested that in America, too, the rising importance to Americans of such nonethnic identities as age, sex, and profession may be undermining the importance of ethnic identity. For an application of this idea to Jewish identity in American society, see Charles S. Liebman, "American Jewry: Identity and Affiliation," in David Sidorsky (ed.), *The Future of the Jewish Community in America* (New York: Basic Books, 1973), pp. 127–152.

there are sharp, often bitter, divisions between the Flemings (of Dutch origin) and the Walloons (of French origin). Sometimes, too, a common nationality does not prevent differentiation of identity along racial or religious lines: white vs. black in the United States, or Protestant vs. Catholic in Northern Ireland.

An important question about ethnicity in any society, then, is the relative importance placed upon racial, religious, and nationality bases of ethnic identity. To illustrate sociological analysis in this vein, we shall consider two contemporary societies that are heterogeneous along racial, religious, and nationality lines: the United States and South Africa.

That the people who populate the United States come from a great variety of national origins is a familiar fact. Also familiar is the "Anglo-conformity" view of American society, whereby immigrants were encouraged, sometimes cajoled, into an "Americanization" process by which they gave up their differentiated national identities.[18] A frequent measure of this progressive elimination of a conscious tie to the "old country" was the increasing tendency of people to marry across lines of national origin. If individuals can ignore their national ethnicity in choosing marriage partners, they presumably can avoid generally any sharp consciousness of national origins.

This conception of the loss of ethnic identity in the United States came eventually to be modified with the discovery that, while intermarriage across lines of national origin is increasingly common in America, there is *no* increase in the tendency to marry across lines of *religious* affiliation. Thus most intermarriage across lines of national origin occurs between people from countries with the same predominant religion: intermarriage, for example, among Irish and Polish and Italians (Catholic); or Germans and Scandinavians and British (Protestant). Kennedy's discovery of such patterns of intermarriage in New Haven, Connecticut, led her to formulate a "triple melting pot" conception of assimilative tendencies in the United States, with each major religious grouping (Protestant, Catholic, Jewish) providing a framework for continuing ethnic identity in the face of the decline of national origins as such a basis.[19]

---

[18]For a description of the Americanization movement, see Milton M. Gordon, *Assimilation in American Life* (New York: Oxford University Press, 1964), pp. 98–104.

[19]Ruby Jo Reeves Kennedy, "Single or Triple Melting Pot? Intermarriage in New Haven, 1870–1950," *American Journal of Sociology,* 58(July, 1952):56–59.

Barron found a similar tendency toward religious endogamy (i.e., marriage within one's religious category) in a small Connecticut town,[20] and Greeley shows that religious endogamy among Protestants is more detailed than simply the marriage of Protestant with Protestant, since most marriages are between persons of the same religious denomination: Baptist, Lutheran, Presbyterian, etc.[21]

The triple melting pot hypothesis was elaborated upon by Will Herberg in *Protestant-Catholic-Jew.*[22] Herberg notes the continuing tendency of Americans to identify themselves by their religion, even when they are hazy or evasive about their national origins. An anecdote that illustrates this point concerns an army sergeant who is interviewing a recruit and asking him about his religious affiliation. After being told "no" when he asked the recruit successively if he were Protestant, Catholic, Jewish, the sergeant exclaimed, "Well, what the blazes *are* you?"[23] Religious identification is so much taken for granted in the United States that those rare individuals who do not so identify themselves are socially excluded in several ways. Recent articles in popular magazines have noted the difficulty encountered by agnostic or atheistic couples who want to adopt children. Political success is probably dependent on having some reputable religious affiliation. When, in the 1960 presidential campaign, the issue of Kennedy's Catholicism was raised, his Republican opponent was asked whether this should be an issue. The "tolerant" answer was, "Of course not; only if a candidate had *no* religion should it be an issue." To ignore one's religious identity is almost tantamount to being relegated to a what-the-blazes-are-you status.[24]

---

[20]Milton Barron, *People Who Intermarry* (Syracuse, N.Y.: Syracuse University Press, 1946).

[21]Andrew W. Greeley, "Religious Intermarriage in a Denominational Society," *American Journal of Sociology,* 75(May, 1970):949–952.

[22]Will Herberg, *Protestant-Catholic-Jew* (Garden City, N.Y.: Doubleday, 1955).

[23]Herberg, *Protestant-Catholic-Jew,* p. 40.

[24]The suspected "un-Americanism" of any American who does not profess some ethnic affiliation is illustrated in Banton's citation of the experience of an eminent American sociologist, Everett Hughes. While a college student, Hughes worked in Chicago during one of his vacations. He was asked by fellow workers, "What are you?" Hughes replied, "American." To his questioners, however, "this answer was not acceptable. 'American' was not an ethnic identity and everyone had to fit into some ethnic category. Eventually they decided that he was an Englishman!" Michael Banton, *Race Relations* (New York: Basic Books, 1967), p. 337.

This notion of the persistence of religious identification and the decline of national origin identification in the United States has many critics. One line such criticism has taken is to show that religious endogamy is not as strong in some places as it was in Kennedy's New Haven of the 1930s. The rate of marriage between Catholics and non-Catholics is considerably higher in many other places, especially where Catholics are a smaller minority in the community.[25] Even when Catholics do marry other Catholics, they may have a strong preference for marriage partners with the same national origin. The hostility between Irish and non-Irish nationality groups has led to a very low intermarriage rate, for example, between Poles and Irish.[26]

Another line of analysis that is implicitly critical of the triple melting pot thesis is the finding that the decline of national origin consciousness is not as complete today as one might have anticipated from that thesis. Ethnic associations—clubs composed of Italian-Americans, American Indians, Chinese-Americans, etc.—flourish today in many parts of the United States, and people identify themselves as half-Polish and half-Italian because their parents were of those two national origins. Political parties still feel constrained to "balance the ticket" by nominating people with names or known national origins that will appeal to the "ethnic" vote in America.[27] Also, as one indication of continued sociological interest in ethnicity in America, several major publishing houses have launched series of sociological analyses of Americans of different national origins. Developments in specific ethnic groups may serve to enhance national origin consciousness, even at the expense of lessened religious consciousness. Thus, in a study of a Christian Arab group from Iraq, Sengstock shows how, under stress of heightened Arab nationalism associated with the Arab-Israeli conflict, these people have come to a new awareness of their Arab

---

[25]John L. Thomas, "The Factor of Religion in the Selection of Marriage Mates," *American Sociological Review,* 16(August, 1951):487–491. Similarly, the marriage of Jews to non-Jews occurs much more frequently in Iowa and Indiana, where the proportion of Jews in the population is very small. Marshall Sklare, *America's Jews* (New York: Random House, 1971), p. 185.

[26]Greeley, *Why Can't They Be Like Us?,* p. 90. For further evidence on lack of intermarriage between Catholics of different national origins, see Harold J. Abramson, *Ethnic Diversity in Catholic America* (New York: Wiley, 1973), pp. 51–68.

[27]Mark R. Levy and Michael S. Kramer, *The Ethnic Factor* (New York: Simon and Schuster, 1973).

origins.[28] All these developments may be symptomatic of a reassessment of a long-standing view that, in American society, one's religious affiliation stands higher than one's national origin in the scale of people's ethnic consciousness.

In South Africa, the main dilemma of ethnic identity is between *racial* identification on the one hand and *national origin* (or tribal origin, in the case of native peoples) on the other.[29] The white vs. black conflict with which the whole world is familiar coexists with national or tribal differences that threaten always to dilute a simple race consciousness. On the white side, there has been a chronic conflict between the original Dutch (Afrikaner) conquerors of the Cape and the English who came later and were able to dominate South Africa (the Union of South Africa became part of the British Empire in 1904). Equally "white," Dutch and English colonists were far apart culturally, as symbolized by the differences in the languages spoken—the Dutch developed an African variant on their native tongue called *Afrikaans*. At times it has appeared that English-Afrikaner conflict would override their sense of racial unity.[30] But the recent militancy of native demands for an end to the historical pattern of native suppression has created an awareness that, after all, the English, who dominate the country economically, have just as much stake in the white supremacy system as do the Afrikaners, who dominate the country politically.[31] According to van den Berghe, white unity is stimulated by a sense of *swart gevaar,* an Afrikaans phrase meaning "black danger."[32]

On the black side, there has been a traditional pattern of "ethnic particularism,"[33] which divides natives into many "peoples" with separate languages and ways of life. The policies of the white governments of South

[28]Mary C. Sengstock, "Traditional and Nationalist Identity in a Christian Arab Community," *Sociological Analysis,* 35(Autumn, 1974):201–210.

[29]The following discussion is based on Pierre L. van den Berghe, *South Africa: A Study in Conflict* (Middletown, Conn.: Wesleyan University Press, 1965).

[30]Peter B. Orlik, "Divided Against Itself: South Africa's White Polity," *Journal of Modern African Studies,* 8(July, 1970):199–212.

[31]For an analysis of this "curious phenomenon" by which the English are able to exploit South Africa economically while the Afrikaners rule it politically, see Julius Lewin, *Politics and Law in South Africa: Essays on Race Relations* (London: Merlin Press, 1963).

[32]van den Berghe, *South Africa,* p. 107.

[33]van den Berghe, *South Africa,* p. 49.

Africa have successively attacked, then attempted to revive this tribal particularism.[34] The recruitment of native labor to mines and factories, the basis of the country's industrial economy, has separated the men from their tribal insulation and treated them as an undifferentiated black or native group. More recently, a policy of "tribalism" has been a major feature of the *apartheid,* or racial segregation, policy of the government. Attempts are made to segregate workers in labor compounds according to tribal origins. The "Bantustan" policy of the government has also encouraged the use of traditional tribal languages, and the establishment of "bush colleges" for "higher education" in the native languages and traditions.[35] It is debatable whether this policy is, as many natives suspect, a deliberate effort of the government to divide and conquer, or, as government apologists claim, a humane respect for native tradition. At any rate, black activists in the struggle against racial domination tend to reject the policy of tribalism and to cast their lot with a Pan-African black identity rather than with their traditional tribal identities.[36] Altogether, recent developments in South Africa have tended to reduce a complex interplay of racial and national or tribal identities to the polarized identity of blacks and whites.

VARIATIONS IN ETHNIC IDENTITY: WITHIN ETHNIC GROUPS

The discussion so far has concerned variations in the intensity and nature of ethnic identification between different peoples and has ignored the fact that there is usually significant variation of ethnic identification *within* an ethnic group. In analyzing this variation, we shall follow the usual sociological procedure of looking at differences in rates or frequency of different kinds of identity among different social structural categories of people. For illustration, we shall consider the variables of *generation,*

---

[34]For a general discussion of "tribal particularism" as it was practiced by European colonial powers in their East African colonies, and of some of the effects of this on pan-tribal unity during and after the period of anticolonial revolt, see P. H. Gulliver (ed.), *Tradition and Transition in East Africa* (Berkeley: University of California Press, 1969), pp. 5–38.

[35]Pierre L. van den Berghe, "Language and Nationalism in South Africa," *Race,* 9(July, 1967):37–46. For a general analysis of the South African Bantustan policy, see Hunt and Walker, *Ethnic Dynamics,* pp. 171–175.

[36]van den Berghe, *South Africa,* p. 234.

social class, and *occupation,* and show how variations in these variables are related to variations in ethnic identity.

Generations

Sociologists have been made aware by Mannheim and others that people of different age categories or generations may have very different social attitudes and behavior. Generational differences may therefore be one of the most significant social structural variables for purposes of sociological investigation.[37] This awareness confirms the popular understanding that a "generation gap" often exists between people of different ages.

The application of the generation variable to the study of ethnic groups has not generally followed the strict definition of a generation as a cohort of individuals born at about the same time. It is certainly possible to study with advantage the differentiated ethnic identities of older and younger members of an ethnic group—older vs. younger American Indians, for example. However, most sociological attention has focused on the situation of *immigrant* peoples and has defined generation in terms of the distance of individuals from the time of their own or their ancestors' immigration. Thus, *first generation* refers to immigrants themselves, *second generation* to the children of immigrants (and sometimes to immigrants themselves if they immigrated as children and spent their formative years in a new country), *third generation* to the grandchildren of immigrants, etc.[38] Numerous sociological studies have been concerned with

---

[37]Karl Mannheim, "The Problem of Generations," in Paul Kecskemeti (ed.), *Essays on the Sociology of Knowledge* (London: Oxford University Press, 1952), pp. 276–320; see also S. N. Eisenstadt, *From Generation to Generation* (Glencoe, Ill.: Free Press, 1956).

[38]In most circumstances there is at least a rough correlation between *generation* so defined and *generation* defined as young vs. old, since most grandchildren of immigrants will be younger than most immigrants. In a situation in which new immigration to a country has been greatly diminished (as in the case of Japanese and Chinese immigration to the United States), this correlation will be very high, and age can practically be substituted for immigrant status in its effect on ethnicity. Where new immigration is still very high—in Israel today, for example—there may be many new immigrants (first generation) who are younger than many children of immigrants (second generation). Where this situation exists at all, it is the research sociologist's task to separate the effects of age and immigrant status (the two conceptions of *generation*) by controlling for the effects of one of these variables while the effects of the other are being examined. For an example of a study that does this, see Sidney Goldstein and Calvin Goldscheider, *Jewish Americans: Three Generations in a Jewish Community* (Englewood Cliffs, N.J.: Prentice-Hall, 1968).

the ethnic identities of people of different generations when conceived in this way. The United States, as a "land of immigrants," has especially been the target of this kind of analysis.

A number of influential historians and sociologists have developed a general scheme for explaining generational differences in ethnic identity, and this scheme is the starting point for most studies in this area.[39] According to this interpretation, immigrants took with them to America identities that were much more regional or local than national. Once in America, these immigrants tended to insulate themselves from the full shock of a new social environment by settling among people from their own village. They often gave the name of their old-country village to the street or the small community in which they lived (often with "New" prefixed to the name.).[40]

Except, perhaps, in some rural communities where a high concentration of immigrants from the same home-country region or town was present, this tendency of the immigrant to maintain a very narrow ethnic identity was eroded under American social conditions. For one thing, they found that native-born Americans were not keenly aware of these finer distinctions of peoplehood, and tended to treat as alike all who spoke a particular language or adhered to a given religion. (The native American was likely to feel that "all Chinamen look alike.") For another, the immigrants often found that they had to widen the scope of their associations to include others of their national origin if they hoped to maintain such institutions as churches, schools, and welfare associations.[41] The overall effect of

---

[39]Oscar Handlin, *The Uprooted* (Boston: Little, Brown, 1952); Herberg, *Protestant-Catholic-Jew;* Marcus L. Hansen, *The Immigrant in American History* (Cambridge, Mass.: Harvard University Press, 1940); Bernard Lazerwitz, "Contrasting the Effects of Generation, Class, Sex, and Age on Group Identification in the Jewish and Protestant Communities," *Social Forces,* 49(September, 1970):50–59.

[40]A similar process among southern migrants to northern cities is noted by Killian. In Chicago, for example, there is a Tennessee Street, so named because so many migrants from that state have settled there. Lewis M. Killian, *White Southerners* (New York: Random House, 1970), p. 105.

[41]The same tendency has been noted in such "internal" migrant situations as the removal of American Indians from rural tribal reservations and their "relocation" in American cities. The relocation policy of the Bureau of Indian Affairs has encouraged a scattering of Indians into many different cities and discouraged the formation of tribal "ghettos" within a given city. The result is an identity-widening effect called pan-Indianism, which occurs for precisely the two reasons suggested in the case of immigrant ethnic peoples: (1) because white people in cities do not recognize and encourage sharp tribal differentiations—"all Indians are alike"

living as strangers in a new land was to lessen some of the insularity that had prevailed among people of the same country but from different regional subcultures.[42] To this enlarged home-country identity, however, the immigrant remained firmly attached.

Members of the second generation, in spite of the best efforts of their immigrant parents to inculcate a strong identity based on national origin, tended to reject this identity, at least according to the scheme of interpretation we are following. For many children of immigrants, the question was raised in a painful way—some variant of "Am I Italian or American?"[43] Children who attended public schools and competed for jobs and marriage partners in the wider American society were likely to feel keenly the discriminations practiced against those adhering to the "strange" ways of their parents. Many children were accordingly ashamed of their parents and ashamed of any such marks of ethnic identification as a foreign-sounding name.[44] Name changing—the Anglicizing of a name (from Pe-

---

—and (2) because any semblance of an Indian "community" must be constituted from among Indians at large, given the paucity in any one urban neighborhood of fellow tribesmen (thus, a Navaho man complained that he could to go every bar in Los Angeles and never find another Navaho). Los Angeles is generally noted for the wide diversity of tribes represented in its population and for the development under such urban conditions of a pan-Indian social identity and community life. John A. Price, "The Migration and Adaptation of American Indians to Los Angeles," *Human Organization,* 27 (Summer, 1968):168–175. For a similar analysis of the situation in San Francisco, see Joan Ablon, "Relocated American Indians in the San Francisco Bay Area: Social Interaction and Indian Identity," *Human Organization,* 23(Winter, 1964):296–304.

[42]It should be noted that the experience of immigration does not always have this identity-widening effect. West Indian immigrants to Great Britain, like other Commonwealth immigrants, have gone to England with a strong sense of themselves as Britons, this identity being engendered by a thoroughly British education at home. Once in England, however, they have discovered by the rejecting reactions of the natives that they represent a special and inferior breed of Briton: the black Briton. West Indian identity is, indeed, bred on English soil, but not because of a breakdown of smaller identities, but rather from a dissolution of a larger one. Philip Hiro, *Black British, White British* (London: Eyre & Spottiswoode, 1971).

[43]Irwin L. Child, *Italian or American* (New Haven: Yale University Press, 1943). For a collection of writings on the problems of second-generation immigrants, see Oscar Handlin (ed.), *Children of the Uprooted* (New York: Braziller, 1966).

[44]The phenomenon of being ashamed of one's parents is not, of course, limited to immigrant situations; many children are ashamed of their parents because their attitudes and behavior reflect the social standards of an earlier generation or of a lower social class. Perhaps our studies of second-generation rejection of parents need to be more careful in differentiating between alienation from old-country ways and alienation from nonethnic sources of differences between parents and children.

trella to Peters, from Rosenberg to Rose)—is one symptom of second-generation rejection of ethnicity.[45]

The ethnic identification of third-generation immigrants is a matter of continuing controversy. Historian Marcus Hansen formulated what has been called the "law of third-generation return" to the effect that ethnic identity, rejected by the second generation, tends to be revived in the third.[46] Herberg took up this thesis in a revisionist analysis that emphasized religious rather than national origin identification.[47] In what is often referred to as the Hansen-Herberg thesis, the grandchild tends to remember and honor what the child of the immigrant has forgotten or rejected: his or her separate national or religious identity. The explanation of this return is found in the threat to individual identity prevailing in American society. While second-generation persons felt the need to strive for 100 percent Americanism for themselves by rejecting the ethnicity of their parents, third-generation persons, secure in their Americanism, find it no longer satisfying just to be an American. The question they pose is, What kind of American? To whom, or to what, do I belong? Many individuals, according to this line of thought, find themselves through identification with a "people"—whether a "people" based on religion, race, or national origin.[48]

The idea of a revival of ethnic identity in later generations has been given considerable attention in recent sociological work. Much of the research on American Jews has seemed to make a case for this thesis. Despite a continuing decline in succeeding generations of the number of Jews who observe the traditional religious rituals, there is an increase in the number of Jews in later generations who are interested in perpetuating a Jewish

---

[45]On the tendency of celebrities—movie stars, etc.—to Anglicize their names, see E. Digby Baltzell, *The Protestant Establishment* (New York: Random House, 1964); on name-changing tendencies among second-generation Slavic Americans, see Louis Adamic, *What's Your Name?* (New York: Harper, 1942).

[46]Hansen, *The Immigrant in American History.*

[47]Herberg, *Protestant-Catholic-Jew.*

[48]Greeley makes the intriguing observation that religious affiliation seems to be highest precisely in those countries in which there is no single or dominant religious denomination, suggesting that religious affiliation can serve the "ethnic" function being discussed only if a person's religion tends to differentiate him from other members of his own society. Greeley, *Why Can't They Be Like Us?,* p. 83. For a contrast to the religious situation in the United States, see R. F. Tomasson, "Religion Is Irrelevant in Sweden," *Trans-action,* 6(December, 1968):46–53, which describes a "one church" society in which religious affiliation is not a basis of qualification for social position.

consciousness in their children.[49] One indication of this is the growing tendency for Jewish children to receive some kind of special Jewish education. This increased Jewish identity is undoubtedly related to events external to American society: to the persecution of Jews in Nazi Germany and to the growth of the state of Israel as a symbol of Jewish identity. A study among university students in England finds that, while there is a decline in most aspects of Jewish activity in later generations, there is an *increasing* identification of younger English Jews with the vicissitudes of the Israeli state.[50] It is really impossible, then, to know how much of the revival of Jewish ethnic identity in the United States is due to the operation of Hansen's "law" and how much to events occurring to Jews in a world perspective.[51]

An ethnic revival is also being noted, and celebrated, among those groups known popularly as "white ethnics"—the predominantly urban Catholic groups in the United States. Novak notes an increasingly keen ethnic consciousness among people who continue to feel rejected by— and increasingly to resent—the snobbery of the Protestant-dominated Establishment.[52] In much the same tone, Greeley describes a pattern of unexpected persistence of ethnic consciousness, including a rather self-conscious effort by many young ethnics to identify with an ancestral tradition through studies of the classic literature of the nation of origin or by sentimental visits to the "old country" to see firsthand the locale of their ancestral homes.[53]

---

[49]Marshall Sklare, *Jewish Identity on the Suburban Frontier* (New York: Basic Books, 1967): Goldstein and Goldscheider, *Jewish Americans;* Lazerwitz, "Contrasting the Effects of Generation, Class, Sex, and Age on Group Identification in the Jewish and Protestant Communities."

[50]Bernard Wasserstein, "Jewish Identification Among Students at Oxford," *Jewish Journal of Sociology,* 13(December, 1971):131–151. Also, see Ernest Krausz, "The Edgeware Survey: Factors in Jewish Identification," *Jewish Journal of Sociology,* 11(December, 1969):151–164. For some reason, Irish-Americans, in the opinion of Father Greeley, have not similarly been moved to emotional identification with their distressed fellow Catholics in Northern Ireland. Greeley, *Why Can't They Be Like Us?,* p. 168.

[51]For an analysis that is sharply critical of the Hansen-Herberg perspective as an explanation of developments among American Jews, see Stephen A. Sharot, "The Three Generations Thesis and American Jews," *British Journal of Sociology,* 24(June, 1973):151–164.

[52]Novak, *The Rise of the Unmeltable Ethnics.*

[53]Greeley, *Why Can't They Be Like Us?,* pp. 148–152. Greeley refers to this kind of self-conscious ethnic revival as a variety of "tribalism."

The Hansen-Herberg thesis, with its recent confirmations, has been challenged by several studies of other American ethnic groups. Herbert Gans's study of an Italian-American community in Boston reports a "straight line" decrease in the salience of ethnic consciousness from the first through the third generations of group members,[54] and Sandberg reports a similar finding in his study of the Polish-American population of Los Angeles.[55] In a foreword to the Sandberg study, Gans suggests that the so-called ethnic revival may reflect a renewed ethnic consciousness among intellectuals, especially those Catholic intellectuals like Greeley and Novak who are experiencing discrimination by the Anglo-Saxon Protestant academic establishment and imagine that their fellow ethnics reflect their own ethnic consciousness.

A recent study of Italian and Irish ethnic groups in Providence, Rhode Island, suggests that this sense of insecurity may be shared as well by the mass of American Catholics.[56] Goering found that, in some respects, there has been a steady decline in ethnic consciousness from the first to later generations. However, ethnic interest has emerged in the third generation in the rather negative sense familiar to analysts of recent political behavior among American "ethnics." White backlash against the demands of the black civil rights movement and, more recently, against the hippie and egghead elements in American society has apparently been concentrated in these groups. Ethnic consciousness may be stimulated by a sense of threat from, or perhaps jealousy of, these groups who are seen as undeserving of the privileges they are claiming, especially in view of the great sacrifices made by their ethnic ancestors to obtain these privileges for themselves and their children. Goering summarized the finding of his study with a criticism of the view, implicit in most of the writings reviewed above, that the ethnic American finds "refreshment" in his ethnic consciousness: "The third generation does, indeed, return to ethnicity, but less as a source of cultural or religious refreshment than as the basis for organizing the skepticism associated with discontent and racial confrontation."[57]

[54]Herbert Gans, *The Urban Villagers* (New York: Free Press, 1962).

[55]Neil C. Sandberg, *Ethnic Identity and Assimilation: The Polish-American Community* (New York: Praeger, 1974).

[56]John M. Goering, "The Emergence of Ethnic Interests: A Case of Serendipity," *Social Forces,* 49(March, 1971):379–384.

[57]Goering, "The Emergence of Ethnic Interests," p. 383.

Glazer's analysis of renewed ethnicity in America develops a somewhat different reason for this revival.[58] After noting the failure of German and other ethnic groups to transplant a European national culture on American soil, Glazer suggests that the recent revival of ethnic consciousness stems from a renewed interest in the national fate of their countries of origin: a strong interest among Polish-Americans in what is happening in Poland, etc. In the same way, O'Connor shows the heightened national consciousness felt by German-Americans at the outbreak of World War I, although it was a consciousness marked by much ambivalence of feeling.[59] Thus, a German conductor of an American symphony orchestra played, as usual, the national anthem on the day of the declaration of war between the United States and Germany in 1917. At the conclusion, the conductor, with tears in his eyes, announced to the audience, "But my heart is on the other side."[60] Traumatic events or the threat thereof were the fate of every European and Asian country during World War II, and immigrants from these countries were unlikely to forget their national origins in the light of what was happening to their compatriots in their countries of origin. This was true whether their hearts lay with America or with their mother country across the Atlantic or Pacific Ocean.

Social Class

Individuals at different levels of social respectability—i.e., social classes —may differ considerably in the degree of importance they attach to their ethnic affiliations. In trying to generalize about this relationship, perhaps the most sensible sociological proposition would be this: When the ethnic group occupies a relatively inferior status position in a society, persons of higher-class positions within that ethnic group will tend to identify with their social class rather than with their ethnic status.

A number of sociological studies of ethnic groups have shown a tendency for higher-class persons in ethnic groups to attempt to dissociate themselves from a derogated ethnic group. This finding is either directly stated or could reasonably be inferred from data reported in studies of the

---

[58]Nathan Glazer, "Ethnic Groups in America: From National Culture to Ideology," in Morroe Berger, Theodore Abel, and Charles H. Page (ed.), *Freedom and Control in Modern Society* (New York: Octagon Books, 1964), pp. 158–173.

[59]Richard O'Connor, *The German Americans* (Boston: Little, Brown, 1968).

[60]O'Connor, *The German Americans,* p. 406.

Irish in "Yankee City,"[61] West Indian immigrants to Great Britain,[62] the Polish-American residents of Los Angeles,[63] Hungarian immigrants to the United States,[64] and Mexican-Americans in the southwestern United States.[65]

Perhaps the best known study that supports the proposition is Frazier's study of the social behavior of the black middle class in the United States.[66] According to Frazier, this black bourgeoisie adopted middle-class American life styles with a vengeance. Sometimes their efforts seemed almost a caricature of the white middle class, since the financial and other resources needed to maintain a middle-class life style are somewhat limited for many black Americans. These middle-class blacks read *Ebony* magazine (sometimes called a black version of *Life*), which features success stories about blacks and advertisements that emphasize the selling of hair straighteners, skin lighteners, and other aids to help the black person develop a more Caucasian physical appearance or life style.

Black Bourgeoisie was published in 1957—before the intensification of the civil rights movement of the 1960s, before blacks began to feel beautiful, before the growth of identification of blacks with the new nations of Africa. (The label "Afro-American" has only recently been popular with blacks.) If these movements have had their intended effects of removing the sense of stigma from black identity,[67] then, according to the proposition with which we started, there should be less tendency for middle-class

---

[61]W. Lloyd Warner and Leo Srole, *The Social Systems of American Ethnic Groups* (New Haven: Yale University Press, 1945).

[62]Ruth Glass, *London's Newcomers: The West Indian Migrants* (Cambridge, Mass.: Harvard University Press, 1961).

[63]Sandberg, *Ethnic Identity and Assimilation.*

[64]S. Alexander Weinstock, "Some Factors that Retard or Accelerate the Rate of Acculturation," *Human Relations,* 17(1964):321–340.

[65]As reflected, for example, in the tendency of middle-class Mexican-Americans to prefer the "Spanish-American" label for themselves, partly because, apparently, it distinguishes them from "Mexicans" of a lower class. Leo Grebler, Joan W. Moore, and Ralph C. Guzman, *Mexican-American People* (New York: Free Press, 1970), p. 386.

[66]E. Franklin Frazier, *Black Bourgeoisie* (Glencoe, Ill.: Free Press, 1957).

[67]There is evidence of some change in black self-conceptions in this direction. For example, a group of black college students were shown pictures of people of different shades of skin color and asked to estimate the degree of ability of the pictured individuals. The students tended to choose as most able those individuals with intermediate shades of skin color rather than those with very light or those with dark skins. Jo Holtzman, "Color Caste Changes Among Black College Students," *Journal of Black Studies,* 4(September, 1973):92–101.

blacks to deemphasize their racial identity in order to maintain their self-respect.

Some modification of the proposition being discussed is indicated by consideration of ethnic identity among people of very high social-class status. It appears that, in many situations, such persons are constrained to emphasize rather than to downplay their ethnic origins. The degree to which this is the case seems to depend on whether the ethnic group in question enjoys any degree of respectable status in the eyes of the dominant group members. Thus, in some New Mexico communities, there is such respect for Mexican-American culture that the highest status members of this group tend to maintain strong identification with their ethnic communities.[68] It has similarly been observed that name changing—a frequent measure of ethnic nonidentification—is quite rare among Italian musicians and artists in the United States (because of the strong reputation of Italians for excellence in these areas), while name changing is quite frequent among scientists of Italian origin (because of the lack of Italian reputation in this area).[69] Similarly, refugee intellectuals of Germanic origins often retain and perhaps cultivate a "thick" ethnic accent because of the high status attributed to German academics.[70]

Occupation

Although a person's occupation is usually treated as a major component of his social-class position, there are often clear-cut differences of social behavior among people who make up a given social class. Although both are broadly upper middle class, the typical college professor and the typical banker tend to be quite different in a number of ways. The question, then, is whether there are some occupations that are particularly favorable or unfavorable to promoting ethnic identity among those who follow that occupation.

Probably the most identity-enhancing occupations are those that have a reputation for being dominated by members of a given ethnic group. A

---

[68]Ronald J. Silvers, "Structure and Values in the Explanation of Acculturation Rates," *British Journal of Sociology,* 16(March, 1965):68–79.

[69]Lawrence F. Pisani, *The Italian in America* (New York: Exposition Press, 1957), chaps. 16 and 17.

[70]Donald Kent, *The Refugee Intellectual* (New York: Columbia University Press, 1953).

Chinese-American who decides to go into the laundry business or a New York Jew who decides to go into diamond merchandising may make their decisions without any consciousness of ethnic affiliation implied in these actions. But the stereotype of the Chinese laundryman or the Jewish diamond merchant is so strong that the chosen occupation will almost certainly be used by others to emphasize the individual's ethnic affiliation. It is perhaps for this reason that third-generation Jews, wishing to disaffiliate themselves from traditional symbols of Jewishness, attempt to avoid lines of work that are considered "Jewish."[71] In the same way, it has been reported that younger Chinese in the Philippines have attempted to avoid the distinctively "Chinese" occupation of tradesman in favor of such occupations as the law or teaching.[72]

This association in the public mind of a given occupation with a certain ethnic group may take a unique form in a given local setting. Thus it is reported that at one time in Chicago there was a heavy concentration of Scandinavians among Great Lakes seamen, of Flemings among apartment house janitors, and of Jews among garment factory workers.[73] Similarly, in New York City, Puerto Rican immigrants have been employed with great frequency by hotels as bellboys, maids, parking attendants, etc.[74] In none of these cases has there been any apparent intrinsic reason for the concentration of ethnic group members in the given occupation. These conditions nevertheless have had the identity-enhancing effects discussed above by virtue of the stereotyping of ethnic group members in given occupational roles.

At the other extreme are occupations that seem to be notably corrosive in their effects on ethnic identity. Much of the writing, both popular and sociological, about ethnicity concerns the effect of an *intellectual* occupation on ethnic identity—an understandable emphasis, since writers are themselves intellectuals. It was Mannheim's position that intellectuals—writers, artists, teachers, etc.—constitute the one exception to the rule that

---

[71]Judith R. Kramer and Seymour Leventman, *Children of the Gilded Ghetto* (New Haven: Yale University Press, 1961).

[72]Hunt and Walker, *Ethnic Dynamics,* p. 110, 111.

[73]Henry Pelling, *American Labor* (Chicago: University of Chicago Press, 1960), pp. 87–88.

[74]Joseph Fitzpatrick, *Puerto Rican Americans: The Meaning of Migration to the Mainland* (Englewood Cliffs, N.J.: Prentice-Hall, 1971).

thought processes are determined by a person's social position.[75] Since intellectuals are drawn from *all* social strata, Mannheim reasoned, there is an interpenetration of special viewpoints that allows intellectuals to, in effect, stand above the partisan ideological strife of those more bound to defend vested social interests.

The same point could be made about the *ethnic* affiliation and consciousness of the intellectual, a point that has often been made implicitly. A study of ethnic identity among engineers, lawyers, and professors, for example, found that professors were the most likely to identify with others of their occupation without regard to the ethnicity of these others.[76] A study of Jewish professors in the Boston area found that, while there was some variability in the matter, the great majority of professors who had to choose between honoring a professional obligation to teach classes, attend a professional convention, etc., and fulfilling the religious obligation to observe a Jewish holiday, would decide in favor of the professional obligation.[77] Gordon characterizes American intellectuals as a "subsociety," drawing its membership, in the manner suggested by Mannheim, from all social elements of the society.[78] Greeley goes a bit further and characterizes intellectuals as an "ethnic group" with a consciousness of itself as a people set apart, and with a great deal of animosity and misunderstanding of "them," the nonintellectuals.[79] Both Greeley and Novak,[80] Catholic priest and Catholic layman, respectively, comment with some bitterness on the tendency of fellow professors and other liberal intellectuals to show a profoundly ethnocentric lack of sympathy with the mentality of members of Catholic ethnic groups, even while lavishing their sympathy on the black American. Both these writers suggest that the well-advertised "antiintellectualism" of white ethnic Americans may be based at least partly on this

---

[75]Karl Mannheim, *Ideology and Utopia,* trans. by Edward A. Shils and Louis Wirth (New York: Harcourt Brace, 1936).

[76]Harold L. Wilensky and Jack Ladinsky, "From Religious Community to Occupational Group: Structural Assimilation Among Professors, Lawyers and Engineers," *American Sociological Review,* 32(August, 1967):541–561.

[77]Norman L. Friedman, "Jewish or Professorial Identity? The Priorization Process in Academic Situations," *Sociological Analysis,* 32(Fall, 1971):149–157.

[78]Gordon, *Assimilation in American Life,* pp. 224–232, 254–257.

[79]Greeley, *Why Can't They Be Like Us?*

[80]Novak, *Rise of the Unmeltable Ethnics.*

"ethnic" snobbery of the American intellectual.[81] Greeley and Novak raise the possibility that the intellectual, rather than being "de-ethnicized," as Gordon suggests, has taken on a hidden "ethnic" identity as a member of an elitist group.

The analysis above refers to intellectuals from the more prestigious ethnic groups. There might be a quite different pattern of ethnic consciousness among intellectuals from the more disadvantaged ethnic groups, such as blacks, Chicanos, and American Indians, in the United States. In all these groups, intellectuals are among the most visible practitioners and articulate spokesmen of ethnic consciousness.[82] Black teachers, clergymen, and writers have been the backbone of the movements to stimulate black identity, whether these movements are expressed through integrationist demands for social equality or separatist demands for racial autonomy. A similar point could be made for the leadership of anticolonial movements in the Third World: the leaders of anti-Western nationalist movements are, ironically, largely men who have been educated in Western universities.[83] Perhaps the experience of being discriminated against is especially productive of intellectual creativity. Perhaps intellectuals find ready markets for their "ideas" in the resentment of oppressed peoples. Whatever the explanation, it seems clear that the removal of intellectuals from ethnic identity is *not* an accurate description for most ethnic groups low on the social-status totem pole.

Intellectuals are not alone among people in middle-class occupations who may experience pressures away from ethnic identity. In his study of

---

[81]Greeley thus comments with some asperity on the tendency of American academics to persist in the belief that Catholics seldom engage in academic careers. This belief is held despite evidence of a rising proportion of Catholics in academic careers, especially among younger men and women. Andrew M. Greeley, "The 'Religious Factor' and Academic Careers: Another Communication," *American Journal of Sociology,* 78(March, 1973): 1247–1255. For further discussion of Greeley's viewpoint as expressed in this article, see Claire Humphreys, "The Religious Factor: Comment on Greeley's Conclusion," *American Journal of Sociology,* 80(July, 1974):217–219, and Greeley's "reply," pp. 219–220.

[82]On Indians, see Robert C. Day, "The Emergence of Activism as a Social Movement," in Howard H. Bahr, Bruce A. Chadwick, and Robert C. Day (eds.), *Native Americans Today* (New York: Harper & Row, 1972); on blacks, see Harold Cruse, *The Crisis of the Negro Intellectual* (New York: Macmillan, 1967); on Chicanos, see Joan W. Moore, *Mexican-Americans* (Englewood Cliffs, N.J.: Prentice-Hall, 1970), pp. 148–156.

[83]Tamotsu Shibutani and Kian M. Kwan, *Ethnic Stratification* (New York: Macmillan, 1965), pp. 450, 451.

Hungarian refugees, Weinstock indicates that occupations can be distinguished by their degree of emphasis on central or peripheral "role elements."[84] A laboratory technician would illustrate an occupational role dominated by central-role elements, since a person's success or failure is pretty much a matter of simple technical performance. However, a salesman or a business executive may find that all kinds of "peripheral" elements enter into the determination of his occupational success: his personal appearance, manner of speaking, maybe even the glamour or lack thereof of his wife. Weinstock accordingly hypothesizes—and tentatively confirms with a sample of Hungarian-Americans—that ethnic identity is most tenuous in those situations in which peripheral role elements are dominant.

---

[84]S. Alexander Weinstock, "Role Elements: A Link Between Acculturation and Occupational Status," *British Journal of Sociology,* 14(June, 1963):144–149; Weinstock, "Factors that Retard or Accelerate Acculturation."

CHAPTER 2
ETHNIC
LIFE
STYLES

THE WAY OF THE PEOPLE

The very term *ethnic group* suggests that an ethnic people can usually be characterized in terms of a culture or life style that is maintained by members of that group. To be a Navaho or an Afrikaner means, among other things, to adhere to a Navaho "way" or an Afrikaner "way" of thinking and acting.

The great variability of these cultural ways among different groups of people has been extensively documented in anthropological and other social scientific studies of human behavior. This is the theme of William Graham Sumner's classic *Folkways*[1] and of Ruth Benedict's more recent study of *Patterns of Culture*.[2]

Part of this variability is undoubtedly the result of the isolation of peoples from one another and of differential adaptations to environmental conditions in these isolated locales. But it can also be shown that ethnic groups

---

[1]William G. Sumner, *Folkways* (Boston: Ginn, 1906).
[2]Ruth Benedict, *Patterns of Culture* (New York: Mentor, 1959).

occupying the same general territory and subjected to very similar environmental conditions may develop or maintain traditional ways that are quite different from one another. An extended study that illustrates this point was the investigation by an anthropologist and a sociologist of an area of New Mexico called "Rimrock."[3] In one small area are found adjacent communities, each dominated by a different ethnic group—Navaho, Zuni, Texan (often called "Anglo" in the Southwest), Mormon, and Mexican-American. These communities vary sharply in the general "value-orientations" that were of interest to the investigators. They differ, for example, in the degree of individualism vs. concern for the welfare of the group that is incorporated in their ways of life. They also differ on the time perspectives that dominate the group's thinking: some ethnic groups are "present-oriented," defining as their ideal the fullest possible degree of day-to-day enjoyment of life, while others are "future-oriented," demanding the deferment of immediate pleasure in the interest of preparing for a better future. Variations in these cultural values had profound implications for the capacity of each group to deal with conditions in the harsh physical environment that all the groups shared. The Texan and Mormon communities, in contrast with the other three, were future-oriented in their life styles. However, the life style of the Texans was much more individualistic than that of their Mormon neighbors so that, while the Texans were equally as interested in projects to improve their future economic condition, they were less able than the Mormons to get together on projects that would accomplish this better future.

In another sort of "community" with several coexisting ethnic groups represented, one can see the same kind of tendency for social experience to be mediated by the perspectives provided by traditional ethnic life styles. In a Veterans Administration hospital in New York City, Zborowski found that members of four ethnic groups—Jewish Americans, Irish-Americans, Italian-Americans, and "Old Americans"—display quite different kinds of "pain behavior," and that these behaviors are symptomatic of general cultural themes in the life style of each ethnic group.[4] The "Old Americans," a future-oriented group of patients, treated their pains as a warning signal to seek medical assistance, and they expressed pain only

---

[3]Florence Kluckhohn and Fred L. Strodtbeck, *Variations in Value Orientations* (Evanston, Ill.: Row, Peterson, 1961).

[4]Mark Zborowski, *People in Pain* (San Francisco: Jossey-Bass, 1969).

when the expression was necessary to help medical people diagnose their ailments. The Jewish patients, though equally future-oriented (i.e., concerned about their future state of health) were more pessimistic about the capacity of medical people to make helpful diagnoses. They also were more prone to express pain as a way of eliciting the sympathetic attention of members of their families. The Italian-Americans, reflecting a "present-oriented" theme in Italian culture, saw the suffering and accompanying incapacitation as spoiling their enjoyment of life (for example, their inability to eat good food). They complained loudly about the pain until something was done to relieve it, after which, in the words of one nurse, they became very "sweet" patients. The Irish-Americans, like the "Old Americans," were relatively quiet about their pain. Their attitude reflected a characteristic stoicism in Irish culture whereby males prove their masculinity by showing that they can "take it" when faced with adversity.

The two studies just reviewed illustrate the fact that differences in ethnic life styles may have many consequences for the social experiences of people who adhere to these life styles. Partly for this reason, an analysis of ethnic life styles, how they differ and how they undergo modification, is a matter of interest to students of human behavior far beyond the interest of the specialist in the study of ethnic groups.

ACCULTURATION

So long as ethnic peoples live in isolation from one another or have only the casual or intermittent contacts of the tourist or the foreign trader, we can expect that ethnic life styles, evolved over long years of reinforcement of the rightness of "the way," will be maintained from generation to generation. When the outside contact becomes more penetrating, as when people who have inhabited a territory are invaded and overwhelmed by a foreign people, or when people of one ethnic group migrate with the intention of permanent residence in territories dominated by other ethnic groups, more radical changes in traditional life styles may be in the offing. This adoption of alien ways, called the process of *acculturation,* has probably been the major focus of interest in the study of ethnic life styles.

One reason for this interest has been the frequent observation that acculturation may have devastating consequences for the capacity of the ethnic life style to fulfill the needs or desires of people who have undergone this acculturating process. According to this view, the traditional life styles represented a delicate adaptation of a people to their conditions of existence. When alien cultural traits are introduced, they are inconsistent with the preexisting integration of cultural elements. American Indian life, for example, may have been seriously disorganized by the introduction of such European cultural traits as the concept of private property, the use of the horse for transportation, the drinking of intoxicating grain liquors, and the use of firearms in the settlement of disputes.[5] The native African, having grown up in a tribal way of life in which there is a careful articulation of meanings of different social experiences, is confused and miserable when introduced to European life styles that he encounters, for example, as an employee in a South African diamond mine.[6]

Selectivity of Acculturation

One of the more obvious facts about the acculturation of any ethnic people is that only some of the alien ways of groups with which they are in contact are adopted as ways of the group. Anthropologists, who have long noted this selective tendency in the acculturation process, point out that "cultural diffusion" is more rapid with some cultural traits than with others.[7] American Indians, for example, borrowed such European traits as the use of the horse for travel and of gunpowder for warfare long before they adopted European styles of religious or political behavior. The usual explanation for this selective acculturation has been the demonstrable utility of different cultural items to an acculturating people. Horses and European firearms were enriching additions to traditional Indian life styles, making possible an expansion on well-established patterns of hunting and warfare.[8] The more subtle aspects of European cultural values did not have this obvious utility for the Indians. In addition to this well-established principle of selectivity in acculturation, this section will describe three other less well-articulated principles, the outlines of which have begun to emerge from the extensive body of research on acculturating processes among specific ethnic groups.

---

[5]This a major theme of most of the studies of the impact of whites on traditional Indian ways that are described in Ralph Linton, (ed.), *Acculturation in Seven American Indian Tribes* (Gloucester, Mass.: Peter Smith, 1963).

[6]A moving account of this situation is given in Alan Paton's novel, *Cry, the Beloved Country* (New York: Scribner, 1948).

[7]Alfred A. Kroeber, *Anthropology,* rev. ed. (New York: Harcourt, Brace and World, 1948), pp. 411–418.

[8]Nancy O. Lurie, "The American Indian: Historical Background," in Stuart Levine and Nancy O. Lurie (eds.), *The American Indian Today* (DeLand, Fla.: Everett/Edwards, 1968).

1. A promising approach to the matter of selective acculturation emphasizes the problems of social adjustment of ethnic peoples who must live in proximity to members of other ethnic groups. Indians and Europeans in the United States and Canada, natives and Commonwealth immigrants in the British Isles—in these and countless other situations, the interethnic problem is partly one of getting along by making whatever accommodations in life style are necessary. If nothing else, linguistically differentiated peoples must find a common language for intergroup communication.

Since these sorts of adjustments in intergroup or interpersonal relations tend to fall most heavily on the weaker parties to the interaction, the problem is largely one of subordinate ethnic groups making necessary adjustments to the life styles of dominant groups. At this point, as elsewhere in this chapter, it will be useful to keep in mind Lieberson's distinction between two kinds of ethnic group contact in the world.[9] In the case of *migrant superordination,* an invading ethnic group establishes its control over the people in an invaded territory, typically subjecting the "natives" to the status of colonial subjects. In these situations, the adjustment problem of the colonized is that of acting—or appearing to act—in a manner that will not bring down the wrath of the powerful colonizers. In the case of *indigenous superordination,* members of an ethnic group come to a new country not as invaders, but as immigrants, subjecting themselves to the control of the "charter groups"[10] who have established their dominance over the territory. The adjustment problem of these ethnic immigrants is likely to be that of adopting enough of the ways of the ethnic "establishment" to enable themselves to make a living, to find their way around a city, etc.

These kinds of "adjustment" motives for acculturation tend toward acculturation of the more superficial or surface elements of a life style. The language, style of dress, and public "manners" of the dominant groups are imitated by the subordinate ones. Among Jews there is a jocular line, "Funny, he doesn't look Jewish!" The fact is, however, that partially acculturated Jews, or other ethnics, tend not to look ethnic (unless there is some strong racial basis to the ethnicity); nevertheless, they do retain important elements of ethnic life style in the matter of basic values, values that are

[9]Stanley Lieberson, "A Societal Theory of Race and Ethnic Relations," *American Sociological Review,* 26(December, 1961):902–910.

[10]John Porter, *The Vertical Mosaic* (Toronto: University of Toronto Press, 1965).

expressed in the privacy of relations with others of their own ethnic group. Outsiders are often unaware of these subtleties of unacculturated ethnic life styles and are surprised, for example, to learn that there is anything like an Indian life style among a people who, to all appearances, are fully acculturated.[11] This lack of appreciation by outsiders of a distinctive ethnic life style is sometimes used to argue, for example, that only a black can understand "soul," or that only a Slavic-American can understand Slavic ethnicity.[12]

Members of a number of subordinate ethnic groups have used this tendency toward a surface level of acculturation to manipulate to their advantage their relations with their ethnic "superiors." Dollard describes a "white folks manner" affected by southern blacks to satisfy the vanity of whites even though among themselves they ridicule white people.[13] Van den Berghe, writing on acculturation among African natives, notes a pattern of native conformity to the ways of their colonial masters as a matter of expediency, a conformity to specific norms without fundamental changes in traditional values.[14]

Occurring as it often does at this surface level, such acculturation frequently produces "bicultural" individuals who can get along quite well in either group by shifting their behavior when in one group or the other. Thus, Mayer describes the African native who can affect Western ways in "town" and revert easily to traditional tribal ways when the occasion demands.[15] Likewise, McFee reports a pattern of behavior in which certain

---

[11]Wahrhaftig and Thomas comment on the striking ignorance of most Oklahomans of the existence in their state of a flourishing traditional Indian culture, an ignorance in which the Indians have acquiesced as a condition of tolerance for their continued existence. Albert L. Wahrhaftig and Robert K. Thomas, "Renaissance and Repression: The Oklahoma Cherokee," *Trans-action,* 6(February, 1969):42–48.

[12]For a critical reaction to what is seen as a "Balkanization of political interests and cultural life," which one critic sees as implicit in such assumptions of the "new ethnicity," see Robert Alter, "A Fever of Ethnicity," *Commentary,* 53(June, 1972):68–73.

[13]John Dollard, *Caste and Class in a Southern Town* (Garden City, N.Y.: Doubleday, 1957).

[14]Pierre L. van den Berghe, "Toward a Sociology of Africa," *Social Forces,* 43(1964):11–18.

[15]Philip Mayer, *Townsmen or Tribesmen: Conservatism and the Process of Urbanization in a South Africa City,* 2d ed. (New York: Oxford University Press, 1971). Suttles describes in a similar way the behavior of some Italian-Americans in Chicago who work some distance from their neighborhood. While at work they are without much Italian consciousness, but upon their return from work they are "obliged to reassume their old world identity." Gerald D. Suttles, *Social Order of the Slum: Ethnicity and Territory in the Inner City* (Chicago: University of Chicago Press, 1968), p. 105.

Blackfeet Indians of Montana retain tribal ways while at the same time adhering to acculturated white ways.[16] Middle-class Mexican-Americans in the Southwest reportedly attempt to develop the "best of both ways" by speaking both good English and good Spanish.[17] Lieberson shows, in the case of French Canadians in Montreal, how this bicultural pattern may be perpetuated over several generations.[18] Although most French Canadians learn English as a second language in order to adjust to Canadian social conditions, those who learn English in this manner typically do *not,* as is true of most ethnic groups in the United States, transmit the newly learned language to their children as a "first language"; rather, the bicultural pattern of French as the primary language is maintained generation after generation.[19]

2. Another basis for selective acculturation is the fact that some traditional ethnic ways can more easily be retained, because the continuation of their practice does not jeopardize the ethnic's accommodation to the dominant culture pattern. American Jews, for example, have learned that the traditional ritual observances (kosher food practices, a non-Sunday Sabbath, etc.) are detriments to easy adjustment to the Gentile social world, and most such practices decline with acculturation.[20] The only exceptions involve those religious observances that fit easily into American social patterns. The increased celebration of Hanukkah, for example, traditionally a minor Jewish holiday, reflects the ease with which this holiday

---

[16]Malcolm McFee, "The 150% Man, a Product of Blackfeet Acculturation," *American Anthropologist,* 70(December, 1968):1096–1103. On a similar theme of bicultural socialization among adolescent boys on a Fox Indian reservation, see Steven Polgar, "Biculturation of Mesquakie Teenage Boys," *American Anthropologist,* 62(April, 1960):217–235

[17]Ozzie Simmons, "The Mutual Images and Expectations of Anglo-Americans and Mexican-Americans," *Daedalus,* 90(Spring, 1961):286–299.

[18]Stanley Lieberson, "Bilingualism in Montreal: A Demographic Analysis," *American Journal of Sociology,* 71(July, 1965):10–25.

[19]A similar pattern for Mexican-Americans in San Antonio, Texas, is reported in R. L. Skrabanek, "Language Maintenance Among Mexican-Americans," *International Journal of Comparative Sociology,* 11(December, 1970):272–282; and for the German-, French-, Italian-, and Romansch-speaking peoples of Switzerland in Kurt Mayer, "Cultural Pluralism and Linguistic Equilibrium in Switzerland," *American Sociological Review,* 16(1951):157–163.

[20]Marshall Sklare and Joseph Greenblum, *Jewish Identity on the Suburban Frontier* (New York: Basic Books, 1967), chap. 3; Sidney Goldstein and Calvin Goldscheider, *Jewish-Americans: Three Generations in a Jewish Community* (Englewood Cliffs, N.J.: Prentice-Hall, 1968), chap. 9.

can be related to the observance of Christmas by American Christians.[21] Another instance of this kind of adaptation of ritual observances to dominant cultural patterns has been found in a Shoshone Indian tribe. Traditionally a very ritualistic people, the Shoshoni have become accustomed to holding a number of their ritual events on the national holiday of the country, the Fourth of July.[22]

3. Acculturation selectivity also arises from the fact that ethnic group members are not equally exposed to all aspects of the life style of other ethnic groups. Colonized people are exposed to a group of colonizers who may be a rather special breed in their countries of origin. Immigrant peoples' first exposure to alien contacts are likely to be immigration and welfare officials or labor contractors.

A case of selective acculturation based on selective exposure to alien ways has been reported for a group of Navaho Indians in the western United States.[23] Navaho men, somewhat ironically in light of the historical cowboy-Indian conflict, tend to affect cowboy dress and manner and to participate actively in rodeo events. This life style is, of course, a part of a western subculture, sometimes referred to as "drugstore cowboys," but Navaho men seem to outdo whites in their interest in this pattern. Downs suggests that this is explainable by the severe isolation of the rural Navaho and the fact that, in their infrequent trips to town, they are likely to be attending a rodeo or some other cultural event celebrating the history of the Wild West. The Indians of the American West may thus be exposed to a biased view of white American life styles, just as many people outside the United States gain a slanted view of American life through the predominance of Westerns among exported Hollywood films.

An extension of this line of analysis should generate the prediction that, when ethnic group members *do* experience a more intimate acquaintance with the day-to-day behavior of persons from other ethnic groups, more fundamental changes in life style will occur. This interpretation could be given to the findings of a study of acculturation of Mandan-Hidatsa Indians

---

[21]Sklare and Greenblum, *Jewish Identity,* pp. 55–59; Goldstein and Goldscheider, *Jewish-Americans,* pp. 201–203.

[22]Jack S. Harris, "The White Knife Shoshoni of Nevada," in Linton (ed.), *Acculturation in Seven American Tribes,* pp. 108, 109.

[23]James F. Downs, "The Cowboy and the Lady: Models as a Determinant of the Rate of Acculturation Among the Pinon Navajo," *Kroeber Anthropological Society Papers,* no. 29 (Fall, 1963), pp. 53–67.

to white ways in a very basic feature of traditional Indian values: the emphasis on interpersonal generosity.[24] Bruner found that in every family in which there was a significant movement away from this value of generosity, there was an intermarriage with a white person. Almost all those Indians who adhered to the traditional generosity ethic had not been exposed to such intimate acquaintance with an "outsider."

Variations in Ethnic Acculturation

Whether an ethnic group preserves its traditional life style or alters it totally or selectively under the influence of contact with alien ways is obviously a matter of great variation. This variation can be analyzed by beginning with two observations: (1) There is variation from society to society in the degree to which ethnic groups are expected to acculturate in the direction of the life styles of the dominant groups. (2) *Within* a given society there is variation in the tendency of different ethnic groups to acculturate or to preserve traditional ways. These two dimensions of variability will now be examined.

Variations between societies. Whether or not an ethnic group undergoes change in the life styles of its members when under the influence of contact with an alien culture depends partly on the willingness or unwillingness of the dominant groups to encourage assimilation by the subordinate ones, and partly on the capacity of the dominant groups to enforce these expectations. Gordon discusses this variation in terms of competing ideologies that have risen and fallen from prominence throughout the history of the United States.[25] The ideology of *Anglo conformity* demands that all ethnic groups acculturate to the dominant Anglo-Saxon life style of the country. *Cultural pluralism* involves the expectation that ethnic peoples will retain their traditional ethnic ways. These contrasting ideologies derive partly from contrasting points of view about the requirements for societal functioning. *Dominant-group conformity* (to use an alternative term to *Anglo-conformity* that will cover other situations) is

---

[24]Edward M. Bruner, "Primary Group Experience and the Process of Acculturation," *American Anthropologist,* 58(1956):53–67. For a broad discussion of the effects of intermarriage on Indian tribes, as well as the reverse process of "Indianization" of intermarried and captured non-Indians, see A. Irving Hallowell, "American Indians, White and Black: The Phenomenon of Transculturation," *Current Anthropology,* 4(December, 1963):519–531.

[25]Milton Gordon, *Assimilation in American Life* (New York: Oxford University Press, 1964).

supported by a view of society that approaches the *totalitarian* in that there can be only *one* basic value system to which all people must adhere. *Consensus* is a vital condition of societal existence, and there must be social control or constraint to insure that "deviant" ways are eradicated or limited. As an ideology, pluralism is most often adhered to by persons with a *democratic* view of society in which the individual members of the society have the freedom to pursue any life style that appeals to them (provided it inflicts no harm on others), and in which all viewpoints are given the opportunity to be represented when decisions must be made on unified social action.[26]

Even though most Americans conceive of their country as a democracy, the expectation of Anglo-conformity has been a recurring feature of the treatment of ethnic groups in the United States. This is perhaps best illustrated at the level of official policy by the legislation that excluded Oriental immigration and, in the 1920s, set immigration quotas aimed primarily at limiting immigration from eastern and southern Europe, the rationale being that such peoples were less desirable because they were thought to be less assimilable to Anglo-Saxon cultural ways.[27] Although this legislation was partly the result of rigorous lobbying by groups with vested interests—labor unions, for example, were opposed to the importation of "cheap labor"—there was broad popular support for this legislation.[28] It reflected with accuracy a trend in the American mentality that surfaced in the late nineteenth century: a fear of the influence of "alien" ways and a belief in the existence of subversive conspiracies organized by those aliens.[29]

The expectation of dominant group conformity is not limited, of course, to the kind of indigenous superordination experienced by immigrants to the United States and other countries. Similar variation can be seen in

---

[26]For a discussion of these contrasting viewpoints, see Pierre L. van den Berghe, "Dialectic and Functionalism: Toward a Theoretical Synthesis," *American Sociological Review,* 28 (October, 1963):685–705.

[27]George E. Simpson and J. Milton Yinger, *Racial and Cultural Minorities,* 4th ed. (New York: Harper & Row, 1972), pp. 114–123.

[28]For a description of the large number of groups in opposition to Asian immigration in California, see Roger Daniels and Spencer Olin, Jr. (eds.), *Racism in California* (New York: Macmillan, 1972), pp. 55–180.

[29]The strongly antiforeign sentiment that attended the riot in Chicago's Haymarket Square in 1886 is described in Stephan Thernstrom and Richard Sennett (eds.), *Nineteenth-Century Cities: Essays in the New Urban History* (New Haven: Yale University Press, 1969), pp. 386–420.

colonizing migrations. The problem for colonizers has been primarily one of gaining sufficient control of the "natives" to make possible an effective exploitation of the human and material resources of the colony. British policy, reflecting perhaps the democratic ethos of the country, favored the practice of "indirect rule." Under this policy, the natives were encouraged to maintain their traditional life styles with, for example, court systems and legislative bodies that made and enforced the laws in terms of the natives' own traditions.[30] Dutch policy has been similar to that of the British, whereas Spanish, Portuguese, and French policies have supported a more direct effort to remake native life styles in the image of their European colonizers. Van den Berghe makes the point, however, that these ideological differences tend to have little effect on actual practice. Portuguese and French colonies in Africa were as "indirectly" ruled as were the British ones; British colonies in the Americas were as thoroughly Europeanized as the Portuguese, French, and Spanish ones.[31] The crucial difference, van den Berghe believes, is that, in Africa, Europeans were never able to overwhelm the natives (except in South Africa), thus cultural pluralism was dictated as a matter of expediency. In the Americas, native populations were quickly decimated by a combination of the white man's military power and his diseases. Europeans therefore had the power as well as the inclination to impose their life styles on the natives.[32]

On occasion, colonizers have vacillated in their policies of dealing with peoples in conquered territories. The attitude of the United States government toward the native Indian population illustrates the possibility of an ambiguous policy and of second and third thoughts about the desirability

---

[30]E. Franklin Frazier, *Race and Culture Contacts in the Modern World* (New York: Knopf, 1957), pp. 191–202.

[31]Pierre L. van den Berghe, "Racialism and Assimilation in Africa and the Americas," *Southwestern Journal of Anthropology,* 19(Winter, 1963):424–432. It might be noted, however, that these policy differences between British and French colonialism may have made a difference in actual practice in, for example, the West Indies, where the assimilationist aims in French Martinique contrast with the more pluralistic tendencies in the former British colonies in the same area. Chester L. Hunt and Lewis Walker, *Ethnic Dynamics* (Homewood, Ill.: Dorsey Press, 1974), chap. 7.

[32]The decimation of native peoples has been shown to have occurred not only among the Indian people of North America but also among the aboriginal inhabitants of Australia and New Zealand. A. Grenfell Price, *White Settlers and Native Peoples* (Melbourne: Georgian House, 1950). The devastating effect on the natives of one kind of "European" disease has led to the grim irony of the observation that what the Europeans brought to the natives was "syphilization."

of a line of policy. For fifty years or so after the "pacification" of the Indians and their confinement to reservations, the Bureau of Indian Affairs pursued a policy of administration that, while ostensibly recognizing the autonomy of Indians to live their own lives within the limits of their treaties with the United States, in fact operated to discourage Indian autonomy and to make the Indians, in effect, wards of the government of the United States.[33] This policy of "deculturation"[34] brought vigorous objection, not the least of which came from those numerous American anthropologists who studied the Indian professionally and developed for themselves a public role as "defenders of the traditionally Indian."[35] The pluralistic side of the American mentality asserted itself in the policies introduced by John Collier, President Franklin Roosevelt's appointee as Commissioner of Indian Affairs. These policies emphasized Indian cultural autonomy and the development of local communities to encourage more Indian people to seek careers within the Indian community.[36] More recently, however, the whole conception of separate Indian reservations has come under attack from Anglo-conformists who claim that it is discriminatory against individual Indians to limit their personal ambitions to the narrow confines of the Indian reservation.[37] As a consequence, a more or less vigorous program of "termination" of government administration of Indian affairs has been pursued. Most Indian leaders have been strongly opposed to the termination policy, seeing it as the latest in a long list of grievances against the American government in violation of treaty provisions with Indian tribes.[38]

The obverse of dominant-group conformity is seen in societies in which acculturating pressures are minimized because there is no one dominant ethnic group. For example, an ethnic group may move into a *frontier* situation where there is either no population or a native population so

---

[33]D'Arcy McNickle, "Process of Compulsion: The Search for a Policy of Administration in Indian Affairs," *American Indigena*, 17(July, 1957):261–270.

[34]Judith R. Kramer, *The American Minority Community* (New York: Thomas Y. Crowell, 1970), pp. 189–212.

[35]Murray L. Wax, *Indian Americans* (Englewood Cliffs, N.J.: Prentice-Hall, 1971), pp. 55, 56.

[36]For a description of what was called a "new day for Indians," see Price, *White Settlers and Native Peoples*, pp. 41–58.

[37]See the exchange between Robert Manners and John Collier reprinted in Deward A. Walker, Jr., *The Emergent Native Americans* (Boston: Little, Brown, 1972), pp. 124–143.

[38]Wax, *Indian Americans*, p. 147.

weak or scattered that acculturation is no issue for the newcomers. Thus, Borrie notes that German migrants to Australia in the nineteenth century found no "Anglo" or other dominant group whose cultural standards were to be adopted, so they had no choice but to set up essentially German institutions on Australian soil.[39] Once British domination was established, however, later immigrant groups such as the Italians were subjected to all the pressures to adopt these Anglo ways. In a study of Italian immigrants to the United States who settled in the West rather than in large eastern cities, Rolle observed the similar point that Italians in the frontier West were relatively free from Anglo-conformity pressures, so that Italian ways persisted in the West for a relatively long time.[40]

Not all frontier situations are equally conducive to resistance to dominant-group conformity. If members of an immigrant group are scattered along a broad frontier, they will be less able to import home-country life styles. Glazer thus contrasts the failure of German-Americans (largely because of their scattered pattern of settlement) to establish much-desired "New Germanies" in America and the relative success of some Norwegian-Americans and of the Mormons in establishing such communities.[41]

In other societies noted for their tolerance of ethnic differences, the situation may be one in which there are two or more dominant groups, none of which is able clearly to establish its right to provide the standards for acculturation of immigrant peoples. The well-known pluralism of Canadian society is probably related to the bicultural character of Canada with two dominant groups, English and French.[42] Some cities in the United States are noted for having populations so ethnically heterogeneous that there is really no one standard for the acculturation of ethnic groups. According to Glazer and Moynihan, this heterogeneity accounts for the failure of ethnic groups in New York City to "melt" into a homogeneous life style.[43] Similarly, in a study of Mexican-Americans in East Chicago,

---

[39]W. D. Borrie, *Italians and Germans in Australia* (Melbourne: F. W. Cheshire, 1954).

[40]Andrew F. Rolle, *The Immigrant Upraised* (Norman: University of Oklahoma Press, 1968).

[41]Nathan Glazer, "Ethnic Groups in America: From National Culture to Ideology," in Morroe Berger, Theodore Abel, and Charles H. Page (eds.), *Freedom and Control in Modern Society* (New York: Octagon Books, 1964), pp. 158–173.

[42]Anthony H. Richmond, "Immigration and Pluralism in Canada," *International Migration Review,* 5(Fall, 1969):5–24.

[43]Nathan Glazer and Daniel P. Moynihan, *Beyond the Melting Pot* (Cambridge, Mass.: M.I.T. Press, 1970.)

Indiana, it is suggested that one reason for the lack of acculturation of this ethnic group is the city's polyglot mixture of ethnic peoples—European Catholics, blacks, Puerto Ricans—indeed almost everything except the white Anglo-Saxon Protestants who are so often characterized as the upholders of Anglo-conformity.[44]

Variations between ethnic groups. Any generalizations about pluralism or dominant group conformity in a given society will have to be severely qualified by the fact of variation between the different ethnic groups in that society. By way of explanation of these differences, we shall examine three kinds of variables—exposure, sensitivity, and status.

Exposure. Acculturation assumes a degree of *contact* between ethnic peoples with diverse life styles, whether this contact involves direct physical presence or less direct hearsay stories that are told about peoples of alien cultures. It must be noted, however, that even peoples who have the technical means at hand to be informed about the ways of other peoples may be isolated from actual effective contacts. Several typical situations of such isolation are described below.

First, ethnic groups who might provide the model for acculturation of other groups may deliberately conceal basic features of their life styles with the effect, intended or unintended, of preventing their imitation by others. For instance, the relatively few well-educated Africans in a European colony or former colony may find a high degree of exclusion of themselves from intimate contact with colonists of higher status.[45] This European exclusiveness is symbolized, for example, among the French colonial residents of Dakar, Senegal, who found ways of segregating their residences in exclusive parts of the city.[46]

---

[44]Julian Samora and Richard Lamanna, "Mexican-Americans in a Midwest Metropolis," in Bernard E. Segal (ed.), *Racial and Ethnic Relations,* 2nd ed. (New York: Thomas Y. Crowell, 1972), pp. 230–242.

[45]Leo Kuper, *An African Bourgeoisie: Race, Class and Politics in South Africa* (New Haven: Yale University Press, 1965).

[46]Paul Mercier, "The European Community of Dakar," in Pierre L. van den Berghe (ed.), *Africa: Social Problems of Change and Conflict* (San Francisco: Chandler, 1965), pp. 294–296.

Second, ethnic groups may discourage their own acculturation to alien ways by isolating themselves in some degree from contact with people outside their own group. The development of enclaves of immigrants desiring to maintain an "old country" life style can partly be explained on this basis.[47] Even more clearly, radical religious sects (in America, Mennonites, Amish, Hutterites, and Mormons, for example) may feel the need to shield their children from the acculturating influence of attendance at public schools in their areas. Sometimes these sects come into rather vigorous conflict with people from the dominant cultures, the level of conflict depending somewhat on whether dominant group conformity or cultural pluralism prevails in the area.[48] If forced to make concessions to acculturating forces, these groups tend to limit the concession as much as possible.[49] Thus, Hutterites in the United States and Canada are described as satisfying government education requirements by maintaining an "English school" alongside the ethnically oriented "German school," but they maintain a tight rein on the English teacher's relations with her pupils, lest the hapless "school marm" become a source of corruption of the colony's youth.[50]

Third, apart from any specific intention of such isolation, the particular situation of ethnic group members may minimize contact with alien ways. The concentration of Chinese-Americans in the laundry business has been described as having an isolating effect on the laundryman, whose work brings him in contact with non-Chinese only in the stereotyped "no tickee, no washee" relation of customer and small business owner.[51] Likewise,

---

[47]Kramer, *The American Minority Community,* pp. 79, 80.

[48]The search of a Hutterite colony for a congenial environment, which they found and then lost in Canada and Mexico successively, and are now looking for in Central and South America, is described in Harry L. Sawatzky, *They Sought a Country* (Berkeley: University of California Press, 1971).

[49]On the "bending" of Hutterite rules under the pressure for Anglo-conformity, see Joseph Eaton, "Controlled Acculturation: A Survival Technique of the Hutterites," *American Sociological Review,* 17(June, 1952):331–340.

[50]John A. Hostetler and Gertrude E. Huntington, *The Hutterites in North America* (New York: Holt, Rinehart and Winston, 1967), pp. 98–100; John W. Bennett, *Hutterian Brethren* (Palo Alto, Calif.: Stanford University Press, 1967), p. 101.

[51]Paul C. P. Siu, "The Isolation of the Chinese Laundryman," in Ernest W. Burgess and Donald J. Bogue (eds.), *Contributions to Urban Sociology* (Chicago: University of Chicago Press, 1964), pp. 429–442.

the "gang employment" of Mexican-Americans as migrant labor or for other kinds of employment has had such an isolating effect.[52]

Sensitivity. As any frustrated professor knows who exposes his students to reading and lecture material only to discover that the exposure did not take, exposure is a necessary but not a sufficient condition of learning. In addition, there must be a sufficient level of motivation to learn and an identification with the learning process.

Members of many ethnic groups maintain a greater identification with the ways of their ethnic group than with the new ways to which they are being exposed. A number of observers of efforts to teach English and other aspects of middle-class Anglo-Saxon life styles to American Indians on reservations have noted this kind of resistance to acculturation. Educators often err in attributing educational backwardness to the "cultural deprivation" in the homes of Indian children when, in fact, their homes may offer a rich cultural heritage to which the Anglo school curriculum is seen as simply irrelevant.[53]

Observers of acculturation among immigrant groups to the United States have often commented on the variation in degree of receptivity to efforts at Anglo-conformity. One factor in this variation can be found in the different intentions of ethnic groups in immigrating to the United States or to another country. Some, like the Jews, Armenians, and Russians in "Yankee City," have "burned their bridges behind them" with no serious intention of ever returning to their countries of origin.[54] Others, like the Italians, Greeks, Poles, and French Canadians in "Yankee City," the French

---

[52]Leonard Broom and Eshref Shevky, "Mexican-Americans in the United States: A Problem in Social Differentiation," *Sociology and Social Research,* 36(January–February, 1952):150–158.

[53]For Canadian Indians, see A. D. Fisher, "White Rites Versus Indian Rights," *Trans-action,* 7 (November, 1969):29–33, and Charles W. Hobart, "Eskimo Education in the Canadian Arctic," *Canadian Review of Sociology and Anthropology,* 7(February, 1970):49–69. For American Indians, see Robert V. Dumont, Jr., and Murray L. Wax, "Cherokee School Society and the Intercultural Classroom," *Human Organization,* 28(Fall, 1969):217–226; and Bruce A. Chadwick, "The Inedible Feast," in Howard M. Bahr, Bruce A. Chadwick, and Robert C. Day (eds.), *Native Americans Today* (New York: Harper & Row, 1972), pp. 131–145.

[54]W. Lloyd Warner and Leo Srole, *The Social Systems of American Ethnic Groups* (New Haven: Yale University Press, 1945), p. 106.

Canadians in Burlington, Vermont,[55] Italian-Americans generally,[56] Puerto Ricans in New York City,[57] the Chinese in California and throughout Southeast Asia,[58] the Irish in Britain,[59] and the Mexican-Americans in East Chicago, Indiana,[60] maintain a "sojourner" attitude toward their residence in a new country. Since they intend eventually to return to the old country to (as in the case of some Italian-Americans) "settle the score" with their rivals back home,[61] these people are little concerned if their alien ways are scorned by the strangers among whom they live.

Another source of continued sensitivity to "back home" styles of life is the continuous influx in some immigrant situations of many "fresh" or unacculturated members of the particular ethnic group. The perpetual arrival of Puerto Ricans in New York City or of Mexican-Americans in many parts of the United States furnishes members of those ethnic groups with recurring reminders of life styles in their countries of origin.[62]

Status.   The likelihood that members of ethnic groups will acculturate to the life styles of the dominant ethnic groups in their area is partly a function of the relative statuses of the ethnic groups in question. Sometimes a reluctance to adopt alien ways is based on a sense of the superiority of one's own ethnic group. The haughty disdain of European colonizers for the "primitive" ways of the natives is a striking example. Long after the United States had attained political independence from Great Britain, many Britons thought of Americans as inferior "colonials," and many

[55]Elin L. Anderson, *We Americans* (New York: Russell and Russell, 1935), pp. 26, 27.

[56]Joseph Lopreato, *Italian Americans* (New York: Random House, 1970).

[57]Joseph P. Fitzpatrick, *Puerto Rican Americans* (Englewood Cliffs, N.J.: Prentice-Hall, 1971).

[58]A number of references to soujourner attitudes of "overseas Chinese" throughout the world and a specific contrast of the attitudes toward immigration of Chinese and Japanese in California may be found in Stanford M. Lyman, "Contrast in the Community Organization of Chinese and Japanese in North America," *Canadian Review of Sociology and Anthropology,* 5(May, 1968):51–67.

[59]John Archer Jackson, *The Irish in Britain* (London: Routledge and Kegan Paul, 1963).

[60]Samora and Lamanna, "Mexican Americans in a Midwest Metropolis."

[61]Lopreato, *Italian Americans,* p. 32.

[62]Fitzpatrick, *Puerto Rican Americans;* Samora and Lamanna, "Mexican Americans in a Midwest Metropolis."

nineteenth-century British immigrants to the United States found the Anglo ways of the Americans to be too un-British to be worthy of respect or imitation.[63]

At the other extreme are ethnic groups of derogated status who, while willing enough to undergo acculturation, find that their attempts to imitate dominant-group ways expose them to ridicule and rejection. In these terms, Shoshoni Indians are more successful than the Northern Arapaho in acquiring the life style of a cowhand on an Anglo-managed ranch.[64] The Shoshoni are thought by the Anglos to be more competent at work tasks, thus Shoshoni are more readily accepted for ranch jobs. A close parallel to this situation is found in Canada, where the acculturating efforts of the Eskimo population are better received than are those of the Indian people, largely, it seems, because the Eskimos are able to command more respect from the "Euro-Canadian" community.[65]

The reaction to such rejection by the dominant groups may well be a defensive reversion to traditional ethnic group ways as a protection against the wounds of rejection. A study of several different groups of foreign students at the University of California, Los Angeles, found that the national status of the country of origin was an important factor in the attitudes of these students toward American life. Those who experienced rejection as citizens of "inferior" countries developed hostile attitudes toward the United States that made their acculturation more unlikely.[66]

In the same vein, Hannerz suggests that the "soul" orientation of American blacks is a reaction to the numerous rebuffs blacks suffer at the hands of whites.[67] Thought to be a life style attainable only by blacks, soul is seen as a superior style that assures the unsuccessful black that he is actually successful. If rejection of acculturation has this kind of effect, then it may

---

[63]Rowland T. Berthoff, *British Immigrants in Industrial America, 1790–1950* (Cambridge: Harvard University Press, 1953), pp. 135–140.

[64]Stanton K. Tefft, "Task Experience and Intertribal Value Differences on the Wind River Reservation," *Social Forces,* 49(June, 1971):604–614.

[65]Robert J. Dryfoos, Jr., "Two Tactics for Ethnic Survival: Eskimo and Indian," *Trans-action,* 7(January, 1970):51–54.

[66]Richard T. Morris, *The Two-Way Mirror* (Minneapolis: University of Minnesota Press, 1961).

[67]Ulf Hannerz, "The Rhetoric of Soul: Identification in Negro Sociality," *Race,* 9(April, 1968):453–465.

be that most of the exclusiveness of life styles among subordinate ethnic groups originated in an earlier situation in which ethnic group members, willing to acculturate to another life style, have been "burned" and have developed the resolve not to repeat the mistake of attempting to imitate alien ways.

REVITALIZATION

Although the purity of ethnic life styles is often diminished in the process of acculturation, sometimes it happens that ethnic groups move in the direction of greater concern with the maintenance or resurrection of a traditional life style. Since these movements usually follow and are a reaction to a period of acculturation, they may be called *revitalization* movements, attempts to recapture some of the traditional ethnic ways that were once taken so much for granted. Some of the impetus for such revitalizations has been discussed in the previous chapter as a matter of "third-generation return." However, such revitalizations are by no means limited to the behavior of third-generation immigrants, as one will quickly realize in observing such recent developments in the United States as the renewed interest of blacks in "black culture," of American Indians in Indian traditions, of Chicanos in "La Raza."

Like acculturation, revitalization is a process that tends to be highly selective in those traits that are emphasized in the revival.[68] When several "tribes" or subsections of an ethnic group develop a common ethnic tradition, they often must choose among several rather diverse ethnic traditions. For instance, the recent Pan-Indian revitalization movement took as the symbol of what is Indian the war-bonneted figure of a Sioux —a Plains Indian—even though many tribes had no traditional experience with that way of life.[69] Perhaps it is because of the romanticizing of this Indian type in the lore of the dominant society that Indians have chosen this highly honorable model as a symbol of a tradition they wish to revive.

In the case of both the American Indian and the black American it can probably be said in fairness that most of the members of these ethnic groups have no direct knowledge of the "tradition" they are revitalizing.

---

[68]Ralph Linton, "Nativistic Movements," *American Anthropologist,* 45(1943):230–240.
[69]Wax, *Indian Americans,* p. 149.

This recalls the recurring joke about the Indian tribe that has forgotten how to dance and, when asked to do so by a visitor, must consult an anthropologist's earlier ethnographic account of this traditional ritual. This is an unexpected role, perhaps, for the "defender of the traditionally Indian," who thought he was studying natives for the benefit of science and found himself the tribe's own chronicler. Likewise it would seem that few American blacks have more than the vaguest notion of the content of the traditional "Afro" culture with which their own life style is being identified. All of which points up the fact that revitalization may be more than just a repetition of the ethnic past of a group. The filter of time is likely to produce a new ethnic person who is proud of his or her heritage but who resembles only slightly the dead heroes being honored.

How and why do revitalization movements occur? Usually they develop following a period of serious disorganization resulting from recent acculturation by a group. A typical case is the formation of the Long House religion, which centered around the vision of a Seneca Indian named Handsome Lake who, apparently in a drunken frenzy, received a number of supernatural messages commanding Indians to give up such evil white ways as the use of intoxicants and to return to a purified Indian way of life.[70] The Ghost Dance religion, which swept in two waves through western tribes in the 1870s and again in the 1890s, carried a similar message of renunciation of white ways. The new religion tended to be most widespread among those tribes that had experienced the most radical acculturation to white ways and the most severe disruption of their traditional life styles.[71]

Another explanation, which involves more subtle psychological considerations, is Mason's view that the acculturating native in colonial situations is subjected to a disillusioning process of "betrayal" when he adopts Western ways on the implicit promise of personal advancement, only to find ultimately that his Western mentors no longer believe in the values they are espousing for him.[72] This leads the acculturated native—much as

---

[70]Wax, *Indian Americans,* pp. 136–138.

[71]Bernard Barber, "Acculturation and Messianic Movements," *American Sociological Review,* 6(1941):663–669. A more recent study similarly indicates that "cultural deprivation" (as measured, for example, by the loss of the buffalo as a cultural resource) was a frequent experience of those Plains Indian tribes in which the Ghost Dance flourished. Michael P. Carroll, "Revitalization Movements and Social Structure: Some Quantitative Tests," *American Sociological Review,* 40(June, 1975):389–401.

[72]Mason, *Patterns of Dominance,* chap. 3.

it has led the black American disillusioned with "civil rights" movements on his behalf—to launch a "search for a pedigree." This search may culminate in "traditionalist" movements that may generate mythical versions of the ethnic past, such as the fantasies of Black Muslims and Black Jews that blacks are descended from Islamic or Jewish origins.[73]

---

[73]C. Eric Lincoln, *The Black Muslims in America* (Boston: Beacon Press, 1961); Howard Brotz, *The Black Jews of Harlem: The Dilemmas of Negro Leadership* (New York: Free Press of Glencoe, 1964).

CHAPTER 3
ETHNIC COMMUNITY

Ethnic groups, like any other kind of human grouping, can be looked at from a perspective that emphasizes the quality of relationships among group members. In our understandable preoccupation with intergroup relations—what happens, for instance, when black meets white or Jew meets Gentile—we are sometimes prone to forget that it may be just as interesting to understand some reasons for the great variety of ways in which people relate to their ethnic peers. The sociological concept of *community* seems to provide a good starting point for the analysis of ethnic intragroup relations. A human community, ethnic or otherwise, involves at least two major notions about what constitutes a community: (a) a degree of *unity* among community members, reflected in feelings of comradeship and, often, feelings of hostility toward members of other communities; and (b) a strong *self-sufficiency* in the lives of community members, that is, a dependence of community members on one another and a relative independence from agencies outside the limits of the community.

These features of a human community represent conditions that are found in varying degrees among different groups of people. No ethnic group seems to fulfill all the criteria of community if these criteria are applied stringently. On the other hand, no ethnic group is so lacking in unity and self-sufficiency that it has none of the features of community. Ethnic community is thus a *variable,* and the sociological problem is that of generalizing about those conditions that encourage or discourage community relationships among members of an ethnic group.

ETHNIC UNITY AND CLEAVAGE

If there is a tendency—as we shall discuss in Chapters 5 and 6—for ethnic groups in contact with one another to establish relations of dominance and subordination between themselves, there should be a correlative tendency for members of an ethnic group to be drawn together by the fact of their common persecution or by their common need to preserve a united front to maintain their dominance. This expectation is in line with a familiar sociological principle: that outgroup conflict tends to produce ingroup solidarity.[1] Benjamin Franklin gave classic expression to this motivation for cohesion in time of crisis: "We must all hang together, else we shall all hang separately." On this consideration, we should expect strong ingroup feeling among peoples who nourish long histories of persecution —for example, European Jews for many generations, or American Indians with their grievances arising from unfulfilled treaties with the United States. Likewise, people with a long history of colonial domination, such as the British, would be expected to feel strong solidarity as a group bearing the "white man's burden."

That the matter of differential ethnic solidarity is more complicated than this is illustrated in the case of American Jews. Lewin described a typical pattern of feelings of Jewish people toward one another as involving a degree of "self-hatred," as evidenced by the fact, for example, that many Jewish people feel uncomfortable in the presence of other Jews, especially if they perceive the latter's behavior as somehow "objectionable."[2] A study of "identification" of Jews with their Jewishness as related to their positive or negative feelings toward fellow Jews found not only that many people with a strong Jewish consciousness had negative feelings toward

---

[1] Georg Simmel, *Conflict,* trans. by Kurt H. Wolff and *The Web of Group-Affiliation,* trans. by Reinhard Bendix (Glencoe, Ill.: Free Press, 1955); see also Lewis A. Coser, *The Function of Social Conflict* (Glencoe, Ill.: Free Press, 1956).

[2] Kurt Lewin, *Resolving Social Conflicts* (New York: Harper, 1948), pp. 186–200.

other Jews, but also that there was even a slight positive correlation between Jewish identification and anti-Semitic feelings.[3] Indications of "anti-
Semitic" feelings have also begun to emerge in the state of Israel. In that
country, it has been noted, the early arrivals experienced a strong sense
of Jewish solidarity by virtue of the extreme threat to the life of the young
state. With some degree of "normalization" of life in that country, however, there has developed increased hostility between, for example, Jews
of European and of non-European (mostly North African) origin.[4]

Similar findings of negative or ambivalent attitudes toward ethnic peers
have been reported for other "persecuted" ethnic groups. In the African
kingdom of Ruanda, numerically dominant Hutu people share with the
socially dominant Tutsi the view that the Tutsi monopolize most of the
better human qualities and the Hutu most of the worst.[5] Psychologists
studying American Negroes have developed a substantial literature on
ethnic preference. Earlier findings showed, for example, that black children preferred white rather than black dolls when given the choice.[6] More
recent evidence has indicated a change in this pattern, as black children
begin to prefer black dolls, reflecting, perhaps, the impact of the recent
"black is beautiful" theme in this ethnic group.[7] When ethnic groups
continue to see themselves as occupying a derogated status, they tend to
hold quite realistic views of the value imputed to their ethnic group. Thus,

---

[3]Joseph Adelson, "A Study of Minority Group Authoritarianism," in Marshall Sklare (ed.),
The Jews: Social Patterns of an American Group (Glencoe, Ill.: Free Press, 1958), pp.
475–492.

[4]Judith T. Shuval, "Emerging Patterns of Ethnic Strain In Israel," *Social Forces,* 40(May,
1962):323–330; Percy Cohen, "Ethnic Group Differences in Israel," *Race,* 9(January, 1968):
303–310.

[5]Philip Mason, *Patterns of Dominance* (New York: Oxford University Press, 1970), pp.
13–20.

[6]See, for example, Mary Ellen Goodman, *Race Awareness in Young Children* (Cambridge,
Mass.: Addison-Wesley, 1952). In a similar way, Indian children on an Ontario reservation
have shown these feelings of inferiority in their preference for white over Indian dolls. Carl
F. Grindstaff, Wilda Galloway, and Joanne Nixon, "Racial and Cultural Identification Among
Canadian Indian Children," *Phylon,* 34(December, 1973):368–377.

[7]Joseph Hraba, "The Doll Technique: A Measure of Racial Ethnocentrism," *Social Forces,*
50(June, 1972):522–527. For another indication of changed intragroup feelings among
blacks, in this case a group of black college students who placed a higher evaluation on
"blacks" than on "white Protestants," see Craig K. Polite, Raymond Cochrane, and Bernie
L. Silverman, "Ethnic Group Identification and Differentiation," *Journal of Social Psychology,*
92(February, 1974):149–150.

Fishman and Nahirny report that there is a tendency among most teachers of foreign languages in the United States to rate French, Spanish, and German as the more honored foreign languages, and not to include the language they teach, if other than one of these three, in a roster of respectable languages.[8]

Self-hatred—or some milder variant of this attitude—seems to describe well enough how many ethnic group members feel toward their fellow ethnics. There is certainly enough variability in this feeling to justify a concern with those factors or conditions that give rise to friendly or hostile attitudes of ethnic group members toward their peers. Sociological approaches to this problem have emphasized the various sorts of cleavage or factionalism that have caused disunity in some ethnic groups. Several of these sources of cleavage will now be discussed.

Home-Country Factionalism and Immigrant Ethnics

The unity that one might expect in an ethnic group by virtue of the underprivilege they share as immigrants in another country is often inhibited by the importation of home-country factional feelings into the immigrant situation. Various Asian groups in Africa—Indians, for example—have occupied a precarious middle position of being disliked by both the black natives and the European colonizers. However, as van den Berghe points out in writing about Indians in Africa, there is a sectarianism within the Indian community that reflects a microcosm of Indian political cleavages, such that "common victimization and stigmatization were not enough to draw people together."[9] Similarly, the contemplated establishment following World War I of the nation of Yugoslavia led to bitter division between Croatian-Americans who favored unification with the Serbs and those who advocated an independent Croatia.[10]

The effect of home-country factionalism on immigrant peoples can perhaps best be seen at its extreme, when the country of origin becomes

---

[8]Joshua A. Fishman and Vladimir C. Nahirny, "The Ethnic Group School and Mother Tongue Maintenance," in Joshua A. Fishman, et al., *Language Loyalty in the United States* (The Hague: Mouton, 1966), pp. 92–136.

[9]Pierre L. van den Berghe, "Asians in East and South Africa," in van den Berghe, *Race and Ethnicity* (New York: Basic Books, 1970), pp. 276–303.

[10]George J. Prpic, "The Croatian Immigrants in Pittsburgh," in John E. Bodner (ed.), *The Ethnic Experience in Pennsylvania* (Lewisburg, Pa.: Bucknell University Press, 1973), pp. 281–282.

embroiled in conflict with the country of immigration. Attitudes for or against the home-country political regime that is carrying on the conflict become the source of bitter division in the immigrant ethnic group. Granting Shibutani and Kwan's point that "overseas Germans" tended to have their sense of German ethnicity stimulated by the rise of Hitler's Fascist regime,[11] this development had also the effect of placing many German-Americans with more pro-American feelings at odds with their fellow ethnics who were more sympathetic to the Hitler regime.[12] In a somewhat different way, the growth of Israel as a Jewish state has, as we noted in Chapter 1, stimulated Jewish ethnicity throughout the world. However, the different attitudes adopted by Jews toward a Zionist movement of active support for the Israeli nation have become a source of cleavage.[13] This may be especially true in the USSR. Given the extreme hostility of Soviet official policy toward Zionism, the adoption of a Zionist position must be an especially group-threatening attitude among Jews in that country.[14]

Subethnic Provincialism

The point was made in Chapter 1 that many immigrant peoples take with them to their country of destination identities that are closely confined to a province or even a town or village within that province, but that the immigrant experience tends to wipe out the significance of these more narrow ethnic identities. While this is the general tendency, there is much variation in the extent to which the persistence of localistic identities inhibits the development of a sense of a wider ethnicity. Several immigrant ethnic groups continue to show the effects of their differentiated local origins long after they have settled among people who tend to see them as an undifferentiated entity. Japanese-Americans have shown a tendency toward organization on the basis of common regional origins in Japan. So-called *kenjinkai* organizations were maintained for the association of people from the same local area in Japan. Kitano notes, however, that such

---

[11]Tamotsu Shibutani and Kian M. Kwan, *Ethnic Stratification* (New York: Macmillan, 1965), p. 495.

[12]Richard O'Connor, *The German-Americans* (Boston: Little, Brown, 1968).

[13]Marshall Sklare, *America's Jews* (New York: Random House, 1972), p. 221.

[14]As Hunt and Walker note, while anti-Semitism is a crime in the Soviet Union, anti-Zionism is not only legal but vigorously pursued by the press and other governmental agencies. Chester L. Hunt and Lewis Walker, *Ethnic Dynamics* (Homewood, Ill.: Dorsey Press, 1974), pp. 77–80.

organizations had their major influence in the past, and that their main significance to younger Japanese-Americans is that they sponsor an annual picnic at which the principal attraction is a plentiful supply of games, food, and soda water.[15]

A more familiar case in the United States is that of Italian-Americans, who have tended to be acutely aware of the differences in regional origins among themselves. At the broadest level, there is a sharp distinction that North Italians have made between themselves, whom they see as middle-class educated bearers of the "classic" Italian civilization, and the South Italians, whom they see as ignorant peasantry.[16] Italian provincial cleavage goes much further than this, however. Italian rural life has been characterized by the notion of *campanilismo,* the view that a person moves into a world of strangers when he moves outside the range of sound of the church bell of his home village.[17] Although these localistic differences are now "hardly more than a memory among the few surviving old-timers,"[18] they persisted long enough, in Lopreato's view, to retard the development among Italian-Americans of as much political power as one might have expected in places like New York City, where they have represented so large a part of the population.[19]

An interesting contrast can also be found in the degree of consciousness of local origins held by white and black southerners who have migrated to northern American cities. White southerners—often treated as an undifferentiated "hillbilly" element by the native northerners—maintain more differentiated associations with fellow Kentuckians, Virginians, etc.[20] Rural blacks who move to northern cities show far less tendency to cluster by their state of origin; rather, their origin is seen as more broadly "south-

---

[15]Harry H. L. Kitano, *Japanese-Americans: The Evolution of a Subculture* (Englewood Cliffs, N.J.: Prentice-Hall, 1969), p. 94.

[16]This North vs. South Italian cleavage was, for example, strikingly displayed in New York's Greenwich Village area during the 1920s. Caroline Ware, *Greenwich Village, 1920–1930* (New York: Harper & Row, 1965).

[17]Joseph Lopreato, *Italian Americans* (New York: Random House, 1970), p. 104.

[18]Lopreato, *Italian Americans,* p. 15.

[19]Glazer and Moynihan similarly indicate a lack of political power of Italians in New York City, but they attribute this political retardation to a slightly different factor: the failure of Italians, as opposed to Irish, to rise rapidly from lower to middle social-class positions. Nathan Glazer and Daniel P. Moynihan, *Beyond the Melting Pot* (Cambridge, Mass.: M.I.T. Press, 1963).

[20]Lewis M. Killian, *White Southerners* (New York: Random House, 1970), p. 105.

ern," as is the "soul" life style that tends to prevail among blacks both north and south.[21] Thus is laid the basis of a unified "black community" without the inhibiting effects of differentiated regions of origin.

Another interesting contrast has been suggested between the community orientations of Italian-Americans and black Americans. Suttles has described a set of "communicative devices" employed by Italian-Americans on Chicago's West Side that indicate a new kind of "provincialism" of the group: a language and a personal style that are oriented toward a particular neighborhood without much connection to trends in the wider American or Italian-American communities.[22] Blacks are far more cosmopolitan in their life styles, employing a language of "jive" that can be understood by almost any other black in the country, and showing a greater sensitivity to fads and fashions in the wider community.[23] In somewhat the same way, Williams has commented on the tendency of urban blacks to identify themselves with a general "black community" that transcends local community limits. A symptom of this cosmopolitanism is the tendency, reported by Williams, for blacks to prefer a visiting sports team with black players over a hometown team with white players.[24] Although, as is frequently pointed out, "black community" in the United States has many weaknesses, the provincialisms that have retarded ethnic unity among other groups do not seem a major problem in this case.

Degree of Acculturation

One of the more universal sources of cleavage within ethnic groups arises from the differences in the degree of acculturation of ethnic group members to the life styles of the dominant groups. The more acculturated

---

[21]The cosmopolitanism of the black community in Washington, D.C., is indicated in Ulf Hannerz, *Soulside: Inquiries into Ghetto Culture and Community* (New York: Columbia University Press, 1969).

[22]Gerald D. Suttles, *The Social Order of the Slum* (Chicago: University of Chicago Press, 1968).

[23]For a similar analysis, see Hannerz, *Soulside*.

[24]Robin M. Williams, Jr., *Strangers Next Door* (Englewood Cliffs, N.J.: Prentice-Hall, 1964), p. 238. There may be a parallel sense of "white community" among sports fans as illustrated, for example, in the reluctance of white fans to support black-dominated teams. Thus, when the decision was made to reduce the number of black players on the Dallas franchise of the National Basketball Association, the head coach of the team was quoted as saying: "Whites in Dallas are simply not interested in paying to see an all Black team and the Black population alone cannot support us." Harry Edwards, *The Sociology of Sports* (Homewood, Ill.: Dorsey Press, 1973), p. 214.

ethnic members tend to be ashamed of the "primitive" ways of their unacculturated peers. Blacks in the cotton-mill town of Kent, for example, are described as being divided fundamentally between the "respectable" and the "unrespectable," respectability being defined largely in terms of middle-class white standards.[25] Members of an outcaste group in Japan, the Eta, who are more acculturated to middle-class Japanese life styles are embarrassed by the ways of their more traditional fellow castemen.[26] Middle-class Mexican-Americans tend to hold the same negative stereotypes of lower-class Mexicans that are held by the middle-class Anglos.[27]

Ethnic group members with more positive attitudes toward their traditional life styles reserve some of their bitterest epithets for the ethnic "sellouts," who are seen as adopting dominant group ways for the advantages to be gained for themselves. Black loyalists castigate the "Uncle Toms" among them; American Indians, who have adapted the epithet, refer to acculturated Indians as "Uncle Tomahawks."[28] More colorful terms of derision are sometimes found. For example, an acculturated black is referred to as an Oreo cookie—black on the outside, white on the inside. Similarly, the ardently Chinese among Chinese-Americans have referred to their more acculturated kinsmen as bananas—yellow on the outside, white on the inside. The author has likewise heard some Indians who are "too white" in their attitudes referred to as apples.

An ethnic group that is aggressively seeking improved social status seems especially subject to this sort of cleavage. American Jews furnish a good example. According to a common interpretation of the Jewish experience in America, Jewish immigrants were forced into menial labor but maintained high ambitions for an improved status for their sons and daughters, especially through the route of better education.[29] They succeeded

---

[25]Hylan G. Lewis, *The Blackways of Kent* (Chapel Hill: University of North Carolina Press, 1955).

[26]George DeVos and Hiroshi Wagatsuma, *Japan's Invisible Race* (Berkeley: University of California Press, 1966).

[27]Ozzie G. Simmons, "The Mutual Images and Expectations of Anglo-Americans and Mexican-Americans," *Daedalus,* 90(1961):286–299.

[28]Robert C. Day, "The Emergence of Activism as a Social Movement," in Howard H. Bahr, Bruce A. Chadwick, and Robert C. Day (eds.), *Native Americans Today* (New York: Harper & Row, 1972), p. 514.

[29]Thus, Herberg refers to the one-generation "proletarianization" of Jewish immigrants to America. Will Herberg, *Protestant-Catholic-Jew* (Garden City, N.Y.: Doubleday, 1955).

to the extent that their children tended to acquire wealth, but perhaps at the expense of getting a reputation for being overly ambitious or "pushy." The third generation, hoping to dispel this bad reputation, are oriented toward imitating the "tasteful" life style of their Gentile peers who have already "made it" in prestige terms.[30] Part of the making-it process has consisted in a status-conscious move from a Jewish ghetto in the central city to a suburb where Jews live an acculturated life style that does not emphasize their "Jewishness," thus enabling them to gain a measure of acceptance by Gentiles. The difficulties in this tactic of status acceptance became apparent in the much accelerated exodus of Jews to the suburbs following World War II. In a study of the midwestern suburb of "Lakeville," Ringer found a pattern of rejection of the recently arrived Jews by those who had been established in the community for some time.[31]

There were several related reasons for this rejection of the newer by the older Jewish residents. One was that the old-timers were mostly German Jews, while the newcomers were from southern and eastern Europe, a situation that mirrored the familiar prejudice of native Americans in favor of the "old immigration" from northern and western Europe.[32] Another was that the newcomers, city bred and perhaps new to affluence, followed life styles that were more those of the urbanite and nouveau riche than those of a more mellowed suburban style (some of "those women" were described as wearing scanty or flashy clothing more appropriate to Miami Beach than to "Lakeville"). Finally there was the objection to the *number* of Jews moving in,[33] the fear being that the community would be defined as a "Jewish" community, with attendant loss of prestige associated with living in an ethnically integrated community. All of these reasons converge on a single point: the old timers' fear of losing the delicate and none-too-certain status acceptance by Gentiles built up over a long period of cau-

---

[30]Judith R. Kramer and Seymour Leventman, *Children of the Gilded Ghetto* (New Haven, Conn.: Yale University Press, 1961).

[31]Benjamin B. Ringer, *The Edge of Friendliness* (New York: Basic Books, 1967).

[32]Nathan Glazer, *American Judaism,* rev. ed. (Chicago: University of Chicago Press, 1972).

[33]It seems to be one symptom of anxiety about changes in composition of a group to *overestimate* the rapidity of the change that is taking place. Thus, most white policemen in Philadelphia overestimated the number of blacks on the force, perhaps as an expression of this kind of anxiety. William M. Kephart, "Negro Visibility," *American Sociological Review,* 19(August, 1954):462–467. It might be suggested, by extension, that many anxious Jews in "Lakeville" overestimated the degree of this Jewish "influx" into their community.

tious living in the community. The negative feelings of the old-timers toward the new arrivals can probably be evoked for most readers by remembering or imagining their feelings toward some situation or person that has kept them from some personal triumph. The feeling against the albatross of one's unacculturated ethnic peers may well match in intensity the reverse feeling against the ethnic "traitors" who are believed to have sold out the collective interest for their private advancement.

INSTITUTIONAL INDEPENDENCE AND DEPENDENCE

Institutions are those established procedures in a community that provide socially approved mechanisms for the satisfaction of basic human needs. Familiar examples are the institutions of the family, education, economy, religion, government, recreation, medical care, and welfare. Since these areas represent vital human needs, we can expect that all or certainly most human beings of whatever ethnic group will make use of some set of institutional mechanisms in each of these areas. According to one conception, *community* represents the level of social organization at which all the basic institutions are maintained for the benefit of group members. Social units such as military garrisons or college campuses are usually not communities because there is at least one area of basic need not being provided by that unit.

Do ethnic groups constitute communities in this sense? There is no clear-cut answer to this question because there is considerable variability among ethnic groups. On the one hand, there are ethnic groups that can be characterized by what Breton calls *institutional completeness:*

> Institutional completeness would be at its extreme whenever the ethnic community could perform all the services required by its members. Members would never have to make use of native institutions for the satisfaction of any of their needs, such as education, work, food and clothing, medical care, or social assistance. Of course, in contemporary North American cities very few, if any, ethnic communities showing full institutional completeness can be found.[34]

Granting the validity of Breton's "few if any" point about institutional completeness, it can still be observed, as Breton does, that there is much

---

[34]Raymond Breton, "Institutional Completeness of Ethnic Communities and the Personal Relations of Immigrants," *American Journal of Sociology,* 70(September, 1964):194.

variability in the degree to which different ethnic groups approach the "extreme" of institutional completeness. In analyzing this variability, there seem to be two major strategies. One strategy would be illustrated by Breton's procedure of taking a sample of members of the various ethnic groups in Montreal and obtaining data to show which ethnic groups are "high" or "low" in overall institutional self-sufficiency. The other strategy is illustrated by the kind of analysis immediately following. We shall consider only two institutional areas here; however, many other institutions could be treated in this fashion. From these two areas we shall try to glean what generalizations we can about the conditions that encourage or discourage ethnic self-sufficiency.

Marriage

Marriage as a social institution deals with the regulation of sexual activity and the attendant concomitants of cohabitation of men and women. An ethnic group would be "institutionally complete" in this respect if the ethnic group was able to provide spouses or other sex partners for each member drawn exclusively from other members of the ethnic group.

Most ethnic groups show a strong preference for *endogamy*—marriage within one's ethnic group—and more or less resistance to intermarriage with outsiders. American Jews are an example of an ethnic group in which there is a deep fear for "Jewish survival" arising from increased intermarriage with Gentiles. The troubling thought to many is, Can the members of the next generation be thoroughly Jewish in identity if they have only one Jewish parent? More disturbing still, How much Jewish identity can be passed on by "half Jewish" parents to *their* children?[35]

In the ethnic situations that usually capture the attention of sociologists —that is, immigration movements in which the newcomers are subordinate to the native population, and colonizing movements in which the newcomers are dominant over the native population—the confinement of marriage and other sexual relations to ethnically endogamous unions is likely to be a serious problem. Ethnic migrations of either type are likely to be adventurous affairs, at least in the pioneer phases of movement, and tend to attract primarily males. As a result, there has been a heavily

---

[35]Sklare, *America's Jews,* chap. 6.

unbalanced sex ratio (proportion of males to females).[36] The impact of this situation on the sexual relations of ethnics has tended to take different courses for colonizing peoples and for subordinate immigrants.

Colonists have, by definition, established a relation of dominance over the native peoples of the colony, and the shortage of women among the colonists has tended to be solved by the colonial men having sexual relations with native women, a situation that native men have been powerless to prevent.[37] Thus, a practice that is a "solution" for a colonizing people becomes a problem for the colonized: native men are denied sexual access to women of their own ethnic kind who enter relations of marriage or concubinage with colonizing men.

If the shortage of women in frontier colonizing situations encourages ethnic miscegenation, other factors influence the degree to which this tendency is carried out. For instance, the rate of intermarriage and extramarital sexual contact between European colonizers and native Indian women (and slave women) was much higher in Central and South America than in North America.[38] The difference lies partly in the different settlement patterns in the two areas: the English in North America came primarily as agriculturalists and more often with wives, while the Spanish and Portuguese, who dominated South and Central America, came mostly as soldiers, traders, miners, and other adventurers. But, as Degler suggests, there may have been another factor at work: the traditional structure of the English family as compared with that of the Iberian family.[39] Spanish and Portuguese husbands tended to have mistresses, a practice condoned

---

[36]On the very high ratio of males to females in the Japanese immigration to the United States at the turn of this century, see Petersen, *Japanese Americans,* p. 196. Considering sex ratios of *all immigrants* to the United States at about the same time, it is shown that there were some 229 male for every 100 female immigrants. Ernest Rubin, "The Demography of Immigration to the United States," *Annals of the American Academy of Political and Social Science,* 367(1966):17.

[37]This practice has, of course, been responsible for the production of a number of peoples of mixed ethnic ancestry: the Meti children of European and native Indian peoples in Canada, the Babu population of Malaysia (descendants of Malay natives and Chinese immigrants), the "coloured" population of South Africa, etc.

[38]Pitt-Rivers thus indicated that even today "intermarriage is not regarded with horror" in Latin America. Julian Pitt-Rivers, "Race, Color, and Class in Central America and the Andes," *Daedalus,* 96(Spring, 1967):542–559.

[39]Carl N. Degler, *Neither Black Nor White* (New York: Macmillan, 1971).

by wives accustomed to patriarchal dominance and a double standard that permitted extramarital involvements for men but not for women. The English wife, by contrast, was much more powerful if not dominant in the marital relation. In the American South, lower-class white men still say, "My old lady would raise hell" if she knew or suspected extramarital involvement, especially with a black woman. It may be that, in North America, marriage and/or sexual relations between Europeans and blacks or Indians were largely confined to: (a) large southern plantation owners, whose upper-class position could withstand the pressures of both "society" and their wives, and (b) the trappers and traders of the West during its "wild" stage, when there was much miscegenation between European men and Indian women, as well as other kinds of "lawlessness." Not until white women arrived in large numbers was the West civilized (or perhaps more accurately, domesticated).

Men of subordinate immigrant groups were not, of course, in any position to solve their woman shortage by sexual relations with women of the dominant indigenous groups. An occasional Italian-American man of great wealth or other success might hope to marry an "Anglo" girl of poor background who was willing to have a husband of inferior ethnic status if his class standing was favorable.[40] But a typical male of mediocre standing could realistically hope for one of the following:

1. He might hope to obtain a wife from his own ethnic group back home, one whom he had his eye on before he left or who could be found for him by friendly intermediaries in the home country. In a study of Hungarians in Canada, Kosa shows that this tactic could work well only for those men who had good contacts with friends and relatives in Hungary and who had enough wealth or other social standing to be attractive to a Hungarian girl who might be willing to emigrate if she could obtain a wealthy husband in Canada.[41] The impecunious and those isolated from primary group contacts in the country of origin—and emigration may have tended to be selective of just these kinds of persons—were relatively out of luck in finding spouses from back home. Another condition inhibiting this solution may be the hostility of the host country to the importation of women under these circumstances. The publicity in the United States surrounding the

---

[40]Lopreato, *Italian Americans,* p. 123.

[41]John Kosa, *Land of Choice: the Hungarians in Canada* (Toronto: University of Toronto Press, 1957).

practice by Japanese men of bringing in "picture brides"—wives who had been found for them by agents in Japan—was a factor in eventual exclusion of further Japanese immigration.[42] The immigration legislation of the 1920s must have similarly frustrated the hope of many immigrant men of southern or eastern European origin of bringing brides from the home country.

2. Unable to develop more permanent sexual liaisons with a woman of his own ethnic group, the immigrant man in such situations may confine his sexual contacts to the few women of his ethnic group who specialize as prostitutes. The prevalence, for example, of Japanese prostitutes on the West Coast of the United States when first-generation Japanese immigrants predominated can be explained in terms of the inability or reluctance of Japanese men to import wives from Japan. As a result, there was an extremely high ratio of males to females among Japanese immigrants to America.[43] This situation must have been all the more true for Chinese men in the same area in light of Lyman's observation that the Japanese were much more likely than the Chinese to "sojourn with their wives" during their temporary residences in an "overseas" location.[44]

Education

The schooling of ethnic group members is often as controversial and emotional an issue within an ethnic group as it is between the ethnic group and the wider society. The fact is understandable when one reflects on how much people depend on their schools to build the kind of "character" that is prized in that society. Ethnic groups may have their own ideas about character that are somewhat at odds with the prevailing ideas in the dominant society. As we noted in an earlier discussion of radical religious sects such as the Hutterites, the question of who educates Hutterite children—the Hutterites themselves or educational agents from the wider society—may become a major issue between the ethnic group and the dominant society. Educational autonomy for ethnic groups is thus frequently demanded, and frequently resisted. The willingness of ethnic out-

---

[42]Petersen, *Japanese-Americans,* pp. 43, 44.

[43]Petersen, *Japanese-Americans,* p. 196.

[44]Stanford M. Lyman, "Contrasts in the Community Organization of Chinese and Japanese in North America," *Canadian Review of Sociology and Anthropology,* 5(May, 1968)· 51–67.

siders to encourage or inhibit ethnic education, and the degree of effort by ethnic groups to maintain an ethnically exclusive instruction are matters of considerable variability, however.

The differential tolerance for ethnic educational autonomy by the more powerful groups in a society is one such area of variability. If the attitudes of ethnic group members themselves or of people in the wider society are such that there is relative indifference to the inclusion of ethnic members as full-fledged "citizens" of the country, there may be a disposition to leave the education of ethnic group children to the ethnic group itself. Chinese residents in such southeast Asian countries as Indonesia and Malaysia furnish good examples of such attitudes.[45] Because of the "sojourner" attitude of nonpermanent residence outside China held by most Chinese, there has been a tendency for Chinese children to be educated within exclusively Chinese schools. Sometimes, however, the amount of hostile feeling toward ethnic group members becomes such that the hands-off policy toward ethnic education is abandoned by the dominant group. Thailand illustrates this situation. Although there was an earlier tendency toward exclusively Chinese education for Chinese children, as was the case in Malaysia and Indonesia, the long tradition of hostile relations of Thai and Chinese peoples asserted itself after 1928 in the form of a concerted attack on the ethnically Chinese character of Chinese schools. In the United States, with its ideology of assimilation of all ethnic group members as citizens, there was never any serious question of autonomous Chinese schools in American Chinatowns, and the public schools have had the same corrosive effects on Chinese ethnicity that they have had for virtually all other immigrant ethnic groups.[46]

Another area of variability is the degree to which ethnic groups are determined to maintain an ethnically exclusive school system. A consideration of the experience of ethnic groups in the United States will indicate some of the various compromises that ethnic groups have made in an attempt to maintain an ethnic education for their children in the face of the assimilating expectations in the wider society. One pattern of compro-

---

[45]Maurice Freedman, "The Chinese in Southeast Asia," in Andrew W. Lind (ed.), *Race Relations in World Perspective* (Honolulu: University of Hawaii Press, 1955), pp. 388–411; Lea E. Williams, *The Future of the Overseas Chinese in South East Asia* (New York: McGraw-Hill, 1966).

[46]Stanley F. M. Fong, "Assimilation of Chinese in America: Changes in Orientation and Social Perceptions," *American Journal of Sociology,* 71(November, 1965):265–273.

mise has been to allow ethnic groups to maintain ethnically sponsored schools at their own expense, providing that (a) they bear the citizen's obligation to support the public schools, and (b) they maintain in their ethnic schools certain standards in such matters as curriculum and qualifications of teachers that are set by government agencies. The familiar pattern of parochial education sponsored by American religious groups is a major instance of an attempt to maintain this kind of compromise—and is a good example of some of the tensions that can develop when such a pattern is followed. A comparison of Catholic, Protestant, and Jewish religious groupings will indicate some of the considerable variation in the way ethnically self-sufficient education has worked in the United States.

In this country, the term *parochial education* is usually associated with the very extensive system of Catholic schools at all levels from elementary school to college. The church hierarchy has often been suspicious, perhaps rightly so, of the secularizing or Protestantizing tendencies of the country's public schools. The development of Catholic parochial education in New York City illustrates the national pattern.[47] Early formal education in New York, as elsewhere, was thought to be a church function with religious purposes. This was so much the case that, in 1805, there was established a Free School Society to provide education for those "poor" people who were not members of or not provided for by the established churches. As the idea of nondenominational public education began to grow in the state of New York, public money was allocated to the Free School Society; and, as the society (soon renamed the Public School Society) was dominated by Protestants, the Catholic church began to establish its own schools and to make the same demand for public funds for the support of these schools. A period of controversy between the parochial Catholic schools of New York City and the Protestant-dominated state legislature followed, culminating, in 1842, in the passage of a law articulating the familiar principle of separation of church and state, in which the state was forbidden to dispense public funds to religiously sectarian schools. From this point, the church developed its system of education at its own expense. With the more recent advent of federal aid to education, the financial plight of Catholics, required to pay for two

---

[47]The following discussion of parochial education in New York City is based on Glazer and Moynihan, *Beyond the Melting Pot.*

school systems if they choose to send their children to parochial schools, has been brought forcibly to the attention of the American public. Various devices have been tried to provide aid without violating the Constitution. Even without such assistance, Catholic parochial schools at the elementary and secondary levels have flourished in most parts of the country. In New York City, for example, approximately one-third of the total school enrollment is in Catholic schools.[48] In the area of higher education and with certain nationality groups, the church has been less successful in establishing parochial schools. In spite of the rather large number of Catholic colleges and universities—Fordham, Loyola, Notre Dame, etc.—their enrollment is very small compared with the total number of Catholic students in higher education.[49] Providing educational facilities for the very large Mexican-American population has also proved to be a problem. Most immigrants from Mexico brought with them some of the anticlericalism of revolutionary Mexico, or at least an unfamiliarity with the pattern of parochial education and with the need for financial support for the church. The church has made vigorous efforts, most notably in the Los Angeles area, to establish parochial schools among Mexican-Americans, partly, again, to counter the felt pressure of Protestant competition. Only a relatively small proportion of Mexican-Americans living in the Southwest are enrolled in parochial schools, however.[50]

Parochial education for Jewish Americans has tended to be much less well-developed. Students of the Jewish experience in America have commented on the tendency of Jews to value secular learning alongside the religious learning that was traditionally valued. Jewish immigrants were grateful to America for making available at last such civil rights as voting and access to public education, and they were thus enthusiastic supporters of the public schools.[51] Any tendency toward parochialism in educational practice would, it was feared, indicate some degree of disloyalty or ingrati-

---

[48]Glazer and Moynihan, *Beyond the Melting Pot,* p. 280.

[49]It is estimated that, in 1965, only about one-third of American Catholic students were attending Catholic colleges. James W. Trent, *Catholics in College* (Chicago: University of Chicago Press, 1967), p. 45.

[50]Joan W. Moore, *Mexican-Americans* (Englewood Cliffs, N.J.: Prentice-Hall, 1970), pp. 86, 87. On the Protestant-Catholic competition among Mexican-Americans in Texas, see William Madsen, *The Mexican Americans of South Texas* (New York: Holt, Rinehart and Winston, 1964), pp. 62–65.

[51]Sklare, *America's Jews,* pp. 19, 20.

tude to the country that had provided these opportunities. Accordingly, in 1917 there were only about one thousand Jewish students in full-time parochial schools. By 1935, parochial enrollment still represented only a tiny fraction of school attendance by Jewish children.[52] More recently, there has been something of a resurgence of Jewish parochial schooling. By 1953, some 6 percent of Jewish children attended such schools and the estimated total enrollment was sixty thousand.[53] The new interest in this form of Jewish education is partly the result of the influx of Orthodox Jews into the United States following the Jewish displacements from Europe after World War II. (The Orthodox Jews have always been the major sponsors of parochial schools.) The upsurge may also be partly the result of an increased interest in Jewish education as a matter of "Jewish identity," as we suggested in Chapter 1. The degree of interest declines sharply with the increasing level of education involved, however. One estimate has it that some 70 percent of children eight to twelve years of age are receiving some kind of Jewish education (most of it not, however, in full-time parochial schools), but only 16 percent of those aged thirteen to seventeen are receiving a Jewish education.[54] Perhaps it is felt by Jewish parents that Jewish education has accomplished its work if it succeeds in bringing their children willingly to the identity-establishing Bar Mitzvah (male) or Bas Mitzvah (female) ceremony at about the age of twelve. At any rate, the "Jewish" college or university is virtually unknown (outside the Yeshivas, which provide special religious training), although it is said that some institutions, such as City College of New York or Brandeis University, are, in effect, "secular Jewish" institutions by virtue of the dominance of Jews in their student bodies and faculties.[55]

Among Protestant Americans, the interest in parochial education seems to be very nearly the reverse of that of Catholic and Jewish Americans, particularly in terms of the level of education. Parochial education at the elementary and secondary levels has never really taken hold among Protestant Americans (except for certain "radical" sects such as the Amish),

---

[52]Nathan Glazer, *American Judaism* (Chicago: University of Chicago Press, 1957), p. 86.

[53]Glazer, *American Judaism,* pp. 109, 110.

[54]Sklare, *America's Jews,* p. 173.

[55]In the case of City College, the recently instituted "open admissions" policy has, according to recent news accounts, drastically altered the nature of the college as one dominated by a Jewish intellectual elite.

if only because their numerical predominance in the public schools guarantees that Protestant children will not be "seduced" by one of the alien religions. Higher education is a somewhat different story, however, as there have been denominationally sponsored colleges established by virtually every Protestant denomination and in all parts of the country. It may well be that the confidence of Protestant parents in their ability to keep their children loyal to the faith of their fathers is somewhat shaken when they consider sending these children away to college and to the possible influence of non-Protestants or, worse, of non-Christians or, worse yet, of such "godless" collegiate types as the hippie and the political radical. Denominational colleges may accordingly thrive on the presumption that they will be able to provide, *in loco parentis,* the needed reinforcement of the traditional religious affiliation.

The discussion above has been primarily about full-time parochial education. It appears, however, that all ethnic groups depend to some extent on less ambitious programs for the ethnic education of their children. In the United States, in line with the "triple melting pot" thesis discussed in Chapter 1, it appears that ethnicity based on national origin has weakened to the point where we should not expect to find much parochial education based on national origin. Instead, such ethnic groups must rely almost exclusively (and religious groups must rely to a greater or lesser extent) on such alternatives as the following.

First, an ethnic group may sponsor "afternoon schools," or Saturday or Sunday or vacation schools to supplement the nonethnic character of the education received in the public schools on weekdays. The Hebrew schools for the religious education of Jewish children were, for many years, the mainstays of Jewish education in the United States.[56] Similarly, Japanese language schools for after-hours education in Japanese life styles have been common in this ethnic group. A long-time student in such a school, Kitano, remarks that few of his Nisei (second-generation) colleagues ever developed any lasting understanding of Japanese language or culture from such schools.[57] However, Kitano points out, these schools did serve functions that have been noted for other ethnically supplementary schools. First, they provided a group of peer associates with whom the ethnic child could feel more identity than he could with the children in ethnically

---

[56]Sklare, *America's Jews,* pp. 162–165.

[57]Harry H. L. Kitano, *Japanese-Americans: The Evolution of a Subculture* (Englewood Cliffs, N.J.: Prentice-Hall, 1969), pp. 24, 25.

mixed public schools. Highly acculturated suburban Jewish children are similarly described as feeling more "at home" or easygoing with Jewish peers, a result that may be highly desirable if the aim is to provide friends and especially spouses from among one's own ethnic group.[58] Second, they served a useful "baby sitting" function for parents. For socially ambitious parents, especially those self-employed parents who must keep long working hours, it may be highly functional economically if children remain away from home for two or so more hours after school.

Second, ethnic group members may successfully demand that material related to their ethnic history or present situation be included in the curricula of the public schools. At the very least, parents and other concerned adults may request that school textbooks and other instructional materials stop fostering self-hatred among their own children by depicting members of their ethnic group in unfavorable lights. Thus, blacks have demanded a more "fair" presentation of the role of Negroes in southern governments during Reconstruction; American Indians have urged a more sympathetic treatment of their ancestors who were too often shown as savage inhibitors of the "civilization" of the West. At another level, ethnic groups such as Mexican-Americans have demanded, with little success, that public schools in areas of heavy Mexican-American concentration devote more attention to the study of the Spanish language and traditional Mexican culture. It is often understood that such revolutions in public school curricula are dependent on the ability of the locally dominant ethnic group to gain a measure of "community control" of the schools in the area. The New York City school crisis of 1968–1969 centered around the efforts of blacks in ghetto areas to gain this kind of capacity to give a desired ethnic slant to the educational program in their communities.[59] It is generally thought that the inability of American Indians to secure an education for their children that will emphasize Indian cultural tradition is related to their chronic lack of community control in the reservation situation. Reservation schools, along with other institutional services, are largely a "gift" to the Indian from the paternal white government, with the customary strings attached to such gifts.[60]

---

[58]Ringer, *The Edge of Friendliness.*

[59]Maurice R. Berube and Marilyn Gittell (eds.), *Confrontation at Ocean Hill-Brownsville: The New York School Strikes of 1968* (New York: Praeger, 1969).

[60]Robert K. Thomas, "Powerless Politics," *New University Thought,* 4(Winter, 1966–67): 44–53.

Finally, and especially at the level of higher education, there may be efforts to institute ethnic studies programs as optional courses for those ethnic group members or interested outsiders who might wish detailed information about the group. The black studies programs that have become common in colleges and universities throughout the United States are the most prominent example. However, one finds ethnic studies programs being established at institutions wherever there is a high concentration of members of some ethnic group: Mexican-American studies at UCLA and the University of New Mexico, Scandinavian studies at the University of Minnesota and the University of Wisconsin, etc.[61] According to Greeley, the increasing demand for such ethnic studies programs is part of a new "tribalism" that he sees emerging in the United States. He does note, however, that few ethnic group members or study programs show any strong involvement in the tedium of learning a *language* that had been allowed to lapse during a period of ethnic indifference.[62]

---

[61]For an evaluation of an ethnic studies program for Mexican-Americans, see Refugio I. Rochin, "The Short and Turbulent Life of Chicano Studies: A Preliminary Study of Emerging Programs and Problems," *Social Science Quarterly,* 53(March, 1973):884–894.

[62]Greeley, *Why Can't They Be Like Us?,* pp. 148–152.

PART 2
ETHNIC RELATIONS

OVERVIEW

In the first part of this book, we concentrated on the nature of ethnic *groups* in several relevant sociological dimensions. In this section, we turn our attention to the matter of ethnic *relations,* the nature and quality of relationship between members of several ethnic groups coexisting in the same social environment.

The key to the analysis in this part is found in the twin sociological concepts of *social interaction* and *social relationship.* We shall follow Max Weber's definitions. According to Weber, human action is *social* (and therefore interactive) when the behavior of a person is "oriented in its course" toward the behavior of other people.[1] A left hook to the chin of an opponent in a fight and a kiss to the mouth of a lover are equally "social" by this definition, since both actions are "oriented" toward another person, whether enemy or lover. A *social relationship* exists, according to Weber, when there is a high "probability" of a given kind of

---

[1]Max Weber, *The Theory of Social and Economic Organization,* trans. by A. M. Henderson and Talcott Parsons (New York: Oxford University Press, 1947), p. 88.

interaction occurring between the interactants.[2] Thus, "friends" are those persons among whom many friendly interactions occur; "enemies" are those persons between whom recurring interactions involve hostility or efforts to do harm.

To say that human behavior is "oriented" to the behavior of others is to raise the problem of the near-infinite complexity of human social behavior. A man works hard at a job in anticipation that the work will provide an income and maybe earn the appreciation of his employer or his wife, or (perhaps) even the respect of future generations. In more general terms, the "other" individuals whose responding behavior is anticipated may represent a great variety of possible respondents, which is another way of saying that the *motives* of human social behavior are greatly varied and complex. It is in the context of this immense complexity that the sociologist, together with other social scientists—and, indeed, every person in every day of his or her life—must attempt somehow to make sense or, alternatively, to make predictions about how persons will orient their behavior to other persons in different social situations.

One starting point for an analysis of social relationships is the distinction between *interpersonal* and *intergroup* levels of social relationship. A woman's interaction or relationship with her husband, children, parents, friends, employers, employees, etc., refers to the *interpersonal* level. Her *participation* as a member of a group of employees, of an organization of women devoted to women's liberation, of a group of parents of school children, etc. refers to the *intergroup* dimension of social interaction— especially where that participation is "oriented" to the anticipated responses of such collective entities as management, male chauvinists, or the school system. Of course the point has often been made that, in a sense, much of so-called intergroup behavior can actually be reduced to the level of interpersonal relations: that, for example, what are often called race relations are nothing more than the summation of many interpersonal situations in which, for example, a white person either accepts or rejects actions that imply equality of status with a black person.

Why insist, then, that human behavior has an *intergroup* dimension, a point that is emphasized in this book, as it is in every other sociological treatise on ethnic relations? An explanation of this insistence involves some analysis of the nature of "participation" in group activities. With even a

---

[2]Weber, *Theory of Social and Economic Organization.*

minimum of *identification* (of the kind discussed in Chapter 1) with one's ethnic group, a person is likely to feel that his or her interpersonal actions toward individual members of other ethnic groups are somehow of concern to fellow ethnic group members. Thus, individual whites or blacks may feel (and sometimes are forcibly made to feel) that they are "representatives" of their race and that their actions in the interpersonal situation must reflect the intergroup *position* of their group whenever encounters are had with members of the other race. This "position" may, for example, be a collective definition of whites as people who must bear the "white man's burden" relative to "primitive" people, or the more directly exploitative relation implied in a "white supremacy" position. On the black side, the racial "position" may be a "black is beautiful" self-presentation in the presence of whites or, alternatively, a kind of accommodative attitude toward whites expressed by the adoption of a "white folks manner."[3]

The poet's insight that "no man is an island" is, of course, an overgeneralization to the extent that there are all degrees of personal identification with or isolation from one's ethnic group. But the insight remains valid: there are often such identities, such feelings of shared fate, and there exist many social forces designed to engender loyalty in one's individual behavior toward some conception of the collective position of the ethnic group. In focusing on the influence of these "collective positions," we remain firmly within the orbit of the genius (some think an evil genius) of sociology that emphasizes group constraints on individual behavior.[4]

---

[3]The use here of the term *position* to indicate *any* stance that an ethnic group expects its members to adopt when dealing with other ethnic group members is broader than that of Blumer. Blumer's view of race prejudice as a "group position" emphasizes those stances vis-à-vis other groups that involve a sense of status superiority imposed by the group on its individual representatives. It is just as possible, from the present perspective, for the collective position of a particular ethnic group to be one of treating other ethnic group members as equals, as superiors, or (perhaps) as "separate but equals." Otherwise, the notion of ethnic group position here entertained is identical with Blumer's view that ethnic relations are defined not by individual feelings but by a "collective process" by which an ethnic group defines itself in relation to other ethnic groups. Herbert Blumer, "Race Prejudice as a Sense of Group Position," *Pacific Sociological Review*, 1(Spring, 1958): 3–7.

[4]Whether this constraint is exercised by "external" sanctions such as the social boycotting by fellow whites of one who violates the group position by being a "nigger lover," or whether the constraint is exercised by the internalization of prejudices learned from childhood in a particular interracial milieu is not at issue here. In either case the "group" (one's own ethnic group, reinforced perhaps by other ethnic groups) is the dominant influence on the behavior in question.

In analyzing the collective positions taken by ethnic groups regarding the relationships of their members with members of other ethnic groups, we can derive some aid from a look at two features of all human relationships. One such feature would emphasize the *closeness* or *distance* that is maintained in interpersonal relations. Some relationships are intimate in the sense of a close emotional involvement of people with one another and a great deal of mutual knowledge about one another by all the interactants. Other relationships are marked by distance or strangeness of people to one another. Just so, an ethnic group position may demand of its members familiarity with or isolation from members of other ethnic groups. Such positionings of ethnic groups in the matter of *social distance* will be the subject of analysis in Chapter 4.

A second ubiquitous dimension of variation in human relationships involves the distribution of *power* between the participants in the relationship. The concept of power is used in the sense defined by Weber, that is, a person's power is measured by the probability of the successful exercise of his will against the opposing wills of any other persons.[5] Defining the power element in human relationships in "probability" terms allows for all degrees of equality or inequality in a social relationship, from the absolute certainty of the despot's power to see that his will prevails, through various compromises by which subordinates are allowed some minor degree of power in the relationship, to completely equalitarian or "stand off" situations in which sometimes the will of one, sometimes the will of another party to the relationship prevails. The sociological concept of social stratification emphasizes this power dimension in human social organization. (*Social strata* are defined as groups or categories of persons who have either a high or low "probability" of having their wills prevail in any struggle for the enjoyment of social privileges.) Ethnic groups often may be seen in such stratified relationships of dominance and subordination: *minority groups* are ethnic groups inhabiting the lower strata of power. The analysis of *ethnic stratification*—the complexity and variety of modes and degrees of dominance and subordination between ethnic groups—is the subject of Chapters 5 and 6.

While Chapters 4, 5, and 6 will emphasize the variation in degrees of social distance or the ethnic stratification in different human situations, Chapter 7 will deal more directly with changes in these aspects of ethnic relationships over a period of time. Such changes may be the result of

---

[5]Weber, *Theory of Social and Economic Organization,* p. 152.

some kind of social planning by officially powerful persons in a society: the efforts of the United States government, through civil rights legislation, to lessen the subordination of minority groups; or the official *apartheid* policy of South Africa designed to enforce greater social distance between peoples of European and native origins. Other changes may occur "spontaneously" as the result of broad social changes that either are not officially planned or have unplanned consequences for ethnic relations. Thus, urbanization and industrialization, processes that are only more or less planned social developments, may profoundly affect ethnic relations in ways not intended or even in ways actively resisted by planners. Attention will also be given to *social movements* undertaken by or on behalf of ethnic group members, wherein attempts are made to bring pressure to bear—this pressure taking all forms from gentle "moral suasion" to violent revolution—to change the positioning of ethnic groups vis-à-vis one another. In Chapter 7 we shall have occasion again to note the distinction between distance and stratification as fundamental dimensions of variation in ethnic relations, observing that such changes, whether planned or spontaneous or the result of social movements, may involve re-positionings either in terms of greater or lesser distance between ethnic groups or greater or lesser amounts of inequality of power between them.

CHAPTER 4
ETHNIC DISTANCE

DISTANCE AND ETHNIC RELATIONS

When individual persons make inventories of their personal relationships, they are likely to think of those persons whom they know intimately, those who are acquaintances, and those who are simply strangers. Similarly, members of various ethnic groups inhabiting the same social space (e.g., a country, a community, a college campus) may display all degrees of acquaintance or lack of acquaintance with members of other ethnic groups. To illustrate one extreme, it has been observed that white people in the state of Oklahoma are almost totally ignorant of the fact that there is a thriving American Indian community in that state.[1] To examine further the element of distance between members of different ethnic groups, we need a closer focus on some of the meanings of intimacy or distance in human relations.

---

[1]Albert L. Wahrhaftig and Robert K. Thomas, "Renaissance and Repression: The Oklahoma Cherokee," *Trans-action,* 6(February, 1969):42–48

Acquaintances and Strangers

Cooley's concept of the *primary group* is useful in suggesting the nature of those relationships in which distance is minimized.[2] Such primary groups as the family, the neighborhood, and friendship groups are characterized by intensive feelings of emotional involvement of people with one another; to be close to someone is to care about that person. The emotion of love (not necessarily but often in a sexual sense) is an ingredient of close relationships. We might be tempted to characterize distant relationships, by contrast, as involving the feeling of hatred between people. However, as Simmel especially has noted, intense love and hatred may coexist in the same intimate relationship.[3] It is probably more accurate, therefore, to characterize distant relationships as those involving indifference or simply not caring. For instance, the ordinary person will experience intense grief upon the death of a loved one but only mild curiosity about the death of a stranger reported in the newspaper obituary column. Likewise, some ethnic relations may come very close to being "love affairs" between members of two or more ethnic groups. In the United States, for example, blacks and Chicanos have recently shown a great deal of sympathy with one another by virtue of their common victimization in American society.[4] On the other hand, relations between ethnic groups may be so distant that the fate of one is of almost total indifference to the other. Thus, a story is told of a king of a primitive tribe who demonstrated to a visiting British official the efficiency of a new rifle by firing at a distant figure. The British official exclaimed that the king had shot an "unfortunate man," to which the king cooly replied, "It is only a washerman."[5] Similar indifference has made it easier for Europeans to carry on warfare against more primitive peoples who were seen not as persons but as "only an Indian" or "only a Chink."

A second feature of social relationships within primary groups that will assist our analysis of ethnic relations is the observation that primary rela-

---

[2]Charles H. Cooley, *Social Organization* (New York: Scribner's, 1909).

[3]Georg Simmel, *Conflict,* trans. by Kurt H. Wolff [and] *The Web of Group-Affiliation,* trans. by Reinhard Bendix (Glencoe, Ill.: Free Press, 1955), pp. 45–48.

[4]Chandler Davidson and Charles M. Gaitz, "Ethnic Attitudes as a Basis for Minority Cooperation in a Southwestern Metropolis," *Social Science Quarterly,* 53(1973):738–748.

[5]Philip Mason, *Patterns of Dominance* (London: Oxford University Press, 1970), p. 1.

tionships are characterized by the members' extensive exposure of all aspects of themselves to one another.[6] More distant relationships are characterized by the interactants' rather narrow range of information about each other. Indeed, such interaction is often based on a few fundamental stereotypes, such as when "the student" confronts "the professor" in terms of some general assumptions about the nature of people in these categories. Members of many ethnic groups complain similarly about being treated as "the Jew" or "the black boy" rather than as unique human beings. Thus the few Jewish families in a small town are often invited by the Gentiles to present "the Jewish viewpoint" on some controversial issue.[7] It has been said that what ethnic groups want and seldom receive is the "right to have scoundrels among us," the right, that is, for individual members to be judged for what they are as individuals rather than in terms of negative stereotypes about how people of their category "generally" are.[8] The prevalence of stereotyped treatment of members of alien ethnic groups is a prominent feature of social distance as applied to ethnic relations. This stereotyping is often referred to as prejudice, and the terms *prejudice* and *social distance* will be used interchangeably in the following analysis.

Maintaining Distance

We turn now to an analysis of some of the reasons why people are reluctant to get close to members of some ethnic groups. In a discussion dealing primarily with race relations in Great Britain, Banton suggests two fundamentally different reasons for white Britons resisting association with

---

[6]Thus, lovers sometimes vow to keep no secrets from one another. A recent popular song describes a love relationship in which "we share each other's pasts" but in which the singer laments that he often wishes that he did *not* know these things about the lover's past. Many years before, Simmel (often rated as our greatest "sociologist of intimacy") had indicated that there is a point beyond which the most intimate of relationships cannot go in the way of mutual knowledge without endangering the relationship. Wolff, *Sociology of Georg Simmel,* pp. 326–329.

[7]Peter I. Rose, "Small-Town Jews and Their Neighbors in the United States," *Jewish Journal of Sociology,* 3(December, 1961):174–191. Reprinted in Peter I. Rose (ed.), *The Ghetto and Beyond* (New York: Random House, 1969), pp. 335–356.

[8]Libby Benedict, "The Right to Have Scoundrels," *Saturday Review of Literature* 28(October 6, 1945):13.

the coloured people around them.[9] One is a sense of status consciousness; the other is a fear of the unfamiliar.

Status consciousness. In Britain, as elsewhere, there is the feeling that a person's status is judged by the people he associates with. A British example cited by Banton is the London landlady who preferred not to rent to coloured people lest her white neighbors assume that her quarters were fit "only" for coloured.[10] Another instance of social distance based on status consciousness involves the idea of *contamination* if too close physical contact is made with members of ethnic groups of inferior status. The Indian caste system, with the Brahmin fear of defilement should any contact be had with "untouchables," is a familiar illustration. Less familiar is the belief held by some Japanese that a Japanese woman having a child by a black man would, should she later have children by a Japanese man, continue to have black children, since her womb has been "stained" by the black man.[11]

The correlation between social-distance tendencies toward an ethnic group and the imputed status of that group is one of the core findings of extensive research using so-called social-distance scales.[12] In the typical such research instrument, subjects are given a list of people of different ethnic groups and asked about their willingness to associate at various levels of intimacy (e.g., common residence in the same community, in the same neighborhood, as coworkers, as marriage partners) with a person from each of the listed groups. In a wide variety of contexts and over a long period of time, most Americans have expressed a preference for intimate association with such higher status ethnic groups as English, French, or Canadians; and a distaste for association with people such as Turks or Koreans even though, in many cases, there has been no actual

---

[9]Michael Banton, *Race Relations* (New York: Basic Books, 1967), chap. 13. In Britain, the term *coloured* is used to refer to all darker skinned people and not just to black Africans.

[10]Banton, *Race Relations,* p. 382.

[11]Hiroshi Wagatsuma, "The Social Perception of Skin Color in Japan," *Daedalus,* 96(Spring, 1967):432.

[12]The journal *Sociology and Social Research* frequently publishes articles on ethnic social distance. For a fairly recent article that refers to much earlier research, see Emory S. Bogardus, "Comparing Racial Distance in Ethiopia, South Africa, and the United States," *Sociology and Social Research,* 52(1968):149–156.

experience with the people about whom preferences are being expressed but only a general notion about the high or low status of such persons.

If one should postulate a general human tendency to act in those ways that would maximize status, one might logically predict that even members of ethnic groups of lower status would show preferences for association with persons from ethnic groups of higher status rather than with members of their own ethnic group. There are some indications of the validity of this prediction in the observation, for example, of the traditional preference among blacks for a marriage partner of lighter skin color than themselves, if not of a white person.[13] The status advantage accruing to the black partner in an interracial marriage is the most apparent explanation for the fact that most racial intermarriages in the United States are between a black man and a white woman.[14] Examination of such intermarriages has shown that they usually involve a black man of higher-class position with a white woman of lower-class position. In such marriages, each partner "gains" something in status through the marriage: *she* gains improved class standing while *he* gains the advantage of sexual association with a white woman,[15] and the probability of having children lighter than himself, thereby encouraging his children's social mobility. The opposite combination—black wife, white husband—could involve no possible gain for the husband, even though the wife were upper class, because the general rule is that the woman takes the status of her husband; therefore, the husband could not gain her class status but could only "degrade" himself in racial terms.

---

[13]W. Lloyd Warner, B. H. Junker, and W. A. Adams, *Color and Human Nature* (New York: Harper & Row, 1970).

[14]Some of the available data on male and female tendencies toward ethnic intermarriage is reviewed in George S. Simpson and J. Milton Yinger, *Racial and Cultural Minorities,* 4th ed. (New York: Harper & Row, 1972), pp. 500–502.

[15]We remarked above on the Japanese belief in the contaminating effect of sexual association with blacks. The other side of this is the very high value placed on whiteness by the Japanese (see Wagatsuma, "The Social Perception of Skin Color in Japan," pp. 407–443). Samuels also notes the Japanese association of whiteness with beauty. To verify this, he says, one has only to go to a beach in Hawaii to see Haole (Caucasian) bathers trying to get a tan and Japanese bathers sitting under palm trees or umbrellas trying to avoid tanning. Frederick Samuels, *The Japanese and the Haoles of Honolulu* (New Haven, Conn.: College and University Press, 1970), p. 76. Wagatsuma ("The Social Perception of Skin Color in Japan," p. 426) reported that many Japanese soldiers found great satisfaction in sleeping with Caucasian women in the belief that their masculinity was enhanced by sexual association with whites.

While there is this evidence in support of the prediction of attraction for association with persons of higher status ethnic groups, there are important limits on the degree to which the point can be generalized. Social-distance scales administered to subjects from ethnic groups of lesser status have shown tendencies for expressing a preference for intimate association with persons of *their own* ethnic groups. Thus, Anglo students at a Texas university whose student body had about equal numbers of Anglos and Mexican-Americans rated Mexican-Americans sixteenth in the order of their preference for association.[16] Mexican-American students, by contrast, placed Mexican-Americans first in their order of preference, even though they otherwise tended to share the Anglo tendency to rate Anglo-Saxon ethnic groups as preferable to Asiatic ones. In a similar vein, Samuels has shown that the Japanese residents of Honolulu are somewhat reluctant to approach Haoles (Caucasians) for intimate association. They participate instead in an "Oriental ingroup" in which, for example, a non-Japanese marriage partner is acceptable as long as the partner is Chinese or Filipino.[17]

A theoretical interpretation of this last set of findings is suggested in a study by Blau that deals with "social integration" in a nonethnic setting, specifically the relationships between different people in a bureaucratic organization.[18] Blau argues that, for an individual to be well "integrated" (by which Blau seems to mean that social distance by others toward the integrated individual will be reduced), he must not only desire association or be "attracted to" other people (which is about what the traditional social-distance scales have measured) but that he must be "attractive to" the other people in his social setting; that is, intimate association with him must be rewarding to them. In the "exchange" model of human social behavior that Blau favors, each person maximizes his profit from social relationships by gaining the greatest reward at the least cost. A less respected person would certainly gain the greatest reward by associating with the most respected person (he would, for example, gain personal prestige by engaging a highly respected person in conversation at a social

[16]Robert L. Brown, "Social Distance Perceptions as a Function of Mexican-American and Other Ethnic Identity," *Sociology and Social Research,* 57(1973):273–287.

[17]Samuels, *The Japanese and the Haoles of Honolulu.*

[18]Peter M. Blau, "A Theory of Social Integration," *American Journal of Sociology,* 65(May, 1960):545–556.

party). However, the likely *cost* of attempting to associate with one whom one is *attracted to* by virtue of his superior status is likely to be very high, since the person of lesser status is not likely to be *attractive to* the person of higher status.[19]

The rule of "safety first"—of minimizing possible costs in interaction—may thus become the rule for persons of lesser status. While it may not be especially rewarding to dance with the least attractive girl at a dance, it is at least highly likely that she will respond favorably to her few invitations, while the belle of the ball will be turning down many dance partners. Thus, Mexican-Americans in Texas, the Japanese in Hawaii, and minority ethnic groups in many other places will experience or anticipate experiencing some variation of the subtle rejection that Jews in a supposedly "integrated" Gentile-Jewish community experience at the hands of their Gentile neighbors.[20] In the case of the Japanese, the preferential evaluation of whiteness is blocked by the experience of many Japanese boys who find that Caucasian girls are simply not accessible to them.[21] Even in the "equalitarian" racial atmosphere of Hawaii, the "out-marriage" rate of Japanese is noticeably low.[22]

Fear of the unfamiliar.   Banton's analysis of British race relations, which raised the issue of the influence of ethnic group status on social distance, also suggests another general reason for whites maintaining social distance from the coloured population. This is the factor of uncertainty or fear of the unfamiliar, a sense that "they" are different from "us" and that one

---

[19]There are exceptions to the generalization that members of an ethnic group of lesser status are not "attractive to" members of ethnic groups of higher status. A black Briton, Mullard, provides a personal account of a fairly common experience. Born in a rural English town in which he was the only black, he found that whites seemed almost to compete with one another to court his favor, perhaps to prove their personal liberality. Upon his removal to London, Mullard found himself in the more typical British racial situation of intense discrimination against the coloured population. Even in London, though, he participated for a time in international friendship meetings in which white higher status British women lavished attention on their coloured guests. Mullard quickly found, however, that there was a price for this acceptance. The coloured guests were expected to accept the rhetoric of speeches made on these evenings in which the British "white man's burden" was extolled and denial was made of any serious discrimination, past or present, against coloured people. Chris Mullard, *On Being Black in Britain* (Rockville, Md.: Black Orpheus Press, 1974).

[20]Benjamin B. Ringer, *The Edge of Friendliness* (New York: Basic Books, 1967).

[21]Wagatsuma, "The Social Perception of Skin Color in Japan."

[22]Samuels, *The Japanese and the Haoles of Honolulu,* pp. 58, 59.

never knows what one of "them" may do in an interpersonal situation. An instance cited by Banton is that of the British white girl who, at a student party, consents to dance with a coloured student, perhaps because she is genuinely unprejudiced, or perhaps because she sees the action as "doing her bit" for interracial harmony.[23] What she may find, to her distaste, is that the "bit" results in a flood of invitations and the risk not only that her status will be degraded among her peers as she becomes known as the "coloured students' girl," but that some of these coloured students will place the wrong interpretation on her action. Their sexual customs may be such that acceptance of any bodily contact is tantamount to a promise of sexual intercourse, and the hapless girl may find herself in the midst of a messy misunderstanding when her dancing partner walks her home and discovers at her door that, from his perspective, he has been shamelessly "led on." The possibility of such a misunderstanding may lead members of *both* dominant and minority ethnic groups to prefer association with their own kind. As long as a person stays within the well-worn grooves of ethnic custom, he knows where he stands with his fellow ethnics—but with a stranger, he never quite knows.

This line of explanation of social distance needs to be tempered by the knowledge that the supposed "differences" between ethnic peoples that make interethnic misunderstandings likely may be exaggerated for some ulterior purpose. Mason notes in this connection that traditional society in Ruanda was based on a "premise of inequality" between the dominant Tutsi and the subordinate Hutu peoples.[24] Along with and supporting this status dominance of the Tutsi was a general belief in the absolute and inherent difference between these peoples so that there was a denial, for example, that a Hutu boy brought up as a Tutsi could escape his inherent Hutu limitations. Mason thus notes the "desire to emphasize differences."[25] In a study of the history of the English class system, Mason argues that the distinctive Rugby way of life of the English aristocracy of the nineteenth century reflected the threat to the earlier "premise of inequality" in British society posed by the American and French revolutions. This accounts, says Mason, for the fact that "the upper-class of the late

---

[23]Banton, *Race Relations*, p. 379.
[24]Mason, *Patterns of Dominance*, pp. 14, 15.
[25]Mason, *Patterns of Dominance*, p. 19.

Victorian Age gloried in subjecting their sons to rigours which marked their superiority to the lower bourgeoisie."[26]

SEGREGATION AND SOCIAL DISTANCE

It should be clear by now that we have been discussing closeness and distance in ethnic relations in a social rather than in a physical sense. The question now arises whether social distance is expressed in actual physical separation. In other words, is there any tendency of ethnic groups to occupy different territories or pieces of "social turf"?[27] The racial position of white supremacy in South Africa is accompanied by an official policy of *apartheid* or racial separation. As van den Berghe notes, this segregation of natives from Europeans occurs at several levels: (1) a *microsegregation* policy, which requires separate facilities for eating and for toilet needs, etc., in situations where natives must come in daily contact with Europeans; (2) a *mesosegregation* level, which provides native compounds or black ghettos to which city-dwelling natives must retire after work; and (3) a *macrosegregation* policy, which confines the native rural population to certain geographic regions of the country, referred to as native "reserves," or Bantustans.[28]

The territorial concomitant to ethnic distance can be observed in many other social situations. Ethnically segregated neighborhoods are found in many large American cities. Also, instances of informal segregation often occur in officially "mixed" situations, such as when black employees of an integrated hospital or other workplace stake out pieces of social turf in the form of "their" tables in the dining room, etc.

While it is appropriate to note this frequent coexistence of physical separation with social distance, we need to observe that the relationship between these two aspects of ethnic relations is more complex than a simple one-to-one correspondence. Sometimes strong social distance is

---

[26]Philip Mason, *Prospero's Magic* (London: Oxford University Press, 1962). Quotation is from Mason, *Patterns of Dominance*, p. 19.

[27]The term *social turf* is used by Greeley to describe the persisting tendency of ethnics to think of a particular neighborhood as "theirs" and to treat alien intruders as interlopers. Andrew W. Greeley, *Why Can't They Be Like Us?* (New York: Dutton, 1971), pp. 95–102.

[28]Pierre L. van den Berghe, *South Africa: A Study in Conflict* (Middletown, Conn.: Wesleyan University Press, 1965), pp. 119–120.

maintained between people who are in close physical contact: for example, the distance between officers and enlisted men in the tightly confined space of a ship.[29] In analyzing this relationship, much depends upon the particular type of separation or segregation being considered. Where residential segregation is concerned, it has been observed that there may actually be more likelihood of people of different ethnic groups occupying the same neighborhoods when there is a greater amount of social distance between those groups. Thus, various applications of an "index of segregation," a measure of the degree to which members of different groups are residentially intermingled or separated, have indicated that northern American cities are about as racially segregated as are southern American cities.[30] It is also a fact that residential segregation is less pronounced in the rural areas and in the older, antebellum cities of the South, where the strong "sense of position" of whites as the superior race has made residential segregation unnecessary to maintain white supremacy.[31] On the other hand, prior to passage of the 1964 Civil Rights Act, southern segregation patterns tended to be severe in the microsegregation areas as defined by van den Berghe. Although it was taken for granted that blacks and whites would be in physical proximity to one another, efforts were made through segregated schools, toilet and dining facilities, and seating on public transportation to insure against any crossing of the color line in the intimate levels of association. While lacking legal sanction, many of these segregation patterns persist.

The pattern of low residential segregation coexisting with high levels of social distance is not limited to the traditional rural American South, as has been illustrated in a number of studies of other ethnically "integrated" communities.[32] Greeley thus describes an American suburban neighbor-

---

[29]Pierre L. van den Berghe, "Distance Mechanisms of Stratification," *Sociology and Social Research,* 44(January, 1960):155–164.

[30]Karl E. Taeuber and Alma F. Taeuber, *Negroes in Cities* (Chicago: Aldine, 1965); Theodore G. Clemence, "Residential Segregation in the Mid-Sixties," *Demography,* 4(1967): 562–568.

[31]On the distinction between "older" and "newer" southern cities in terms of racial segregation, see Leo F. Schnore and P. C. Evenson, "Segregation in Southern Cities," *American Journal of Sociology,* 72(July, 1966):58–67.

[32]In addition to the cases discussed immediately below, see, for example, the study of a Jewish-Gentile integrated midwestern American suburb in Ringer, *The Edge of Friendliness;* and the discussion of Japanese-Caucasian relations in the largely racially integrated city of Honolulu in Samuels, *The Japanese and the Haoles of Honolulu.*

hood in which Catholics and Protestants live in about equal numbers with little or no segregation of housing. Even the local country club is nonexclusive, with about equal numbers of Catholics and Protestants among the membership.[33] But alongside this residential integration is a high degree of separation of the children between public and parochial schools, with almost no contact between students in the two types of schools (no inter-school athletic contests, for example). Greeley observes also that one might play bridge for years and never sit with a person of the other faith and that, even in the "integrated" country club, there is a striking tendency for Catholics to play golf with Catholics, and for Protestants to play with Protestants. Similarly, in a study of racial patterns in the South Shore section of Chicago, Molotch finds residential integration coexisting with many subtle kinds of racial segregation.[34] For example, public parks and shopping facilities are used by people of both races; however, there tends to be the same kind of segregation of ball games played in the public parks that Greeley noted in the bridge games and golf matches of suburbia. Even that most "impersonal" of social transactions, the buying of goods and services, shows some racial segregation, with whites dominating the shopping scene in the daytime, blacks at night (especially Saturday night), when many whites are apparently afraid to go out.

The complex relationship between residential segregation, school segregation, and interethnic social distance or *prejudice* has been a matter of much concern in recent years in the United States. Although the Supreme Court in 1954 declared that racially segregated schools are "inherently unequal" and therefore unconstitutional, there is to this day great controversy about the way in which school integration should be implemented. Much of this controversy arises from the fact that neither residential segregation nor interracial social distance has been defined as unconstitutional, and both these features persist in American social life.[35] With residential segregation still strong in American cities, school segregation has been generated "de facto" by the pattern of the neighborhood school, which

---

[33]Greeley, *Why Can't They Be Like Us?*, pp. 103–119.

[34]Harvey Molotch, "Racial Integration in a Transitional Community," *American Sociological Review,* 34(1969):878–893.

[35]As we note in Chapter 6, the *form* of white racism in the United States has changed considerably, but not necessarily its intensity. On the persistence of racial segregation in the United States, see Robert E. Forman, *Black Ghettos, White Ghettos and Slums* (Englewood Cliffs, N.J.: Prentice-Hall, 1971).

services all the residents of a given neighborhood. If it "so happens" that nearly all the residents of a neighborhood are members of one ethnic group, then nearly all students attending a given neighborhood school are going to be of one ethnic group.[36] The recent practice of busing white children to schools in black neighborhoods or black children to schools in white neighborhoods has generated much resistance. White parents, especially, protest this assault on the integrity of the neighborhood school or, alternatively, complain that the quality of their children's education suffers by association with black children, who are believed to be more educationally retarded.[37] The interracial violence in Boston is a recent dramatic example of this protest.

Whether opposition to busing to achieve racial balance in schools is really based on such "rational" grounds or on more irrational feelings of interracial distance is a matter of some uncertainty. Skeptics have observed the fallacy of the argument that integration downgrades educational quality. Binzen asserts, for example, that residents of a white section of Philadelphia are perfectly willing to accept a low level of educational quality for their children's schools (it is even suggested that some nearby black schools maintain higher standards) so long as school officials do not try to shift students between black and white schools.[38] On the other hand, Greeley has argued that too many of our intellectuals, themselves lacking firm ties to neighborhoods, fail to recognize the emotional investment of people in "their" neighborhood and the resentment felt when people of an alien ethnicity intrude upon an ethnically homogeneous neighborhood.[39] As Greeley says, his purpose in these observations is not to "canonize" the neighborhood, but to engender some understanding of why ethnic groups resist social experiments that ignore such commitments to "social turf."

---

[36]Pettigrew cites Cincinnati, Philadelphia, Chicago, New York, and Los Angeles as cities in which a majority of students attend schools in which nearly all their fellow students are of the same ethnic group as themselves. Thomas F. Pettigrew, "The Racial Integration of the Schools," in Thomas F. Pettigrew (ed.), *Racial Discrimination in the United States* (New York: Harper & Row, 1975), pp. 224–239.

[37]That even "white liberals" have opposed busing as a solution to the problem of racial segregation is indicated by Judith Caditz, "Ambivalence Toward Integration: The Sequence of Response to Six Interracial Situations," *Sociological Quarterly,* 16(Winter, 1975):16–32.

[38]Peter Binzen, *Whitetown USA* (New York: Random House, 1970), p. 192.

[39]Greeley, *Why Can't They Be Like Us?,* pp. 96–101.

There is, however, a subtle form of racism involved in this emotional commitment to the "neighborhood," as indicated in a study by Pettigrew of the supporters of Louise Day Hicks, a militant leader of antibusing forces in Boston.[40] Although less than 10 percent of her white supporters expressed opposition in principle to racial integration of schools, 64 percent indicated opposition to the idea of sending their children to schools in which a *majority* of students were black.[41] Large numbers of her supporters also expressed attitudes favorable to residential segregation of blacks and whites. Indeed, it is Pettigrew's suggestion that the opposition to racial mixture in the schools is based on the fact that supporters of Mrs. Hicks view school segregation as a "harbinger of residential desegregation."[42] As Greeley suggests, busing opponents *are* genuinely attached to their neighborhoods (Pettigrew reports that more supporters than nonsupporters of Hicks own their own homes and have lived for a long time in their neighborhood), but this is apparently an attachment to the racial status quo of the neighborhood. Their opposition to *extensive* desegregation is perhaps a specification of a general attitude of conservatism, as evidenced by the fact that many more pro-Hicks than anti-Hicks Bostonians agreed with the statement: "Things are pretty good nowadays—it is best to keep things the way they are."[43]

DESEGREGATION AND THE REDUCTION OF SOCIAL DISTANCE

We have just seen that the relationship between physical separation (segregation) and social distance (prejudice) is a complex one. To the extent, however, that social distance is based on fear of the unknown and the tendency to reduce this fear by stereotyping (often in the negative form of prejudice) members of other ethnic groups, it would seem that any events that lead to greater contact (desegregation) between ethnic groups

---

[40]Thomas F. Pettigrew, *Racially Separate or Together?* (New York: McGraw-Hill, 1971), pp. 211–229.

[41]Ringer found a similar reaction among Gentiles living in "Lakeville," a midwestern suburb. Some 20 percent of the Gentiles indicated a preference for living in a community with *no* Jews; only 1 to 2 percent preferred a community with a *majority* of Jews. Ringer, *The Edge of Friendliness,* p. 157.

[42]Pettigrew, *Racially Separate or Together,* p. 223.

[43]Pettigrew, *Racially Separate or Together,* p. 219.

would help to reduce social distance.[44] This so-called *contact hypothesis* has been qualified by a recognition of the influence of one of the two forces encouraging social distance as discussed above: the impact of *status* considerations in intergroup associations. Any forced association of higher with lower status ethnic groups is likely to engender the resistance of "superior" groups to such "contaminating" contacts and resentments by "inferior" groups of the standoffish attitudes of the superiors. The amendment, then, to the contact hypothesis is that this contact must be between members of different ethnic groups who are of approximately *equal status.*[45]

This equal-status amendment will lead to three sorts of predictions or hypotheses about the social distance effects of interethnic contacts: (1) Where there is a system of ethnic stratification in which *all* members of a dominant group are higher in status than *any* member of a minority group, there will be no occasion for equal-status contacts between members of those two groups and contact will therefore never lead to a reduction in social distance.[46] (2) When there is some overlap in the distribution of high-status and low-status positions between two ethnic groups (some blacks, for example, being as high in social status as some whites), reduced social distance will result only from those contacts between members of the two ethnic groups who are of approximately equal status.[47] (3) When

---

[44]Thus Williams and his research associates were able to substantiate this assumption in surveys of a number of American communities: "In all the surveys in all communities and for all groups, majority and minorities, the greater the frequency of interaction, the lower the prevalence of ethnic prejudice." Robin Williams, *Strangers Next Door* (Englewood Cliffs, N.J.: Prentice-Hall, 1964), pp. 167–168. For a useful summary of data on the contact hypothesis, see Simpson and Yinger, *Racial and Cultural Minorities,* pp. 673–684.

[45]It should be added, perhaps, that it is the *perception* of relative status of ethnic groups by the people involved that determines the attitudinal impact of cross-ethnic contact. Among the residents of various integrated and segregated neighborhoods in Dayton, Ohio, those whites who *believe* that blacks are higher in status are those most likely to express favorable attitudes toward blacks. David C. Morris, "Racial Attitudes of White Residents in Integrated and Segregated Neighborhoods," *Sociological Focus,* 6(Spring, 1973):74–94.

[46]In Chapter 5 we shall discuss an "echelon" system of interethnic relations in which all members of one group outrank all members of another group. Under such conditions, according to this hypothesis, interracial contacts such as might occur in "traditional" black-white relations in the United States would not tend to lessen social distance.

[47]Contact would thus be effective in reducing social distance only for those relatively few minority group members whose status position was on a par with that of their dominant-group associates. One reason why the integrated experience in the military services may be of strategic importance to American blacks is that the military replaces external indicators of

considering the overall status of an ethnic group (rather than status differentials among group members), the hypothesis would predict less of a reduction in social distance when high-status groups come in contact with low-status groups than when not-so-high-status groups come in contact with low-status groups. For example, Mexican-Americans coming in contact with blacks or Indians would be more likely to experience a reduction in social distance than would Anglos coming in contact with blacks or Indians.[48]

The only one of these hypotheses to be given much research consideration is the second—the one dealing with the effect on social distance (or prejudice) of contacts between *individual* ethnic group members of equal status. Since residential patterns in the United States tend to cluster people by income or some other index of status, it is understandable that much of the research on equal-status contacts has focused on the effect of integrated housing on the degree of racial prejudice reported by people who have experienced such integration. A series of studies[49] has shown that whites living in integrated housing situations tend to show less prejudice toward blacks as compared with whites living in segregated housing situations.[50]

---

status with its own system of ranks, and *enforces* equality of treatment of all those in the same rank. Thus, all privates, regardless of ethnicity, are reduced to the lowest status and are assigned to menial tasks; all officers, regardless of ethnicity, are accorded whatever privileges their rank in the military hierarchy confers.

[48]See Brown, "Social Distance Perception as a Function of Mexican-American and Other Identity," who shows that Mexican-American students in a Texas University report feeling less prejudice (social distance) than did Anglo students toward blacks, American Indians, and Italians. Similarly for a population of residents of Houston, Texas, see Davidson and Gaitz, "Ethnic Attitudes as a Basis for Minority Cooperation in a Southwestern Metropolis."

[49]Morton Deutsch and Mary E. Collins, *Interracial Housing* (Minneapolis: University of Minnesota Press, 1951); Daniel M. Wilner, Rosabelle P. Walkley, and Stuart W. Cook, *Human Relations in Interracial Housing: A Study of the Contact Hypothesis* (Minneapolis: University of Minnesota Press, 1955). For a recent study contradicting the contact hypothesis, see Morris, "Racial Attitudes of White Residents In Integrated and Segregated Neighborhoods."

[50]There is an obvious problem of serious proportion in arguing that whites in integrated settings are less prejudiced "because of" their experience with integration. It may be, of course, that those who are less prejudiced are more likely to choose to live in integrated surroundings. Several of the studies cited here deal with this problem by comparing racial prejudice in integrated versus segregated environments in which people had not really chosen either integration or segregation; for example, applicants for public housing who were assigned, without consideration of their wishes, to either a segregated or an integrated apartment building.

Critical analysis of the contact hypothesis, especially as applied to the effects of housing integration, has raised a number of recurring doubts about the general validity of this hypothesis. Two major points were raised in a recent reexamination that used data on interracial attitudes in several integrated and segregated neighborhoods in one American city.[51]

First, it appears that most of the earlier studies had focused on racial attitudes of *whites* under conditions of racial integration. In this study, which included interviews with blacks as well as whites, it was found that *blacks* in integrated neighborhoods felt no more favorably disposed toward whites than did blacks in segregated neighborhoods. This finding may reflect the fact that members of traditionally inferior groups have more realistic and less stereotyped ideas about members of dominant groups than dominant group members have about minority group members.[52] Whites thus have further to go in developing a realistic understanding of members of the other race.[53]

Second, a variable not usually dealt with in the earlier studies was whether or not the particular interracial contact was the first experience of people in an integrated situation. In this study it was found that most subjects reporting some prior experience were more likely to have their attitudes "favorably" affected by the current experience. This suggests that, while the initial contact with "aliens" may have been more shocking than enlightening, subsequent experiences may be approached with less trepidation.

An additional source of doubt about the general validity of the contact hypothesis is the observation that there seems to be a fundamentally different reaction of people toward intergroup contact, depending on whether integration or segregation was the originally established "norm" in a particular situation. A newly built residential area with clearly estab-

---

[51]W. Scott Ford, "Interracial Public Housing in a Border City: Another Look at the Contact Hypothesis," *American Journal of Sociology,* 78(May, 1973):1426–1447.

[52]An hypothesis to this effect was suggested in Jerry D. Rose, "The Role of the Other in Self-Evaluation," *Sociological Quarterly,* 10(Fall, 1969):470–479; and was given empirical verification in Darwin L. Thomas, David D. Franks, and James M. Calonico, "Role-Taking and Power in Social Psychology," *American Sociological Review,* 37(October, 1972):605–614.

[53]Dollard observed that, in "Southerntown," it was generally understood that the blacks were the best "psychologists" around, that they "knew their white people" and were able to "work" them accordingly, while the average black was something of a mystery to the average white. John Dollard, *Caste and Class in a Southern Town* (New Haven, Conn.: Yale University Press, 1937).

lished "open occupancy" rules forbidding ethnic discrimination is likely to attract residents who are more disposed to reducing social distance through their interethnic contacts. On the other hand, in an area that was originally segregated, the introduction of ethnic newcomers may exaggerate preexisting feelings of social distance by bringing into play the residents' fear of the unfamiliar or of status contamination. This hypothesis is supported by the findings of an earlier study about the effects of the employment of white workers of southern origin in northern industrial plants.[54] Killian found that some plant managers who already had many black workers were reluctant to hire such "hillbillies" in anticipation of racial trouble. Those managers who *did* hire white southern workers tended to make it clear to them that they would be working alongside blacks and employment under these conditions was offered on a "take it or leave it" basis. The quality of interracial relations appears to depend largely on the conditions prevailing when these relations are initiated. If they are started under a "premise of equality," they seem much more likely to produce the hypothesized reduction in social distance under "equal-status" conditions.

---

[54]Lewis M. Killian, "The Effects of Southern White Workers on Race Relations in Northern Plants," *American Sociological Review,* 17(June, 1952):327–331.

CHAPTER 5
ETHNIC STRATIFICATION: PATTERNS OF DOMINANCE

In the preceeding chapter we emphasized the element of *distance* in human relationships to highlight one phase of ethnic relations. We turn now to another fundamental feature of the orientation of persons to one another: the element of *power* in social relations, and the possibility that, under some conditions, some ethnic groups will establish a relationship of dominance over other ethnic groups. A society in which such relations of dominance and subordination between ethnic groups prevail is one in which *ethnic stratification* prevails. Throughout this discussion, we shall use the terms *dominant group* and *minority group* to designate those ethnic groups that occupy either high or low positions in the system of ethnic stratification.

DIMENSIONS OF STRATIFICATION

Any contemporary sociological analysis of the differential power of various groups is likely to be influenced more or less directly by Max

Weber's famous essay on the subject entitled "Class, Status and Party."[1] The three terms in the title of this essay refer to three different dimensions of power as differentially distributed among people. The *class* position of a group refers to its economic power—its capacity to work its will in the marketplace, to command a favorable income, to possess property, to monopolize consumer goods, etc. Most such distinctions are captured in popular language by those words and phrases that distinguish the rich from the poor. A *status group,* in Weber's usage, is a group of people with a distinguishable level of social power, that is, who have the capacity to command respect or deferential treatment by other persons. *Social respectability* is perhaps the nearest popular term for denoting this dimension of power. Finally, *party* points to the differential political power of groups, their ability or inability to work their wills in the operation of the various organs of government.

Weber's definitions of types of power provide the basis for some fundamental questions about the nature of domination by some groups of human beings over other groups of human beings. In thinking about these three dimensions of stratification with reference to ethnic relations, two alternative models of power relationships come immediately to mind. One model presents the possibility—indeed, often the reality—that group power in one of these dimensions may be used to enhance the power of the group in another dimension, thus suggesting that Weber's three dimensions of power are *interchangeable.* For instance, a group comprised of many wealthy persons may use that wealth to "buy" control (either directly or indirectly) of political office or to secure positions of honor for themselves; the politically powerful may use their power to improve their financial position; and so forth. The other model suggests that these three dimensions of power may not always coincide—may, in fact, be *independent* of one another. For example, persons of great wealth may be denied social honor or political influence if their wealth is thought to be "ill-gotten"; the social elite of a community—its old family "aristocracy"—may not be its wealthiest or most politically influential; and so forth. The question of whether a given ethnic (or any other) group is a *minority group* must at least entertain the possibility that social disadvantage in one area

---

[1]H. H. Gerth and C. Wright Mills (eds.), *From Max Weber: Essays in Sociology* (New York: Oxford University Press, 1958), pp. 180–195.

may not be generalized to a disability in all aspects of the group's social existence.

We take no position here on the relative merits of the interchangeability and independence models of power relationships. A fully rounded description of ethnic relations between groups in a specific context (e.g., French-English relations in Canada, Jewish-Gentile relations in the United States) would probably have to adopt one or the other of these positions. But, since the purpose of this book is not to describe fully any ethnic situation but to furnish some tools for the analysis of specific situations, we limit ourselves in this chapter to a closer examination of some of the considerations involved in Weber's three dimensions of power. Adopting his language, we shall examine below the three types of stratification (economic, social, political) indicated by his analysis.[2]

ECONOMIC STRATIFICATION

The general distinction between "the rich" and "the poor" is often closely related to the interaction of different ethnic groups in the same social environment. Black, Indian, and Chicano Americans, for example, are found in overwhelming numbers among the poor, whereas Japanese and Jewish Americans tend to be among the affluent. So often is this the case that it is sometimes argued that so-called race relations are really "class relations," that the "revolt against inequality," which we shall discuss in Chapter 7, is actually a revolt of the deprived ethnic groups against the economic domination of peoples of European origin.[3] Further support for the importance of considering "class" in any discussion of relationships between ethnic groups was indicated in the previous chapter, where we saw that equal status is probably a necessary condition for harmonious interaction in contact situations. When equal status is only very infrequently the case in interpersonal contact across ethnic lines (the more usual situation being, for example, the unequal-status relation of white

---

[2]With some apology for using the term *social stratification* as one of several dimensions of stratification since, from the author's viewpoint, all forms of stratification are "social" in the broad sense of dealing with socially controlled relationships between people or groups of people.

[3]For a survey of some viewpoints of this type, along with an attempted refutation of the view by showing that the revolutions in Zanzibar and Ruanda were essentially "race" rather than "class" revolutions, see Leo Kuper, "Theories of Revolution and Race Relations," *Comparative Studies in Society and History,* 13(January, 1971):87–107.

employer and black employee), then it would appear that such contact may only engender social distance rather than reduce it.

Sociological discussion of economic stratification has been overwhelmingly oriented toward the area of *employment* since, with rare exceptions, an individual's wealth or income is derived from some gainful employment or job; in the case of inherited wealth, income is based on the job earnings of one's forebears. It seems reasonable, then, to concentrate analysis on three conditions that mark an ethnic group as a minority with regard to its economic position. Economic disadvantage will result if most members of an ethnic group experience one or more of these conditions: (1) unemployment, (2) employment in less remunerative lines of work (underemployment), and (3) less remuneration than dominant-group members in the same line of work (underpayment).

Unemployment

In a tight labor market—one in which there are fewer jobs than there are job seekers—the subordination of a minority group may be indicated by the relative difficulty its members have in getting and holding steady jobs. The unemployment rate of black Americans has been two to three times higher than the unemployment rate of white Americans during the last fifteen years; and black unemployment is especially high among young men.[4] The unemployment situation among American Indians is even worse. In the "full employment" year of 1967, with an overall national unemployment rate of 3.1 percent, the unemployment rate of nonwhites was 6.0 percent, while that of Indians living on reservations was 37.3 percent.[5] At about the same time there were certain reservations on which the unemployment rate among Indian males was as high as 79 percent.[6]

Some of the wider consequences of high unemployment among ethnic group members have been noted. In the case of the American Indian, the high proportion of alcoholics among the Indian population has been related to the frustrations attending the abject poverty in which many Indian

---

[4]Bernard E. Anderson, "Full Employment and Economic Equality," *Annals of American Academy of Political and Social Science,* 418(March, 1975):127–137.

[5]Alan L. Sorkin, *American Indians and Federal Aid* (Washington, D. C.: Brookings Institution, 1971), p.12.

[6]Sorkin, *American Indians and Federal Aid,* p. 14.

people live.[7] In the case of blacks, the well-publicized "matriarchal" tendency in black families is apparently largely the result of the inability of the unemployed (or underemployed) husband to provide economically for his wife and children. This failure to provide weakens the family's power in both a direct economic sense and in a more extended social sense.

Economically, the presence of an unemployed man in the household may be an out-and-out liability. A mother's eligibility for public welfare assistance (Aid to Dependent Children, or ADC) to support her children may be based on the existence of a household without an "able-bodied" man. Thus, many black men are actually discouraged from living with their families in a husband-father role. As Billingsley puts it: "Many low-income Negro families are often forced to choose (due to current ADC procedures) between a father in the home and money in the home, and many make the pragmatic choice for money."[8]

According to the interchangeability conception of power relationships, black economic deprivation, especially among young black men, would tend to generate subordination in the area of social power as well. In a society that emphasizes the male role as breadwinner, a man unable to provide this bread suffers a loss of social respectability.[9] If, for example, he goes on welfare, he is likely to find himself labeled by the "haves" of the society as a "have not" without will or gumption to make it for himself, a parasite who would rather take a handout than get a job. The unemployed male thus has nothing to give his family in the way of a respectable standing in the community. With the loss of social respect there often goes, of course, a loss of self-respect[10] and, perhaps, an attempt to compensate

---

[7]For a study of off-reservation Indian behavior that illustrates this relation between drinking and economic privation, see Theodore D. Graves, "The Personal Adjustment of Navajo Indian Migrants to Denver, Colorado," *American Anthropologist,* 72(February, 1970):35–54.

[8]Andrew Billingsley, *Black Families in White America* (Englewood Cliffs, N.J.: Prentice-Hall, 1968), pp. 156, 157.

[9]Mirra Komarovsky, *The Unemployed Man and His Family* (New York: Dryden Press, 1940; reprint ed., New York: Octagon Books, 1970).

[10]This effect is demonstrated in, among other studies, Elliott Liebow, *Tally's Corner* (Boston: Little, Brown, 1966); David Schulz, *Coming Up Black: Patterns of Ghetto Socialization* (Englewood Cliffs, N.J.: Prentice-Hall, 1969); Ulf Hannerz, "Roots of Black Manhood," *Trans-action,* 6(October, 1969):13–21. Banton comments on "an interesting implication that, in a white supremacy society, the Negro women gain a relative advantage because they suffer less from racial subordination than their men, and because the subordination of the men permits their women to seize greater authority in domestic matters." Michael Banton, *Race Relations* (New York: Basic Books, 1967), p. 186.

for status loss by withdrawing into a hell-raising street corner life with the rest of the "boys."[11]

Underemployment

Data on the rate of unemployment among members of an ethnic group provide, of course, only a relatively small part of the picture of economic disadvantage arising from limited employment opportunities. Most black American men—even young ones—have jobs of some sort, but the jobs tend to be concentrated at levels or in fields that are low paying. To cite a few indications of this: in 1969, although blacks comprised about 11 percent of the population of the United States, only 3 percent of workers classified as "managers, officials, and proprietors" were nonwhite, and only 6 percent of "professional and technical" workers and 7 percent of "craftsmen and foremen" were nonwhite, while fully 27 percent of all "nonfarm laborers" and 44 percent of all "private household workers" were nonwhite.[12]

Ethnic enterprise. The relatively small number of American blacks listed as "managers, officials, and proprietors" suggests an aspect of economic subordination that has been of much interest in the black community itself. The subject has also generated a considerable body of sociological writing.[13] Blacks and those friendly to their situation have encouraged black ownership of business—especially businesses catering to a black clientele. This "black capitalism" is often seen as something of a panacea for black economic ills, since it is widely believed that black employers would be less racially discriminatory in their hiring practices than are white employers and that the profits of black-owned business would be invested in the

---

[11]This compensatory explanation of young black male street behavior is suggested in John H. Rohrer and M. S. Edmonson (eds.), *The Eighth Generation: Cultures and Personalities of New Orleans Negroes* (New York: Harper, 1960). It also follows closely the view of Cohen that delinquent lower-class gang activity represents an attempt by lower-class youths to substitute a delinquent world in which they can succeed for a legitimate world in which they *cannot* succeed. Albert K. Cohen, *Delinquent Boys: The Culture of the Gang* (Glencoe, Ill.: Free Press, 1955).

[12]George E. Simpson and J. Milton Yinger, *Racial and Cultural Minorities,* 4th ed. (New York: Harper & Row, 1972), p. 323.

[13]Some titles in this literature include James M. Hund, *Black Entrepreneurship* (Belmont, Calif.: Wadsworth, 1970); Earl Ofari, *The Myth of Black Capitalism* (New York: Monthly Review Press, 1970); Ronald W. Bailey (ed.), *Black Business Enterprise* (New York: Basic Books, 1971); Edwin M. Epstein and David R. Hampton (eds.), *Black Americans and White Business* (Encino, Calif.: Dickenson, 1971).

"black economy" rather than being used to enrich white financial institutions. The sociologist's questions on this matter seem to be, (a) Why has there been so little self-employment among blacks until this time? (b) To what extent could discrimination in the job market be overcome by putting more ownership of employing organizations in the hands of blacks?

On the first point—the dearth of black entrepreneurial activity so far— there has been a variety of explanations. To illustrate, we will mention four:

1. It has been argued that black Americans—unlike other American ethnic groups such as the Jews or the Chinese—have no "tradition" of self-employment.[14] An aspect of the "communal deprivation" inflicted on blacks by slavery was their enforced inability to engage in *any* autonomous social activity, entrepreneurial or otherwise.[15] A great many successful family businesses are built up over several generations, during which time the business acquires a clientele through the development of a favorable reputation in the community (legally called "goodwill") and children acquire technological know-how and often inherited capital from their parents. Thus any present lack of entrepreneurial activity may reflect the lack of such activity among the forebears of currently employed members of an ethnic group.

2. In contrasting the lack of business ownership among blacks with the entrepreneurial success of some other ethnic groups, it has been suggested that the cultural distinctiveness of a group and the tendency toward perpetuating a unique ethnic life style may have encouraged such activity for other ethnic groups, but not for blacks.[16] Peoples with very different traditional cultures who maintain a "sojourner" attitude of only temporary

---

[14]E. Franklin Frazier, *The Negro in the United States,* 2nd ed. (New York: Macmillan, 1957), pp. 410, 411; Eugene P. Foley, "The Negro Businessman: In Search of a Tradition," *Daedalus,* 95(Winter, 1966):107–144.

[15]Roy Simon Bryce-Laporte, "The American Slave Plantation and Our Heritage of Communal Deprivation," *American Behavioral Scientist,* 12(March–April, 1969):2–8.

[16]Robert H. Kinzer and Edward Sagarin, *The Negro in American Business: The Conflict Between Separation and Integration* (New York: Greenberg, 1950). In a study of Pakistanis in Bradford, England, Dahya points out that Pakistani businessmen, dependent on an ethnic clientele, have a vested interest in their customers *remaining* Pakistani culturally. Accordingly, these businesssmen tend to be very active in promoting community activities that have an ethnic flavor. Badr Dahya, "The Nature of Pakistani Ethnicity in Industrial Cities in Britain," in Abner Cohen (ed.), *Urban Ethnicity* (London: Tavistock, 1974), p. 93.

residence in a country are inclined to resist acculturation in the area of taste in consumer goods. Thus Americans of Chinese or Puerto Rican descent are likely to patronize grocery stores that cater to the unique tastes of people from these countries. Black Americans, however, have little or no connection with native African tastes, and the Americanized version of black culture designated as "soul" has generated little business activity designed to satisfy the consumer demands of that life style.[17] Where such activities do exist—in the rather extensive production of soul music, for example—the pattern of black consumer demands being met largely by white-dominated business interests prevails here, as elsewhere.[18]

3. The foregoing interpretation of why black enterprise is retarded has been criticized by Light, who offers an alternative interpretation in a study in which he compared Japanese, Chinese, and black American communities with reference to their entrepreneurial activities.[19] The two Oriental groups, in contrast with the blacks, have been heavily involved in business enterprise in America. This propensity of the Japanese and Chinese to engage in entrepreneurial activity *cannot,* Light argues, be totally explained by the tendency of such businesses to cater to the special consumer demands of an ethnic clientele. For one thing, the amount of enterprise conducted by Orientals in a given community may be far greater than would be the case if there were sole or principal dependence on an ethnic clientele. The Chinese restaurant or laundry, the Japanese landscaping business—all depend for their success on support from outside the ethnic community. For another, those Oriental businesses with predominantly ethnic clienteles may be heavily involved in consumer demands that do not reflect traditional life styles. Chinese groceries stock evaporated milk as well as ginger root, and when Chinese-Americans "buy Chinese," they may well be buying non-Chinese goods from a Chinese merchant.

---

[17] In New York City, for example, with its proliferation of "ethnic" restaurants—Italian, Greek, French, etc.—the "soul" restaurant is almost totally absent. Baklava is available in any number of restaurants, but where can one buy a serving of turnip greens or black-eyed peas?

[18] This situation may relect the fact that "soul" musical styles tend to be appropriated by whites who are also interested in the soul life style. The three major components of soul music —gospel, jazz, and urban blues (as opposed to "country" music)—have all attracted interest far beyond the black community. Charles Keil, *Urban Blues* (Chicago: University of Chicago Press, 1966).

[19] Ivan H. Light, *Ethnic Enterprise in America* (Berkeley: University of California Press, 1972).

Light suggests that the crucial difference between Oriental and black Americans may be the existence among Orientals, but not among blacks, of a traditional system that makes it relatively easy for the would-be entrepreneur to acquire the capital needed to start up a business. Light describes the operation of the exotic (from an Occidental perspective) custom of the "rotating credit association" that makes it possible for every participant in the scheme to have unrestricted use of the money in a pool generated by the participants. Oriental entrepreneurs in the United States have made much use of this device for capitalization of businesses. Blacks, deprived of this source,[20] have had to depend on banks or other formal lending agencies. If controlled by whites, these lending institutions have tended to be racially discriminatory in their lending policies; if controlled by blacks, they have tended to be unstable in their financial structures.

4. Another explanation for the differences in entrepreneurial activity between Orientals and blacks is suggested in the notion of the social role of the middleman in ethnic stratification systems.[21] Middlemen are intermediaries between the most dominant and the most subordinate groups in a population. This middleman function often takes the form of retail merchandising, the conveying of goods from dominant-group members, who profit from their production, to the masses, who consume the goods. These merchants tend to be rather precariously balanced between the negative reactions of both dominant and subordinate groups: dominants find them too grubby and calculating; subordinates often see them as exploiters who sell shoddy goods at exorbitant prices.[22] In addition to this rejection of themselves in their social environments, middlemen entrepreneurs must face the classic problem of getting started. This involves not only the problem of credit to capitalize a business, as discussed above, but

---

[20]Light indicates that very similar customs were found in traditional African cultures; however, as we have already noted, the experience of slavery in the United States effectively cut off blacks from this ethnic tradition.

[21]Hubert M. Blalock, *Toward a Theory of Minority-Group Relations* (New York: Wiley, 1967), pp. 79–84; Edna Bonacich, "A Theory of Middleman Minorities," *American Sociological Review*, 38(October, 1973):583–594.

[22]For the attitudes of black ghetto residents toward white merchants, and the reciprocal hostile feelings of the merchants, see David Boesel et al., "White Institutions and Black Rage," *Trans-action*, 6(March, 1969):24–31. That so-called black anti-Semitism is largely limited to blacks' resentment of the behavior of Jews in such "middleman" or merchandising roles is indicated in Gertrude Selznick and Stephen Steinberg, *The Tenacity of Prejudice* (New York: Harper & Row, 1969), pp. 117–131.

a willingness to work long hours for a minimum standard of living so that profits can be plowed back into the business to expand it.[23]

Perhaps it requires something of the "sojourner" attitude of some ethnic groups to be able to endure these conditions. People can stand to be "despised and rejected" in the immediate social environment if they believe that eventually they will return home to live among their "own" people after having turned a tidy profit on "overseas" entrepreneurial activity. Such consideration would certainly explain some of the differences in entrepreneurial activity between blacks and Orientals. Most black Americans have always understood that, for better or worse, they are here to stay. Many Oriental immigrants (as well as Italian, Greek, Puerto Rican, Mexican-American, etc.) have assumed, at least in the early stages of their stay in the United States, that they would be returning to their countries of origin. Although probably most Americans of Oriental extraction are also now here to stay, their desire to stay may be one of the ironic effects of their earlier economic success. Having achieved monetary success in their middleman economic roles, they now are loathe to return to a China or a Japan that is about as remote to their personal experience as it is to that of most other Americans.[24]

Ethnics in the labor market.   Self-employment is clearly the "wave of the past" in the occupational scene in the United States and other industrial countries, and most ethnic group members must stand or fall economically on their ability to make themselves "salable" to those who will pay wages for their work. This fact is as true for white-collar occupations such

---

[23] The sociologically educated reader may recognize in this work syndrome a close similarity to Weber's attribution of the influence of a "Protestant ethic" on the capitalistic activities of persons adhering to the Calvinist brand of Protestantism. The parallel is strengthened when we note that Weber also described the early capitalist entrepreneur as being "despised and rejected" among his peers, who still felt commercial enterprise was sinful and should be restricted—a view contrary to the hard-working "sober bourgeois" spirit of the modern capitalist, who saw commercial success as a mark of God's blessing. One can speculate that perhaps today, because there is no religious ethic (except possibly the teachings of the Black Muslims) that gives strong sanction to entrepreneurial activity, ethnic middlemen with sojourner attitudes have taken on these marginal economic roles. Max Weber, *The Protestant Ethic and the Spirit of Capitalism,* trans. by Talcott Parsons (New York: Scribner's, 1930).

[24] As one indication of this, Kitano reports that newly arrived immigrants from Japan can hardly be understood by Japanese-Americans several generations removed from the immigration of their ancestors, and that the newcomers may be objects of derision, as when they are referred to as F.O.B.'s (Fresh Off the Boat). Harry H. L. Kitano, *Japanese Americans* (Englewood Cliffs, N.J.: Prentice-Hall, 1969), pp. 132, 133.

as teaching or scientific research as it is for blue-collar jobs or manual labor. The question to be addressed in this section is, To what extent are minority group members denied opportunities to compete on an equal basis for jobs with members of the dominant ethnic groups?

Any number of sociological studies have indicated the heavy concentration of minority group members in occupations of lesser income and prestige.[25] A typical observation is that there is a dual labor market whereby, for example, native British workers dominate occupations of higher rank while the less desirable occupations are the lot of Britain's Commonwealth immigrants.[26]

There may, of course, be explanations other than discrimination for such occupational distributions (some of these explanations will be suggested in the following chapter). The inadequate education of many American blacks may be a factor in their occupational disadvantage,[27] as may be their tendency toward a "culture of poverty," whereby they become resigned to their low social position. But even when such "explaining away" variables are controlled for, as in a recent study of applicants for disability benefits under social security,[28] it can be shown that blacks of a *given* level of education and a *given* work attitude may be occupationally disadvantaged compared with whites who have a similar level of education and a similar attitude toward work.

Employment opportunities for minority groups are largely a function of the redistribution of residential and employment patterns among members of dominant groups. Traditionally, the movement of earlier immigrant groups away from the central city has opened up job opportunities for more recent migrant groups willing to settle in the core areas of American cities.[29] The rapid suburbanization of the white population in the United

---

[25]A number of such studies of minority ethnic groups in the United States are reviewed in Simpson and Yinger, *Racial and Cultural Minorities,* chap. 11.

[26]Nicholas Bosanquet and Peter B. Doeringer, "Is There a Dual Labour Market in Great Britain?" *Economic Journal,* 83(June, 1973):421–435.

[27]Stanley Lieberson and Glenn V. Fuguitt, "Negro-White Occupational Differences in the Absence of Discrimination," *American Journal of Sociology,* 73(September, 1967):188–200.

[28]Elmer A. Spreitzer and Saad Z. Nagi, "Race and Equality of Opportunity: A Controlled Study," *Phylon,* 34(September, 1973):248–255.

[29]W. Lloyd Warner and Leo Srole, *The Social Systems of American Ethnic Groups* (New Haven, Conn.: Yale University Press, 1945). The same process of occupational advancement of early groups as later groups arrive is described in John Brown, *The Unmelting Pot: An English Town and Its Immigrants* (London: Macmillan, 1970).

States following World War II may have opened up job possibilities for urban blacks, who were generally left behind in the movement to the suburbs. A picture emerges of a lessening gap between black and white in occupational opportunities available to the two races.[30] Nevertheless, a substantial gap remains, partly because employment opportunities for blacks in the inner city have not kept pace with changes in the racial composition of urban neighborhoods.

A study of black ghetto areas in Boston, Chicago, and Washington, D.C. verifies this fact that despite residential turnover in the inner city, job opportunities may still be somewhat limited.[31] In these as in other cities, employers in black ghetto areas tend to be whites who live in suburban locations several miles from their places of business and who employ many white workers who also live outside the ghetto. These white employees are often people who once lived in the area and who have retained their jobs even though they no longer live in the neighborhood. Neither the white owner nor the white wage earner stays in the ghetto necessarily out of a strong desire to hold onto these economic positions. In the case of the white businessman, he may find the cost of starting over elsewhere prohibitive, or he may be willing to sell but cannot find a black buyer with enough capital to buy him out. The white wage earner may simply not be able to find a job closer to home. Even if all businesses in black ghettos were transferred to black owners and if only blacks were employed by these owners, Aldrich shows that only 40 to 50 percent of ghetto residents could be so employed. Black ghetto areas must of necessity be "labor exporters," which means many ghetto residents must seek employment outside the ghetto and contend with all the discriminations that exist in the general labor market.

Underpayment

Even though members of an ethnic minority may achieve some degree of equality of opportunity to secure "better" lines of employment, they may be victims of discriminatory wage-payment practices whereby members of dominant groups are paid more than minority group members even

---

[30]Claire C. Hodge, "The Negro Job Situation: Has It Improved?" *Monthly Labor Review,* January, 1969, pp. 20–28; Reynolds Farley and Albert Hermalin, "The 1960s: A Decade of Progress for Blacks?" *Demography,* 9(1972):353–370.

[31]Howard E. Aldrich, "Employment Opportunities for Blacks in the Black Ghetto: The Role of White-owned Businesses," *American Journal of Sociology,* 78(May, 1973):1403–1425.

though both are doing the same work. To illustrate: in the copper mines of Northern Rhodesia, industrial employers (with the support of all-white labor unions) maintain one wage scale for European workers and a lower scale for native workers.[32] This discriminatory policy is justified by management on the grounds that the standard of living in traditional native economies is lower than that prevailing in the European countries of origin of white workers. Powdermaker indicates the fallacy in this rationalization by showing the bitter reaction to the policy by the native workers, many of whom have acquired quite modern tastes in consumer goods and feel economically deprived relative to the white workers.

In the United States, studies of the earning power of blacks and Mexican-Americans suggest a similar "cost" of belonging to one of these ethnic groups.[33] Siegel found, for example, that when other elements of black disadvantage (poorer education, etc.) were taken into account, it "cost" about one thousand dollars in annual lost income to be a black person in American in the mid-sixties. These studies also show that the economic disadvantage of blacks and Mexican-Americans is especially apparent in higher-level occupations. This suggests that efforts by blacks and Chicanos to prepare themselves for more lucrative occupations (through higher education, for example) are less likely to "pay off" in higher income than are similar efforts made by whites. This latter finding is, however, sharply contradicted by recent evidence of dramatic income gains by blacks at the "professional" occupational level.[34] The demand for blacks to serve black clientele or the "token integration" needs of universities, law firms, social work agencies, etc. has given those relatively few blacks who qualify for such positions a competitive advantage over whites.[35]

These studies of the "cost" of being a member of a minority group do not seem to come fully to grips with the possibility that a lower income

---

[32]Hortense Powdermaker, *Copper Town: Changing Africa; The Human Situation on the Rhodesian Copperbelt* (New York: Harper & Row, 1962), pp. 89–98.

[33]Paul M. Siegel, "On the Cost of Being a Negro," *Sociological Inquiry,* 35(Winter, 1965): 41–57; Dudley L. Poston and David Alvirez, "On the Cost of Being a Mexican-American Worker," *Social Science Quarterly,* 53(March, 1973):697–709.

[34]Richard B. Freeman, "Decline of Labor Market Discrimination and Economic Analysis," *American Economic Review Proceedings and Papers,* 67(May, 1973):280–286.

[35]For an indication of some of the employment advantages associated with minority sexual status (women) and minority ethnic status (blacks), see Cynthia Fuchs Epstein, "Positive Effects of the Multiple Negative: Explaining the Success of Black Professional Women," *American Journal of Sociology.* 78(January, 1973);912–935.

may reflect not so much income discrimination *within* an occupation as it does the continued exclusion of ethnic group members from certain occupations. To show, for example, that white plumbers earn more than do black plumbers *may* be to show that black plumbers are denied access to the status of "master" plumber with its accompanying higher income.

In the case of Mexican-Americans, a careful study of the economic situation of Chicanos in Texas and California reveals that Mexican-Americans earn less money than Anglos in similar lines of work.[36] In California, however, there was only a very slight discrimination in wages against Mexican-Americans. Even in Texas, where income discrimination is much greater, the average income of Chicano workers ranges from about 75 to 85 percent of the average income of other workers in the same job classification. Grebler, Moore, and Guzman feel that the *standardization* of wages, which minority groups are demanding, often through the efforts of a labor union, may indeed lead to the elimination of income discrimination *within* an occupational category without necessarily influencing the degree of access to that occupation. In fact, these authors hypothesize that standardized wage scales may actually work *against* this greater access of ethnics to the "better" jobs: "Mexican-Americans enjoy the benefits of standardized wages at the price of low employment representation in jobs paying these better wages."[37] The authors do not really make clear why "low employment representation" is a necessary "price" that must be paid for wage standardization. It may simply be that Mexican-Americans, like other ethnic minorities, have been more successful in insuring equal treatment for their relatively "successful" members than for their failures, who might have been successes under less discriminatory social conditions. It stretches the imagination, for example, to believe that the lot of the mass of black Americans was retarded by the successes of the civil rights movement, which, as has often been noted, benefited primarily those blacks with enough resources to be in some kind of competitive relationship with whites. Although social movements can often be criticized for their inattention to the needs of the masses of a minority group, it is something else again to suggest that the continued subordination of most minority group

---

[36]Leo Grebler, Joan W. Moore, and Ralph C. Guzman, *The Mexican-American People* (New York: Free Press, 1970), pp. 239–245.

[37]Grebler, Moore, and Guzman, *The Mexican-American People,* p. 242.

members is the "price" that must be paid for the success of these social movements.[38]

POLITICAL STRATIFICATION

The political power of an ethnic group is measured by the ability of its members to influence the course of those governmental actions (passage of laws, arrests by police, sentences by judges, etc.) that affect their daily lives. In this section we shall discuss the position of minority groups in terms of their political power on three levels: (1) political autonomy, the ability of a minority group to establish its own political system without "outside" political interference; (2) political influence, the ability of minority group members to influence governmental decisions that are also being influenced by *other* groups; and (3) civil rights, the ability of minority group members to demand and receive equal treatment from various agencies of government. In discussing each of these dimensions of political stratification, we shall observe some of the great variations in ability of ethnic peoples to exercise these powers.

Political Autonomy

A feature of any fully developed human community is the capacity of people in that community to exercise the political function of self-regulation of their own members. While no political jurisdiction—city, county, state, etc.—is completely autonomous under modern political conditions, because the people in each jurisdiction are subject to laws emanating from some higher level of authority—the national state, for example—there are more or less well-established areas of "local control" built into these political systems. The degree of such local autonomy is often a prime political controversy. The controversy is frequently heightened when most of the residents of a local community belong to an ethnic group composed of people of a race, religion, or national origin different from that of most other people in the society. Black people in Harlem, Catholic residents of Belfast, French-Canadians in Montreal, for example, may feel they are subject to laws not of their own making and not consistent with the interests of their ethnic groups.

---

[38]This is not, of course, to deny that there may be this kind of *feeling* among the masses of an ethnic group who must compare their own lack of advancement with that of a few successful members of their own group.

Probably the clearest examples of ethnic groups deprived of the opportunity for political autonomy are those *colonial* situations in which a foreign people, usually a major European power like Britain or France, establishes its domination over a "native" people and extends over them the authority of the laws of the colonizing power. As we noted in Chapter 2, there is some variation in this practice: "direct rule" substitutes completely the laws of the colonizing power for those of the natives; "indirect rule" leaves intact much of the traditional native political structure. Despite such an important differentiation, a colony by definition involves foreign political domination, and it may be no less complete for being "indirect." Local political figures whose continuation in power is at the pleasure of alien authorities may develop an understandable sensitivity to the necessity of ruling "autonomously" in a way that satisfies colonial officials.

In the last several years, a number of American sociologists have begun to develop the concept of "internal colonialism" to describe the political situations of several ethnic groups within the United States.[39] Although blacks, Chicanos, and American Indians, to a greater or lesser extent, exercise the political rights of citizens of the country, they may have the sense, and perhaps an accurate one, that the communities in which they live are really very much like colonies in that the important decisions affecting their lives are made by people and through political processes over which they have little effectual control. Just as "classic" colonialism eventuated in the movements for liberation of native peoples from foreign domination (with the more or less willing acquiescence of the dominators), the existence of internal colonialism has led to calls for Black Power or Red Power or some other expression of the idea that an ethnic people should exercise political autonomy in their own communities. Since the revolt against internal colonialism has been so prominent a feature of recent social movements, we shall defer further consideration of this drive toward political autonomy and concentrate in the rest of this section on the deprivation of political autonomy experienced by people in true colonial situations.

Colonialism in the classic sense, that is, the political domination of native peoples by the great European powers—British, French, Portuguese, Span-

---

[39]Robert Blauner, "Internal Colonialism and Ghetto Revolt," *Social Problems,* 16(Spring, 1969):393–408. Joan W. Moore, "Colonialism: The Case of the Mexican Americans," *Social Problems,* 17(Spring, 1970):463–472. Robert K. Thomas, "Colonialism: Classic and Internal," *New University Thought,* 4(1966):37–44.

ish, Dutch, etc.—is almost a thing of history, with a few exceptions such as continued French domination in parts of the West Indies.[40] But the legacy of foreign political domination lives on in the political life of newly independent nations. One consequence of colonial withdrawal was to lay bare the artificiality of political jurisdictions imposed on native people by foreign rule. Intertribal civil war followed the removal of Belgian administrators from the Congo (now the Republic of Zaire), for example. Secessionist movements proliferated—the unsuccessful Ibo in Nigeria, the successful Bengalese in Bangladesh—demonstrating that national independence from a colonial power is not enough to satisfy the demands of all ethnic groups for political autonomy if one of the several peoples incorporated into a new nation feels that the country is being politically administered for the benefit of the dominant ethnic group.

The political aftermath of great power colonialism depends to a considerable extent on the process by which colonies attained their political independence. For one thing, there is a difference between independence attained with the acceptance or even active encouragement of the colonial power, and independence won after bitter conflict between colonizer and the colonized. Under British colonial policy, native peoples were considered politically immature but, under British tutelage, capable someday of self-government.[41] This philosophy influenced the willing cooperation of Britain in the independence movements of most of her colonies, although it did not prevent fierce resistance in Cyprus and India, where British reluctance to let go was apparently based on a sense of vital national interest in the continued political domination in these areas. France, on the other hand, operated under an "assimilationist" policy, which assumed that natives would eventually become full-fledged Frenchmen in an extended or "metropolitan" France. This philosophy made it less easy to relinquish colonial control; the long struggles in Indochina and Algeria are well-known results. These variations in policy will influence, if nothing else, the fate of those European "colonials" who remain in the country after independence is attained.

---

[40]For a description of the apparently stable French colonial presence in the West Indian countries of Martinique and Guadaloupe, see Chester L. Hunt and Lewis Walker, *Ethnic Dynamics* (Homewood, Ill.: Dorsey Press, 1974), pp. 207–214.

[41]Philip Mason, *Patterns of Dominance* (London: Oxford University Press, 1970), pp. 81–86, with reference to the "paternalist" tendency in British colonial policy as opposed to the "assimilationist" tendency in French policy.

Another profoundly important variation in the nature of political independence is whether political control passes from the colonial power into the hands of the indigenous people, as was the case in India, or whether, as happened in Rhodesia, it passes into the hands of the European "settlers," whose control of the political apparatus guarantees continued domination over the indigenous people. Very different interethnic relationships will develop in newly independent nations, depending on which group succeeds to political power.

Natives who successfully revolt are likely to use their new political autonomy to make life very difficult for the European settlers among them. The Algerian revolution, for example, was followed by wholesale expropriation of the agricultural holdings of the French settlers;[42] a similar policy was followed by the new native government in Kenya in dealing with British settlers in that country.[43] In colonies that had colonial administrators but very few settlers—as was generally true of British colonies in West Africa—this effect of independence was, of course, greatly reduced.

Another ethnic people who may experience hardship following native revolts are those immigrants who have entered the country at the behest of colonial exploiters to supplement an inadequate supply of skilled native labor. The Chinese entered southeast Asia to fill such specialized occupational roles while this area was under European colonial domination. Their subsequent difficulties in such newly independent nations as Malaysia and Indonesia reflect native feelings against people who are seen as economic competitors.[44] Similarly, a great many people of Asian origin, especially Indians, entered African colonies in such roles and have experienced severe postrevolutionary persecution: the recent mass expulsion of Asians from Uganda is a prominent example.[45]

Settler-sponsored anticolonial revolts are likely to have the reverse effect on the balance of political power between settler and native in postrevolutionary regimes. So long as an imperial power administers colonial affairs through a colonial office, it can afford—indeed, may find it vital—to maintain an "enlightened" or paternalistic attitude toward the native popu-

[42]Eric R. Wolf, *Peasant Wars of the Twentieth Century* (New York: Harper & Row, 1969).

[43]Donald Rothchild, "Kenya's Africanization Program: Priorities of Development and Equity," *American Political Science Review,* 64(September, 1970):737–753.

[44]Lea E. Williams, *The Future of the Overseas Chinese* (New York: McGraw-Hill, 1966).

[45]Pierre L. van den Berghe, "Asians in East and South Africa," in Pierre L. van den Berghe, *Race and Ethnicity* (New York: Basic Books, 1970), pp. 276–303.

lation.[46] If nothing else, the colonial power may be concerned about its "image" on the international stage and, when a democratic ethos of universal human equality prevails, may need to assure itself that it is not using its technological power for the raw exploitation of the natives. Post-revolutionary settler governments, however, while likely to adopt much of the value system of the mother country, are much more concerned with problems of survival and prosperity in their territory of residence.[47] If their population growth makes them either land or job hungry, it is to their immediate interest to deprive the natives of these privileges. Thus a South Africa or a Rhodesia, freed of British colonial restraint, may develop a severely repressive system such as *apartheid.* The policy of "Indian removal," by which the young government of the United States pushed the indigenous Indians from the Atlantic coastal areas into an Indian Territory in the then-remote West, would perhaps have been unthinkable under British colonial rule.

Political Influence

Although an ethnic group may have difficulty maintaining complete autonomy or self-government, they may still gain significant influence over the direction of affairs in their social environment. Indeed, the well-known political theory of pluralism argues that political decisions in a democracy tend to represent a balance (or compromise) among the competing political demands of *all* significant social groupings, ethnic or otherwise.[48] Thus, although blacks or Puerto Ricans in a given community may not be ethnically self-governing by any means, they may be able to influence policies and laws directly affecting their vital interests. They can accomplish this because, if for no other reason, competing political organizations may be rivals for the voting support of members of such groups.

---

[46]Even a country like Spain, which is not usually noted for its "paternalistic" attitudes toward colonized peoples, may have exercised such constraints on its settler representatives, although Spanish control over local policies of powerful Spanish settlers in countries like Mexico was probably slight. Hunt and Walker, *Ethnic Dynamics,* pp. 132, 133.

[47]On the severely repressive policies toward native peoples that followed the independence of the United States and other countries from British colonial control, see A. Grenfell Price, *White Settlers and Native Peoples* (Melbourne: Georgian House, 1950).

[48]Robert A. Dahl, *Preface to Democratic Theory* (Chicago: University of Chicago Press, 1956).

Such political pluralism is not always the case, however, as illustrated by a series of studies of decision-making processes in New York City concerning matters, such as public housing, that *do* directly affect the interests of black residents of the city.[49] These studies all indicate that various political forces in the city have conspired to limit severely the influence of blacks on decisions that directly concern them. For example, the administration of Mayor Lindsay was committed to a policy of "scattered" sites for housing projects rather than to continue the existing policy of locating projects in or near established "black" areas of the city. As it turned out, the vehement opposition of middle-class whites in the areas of the proposed sites made the scattered scheme impossible to implement. Thus, although they were an important part of the coalition of liberals that elected and reelected Mayor Lindsay, blacks found that their support was seldom rewarded with concrete political decisions such as they had expected to receive from the city government.

Some realization of the futility of advancing their political interest through the support of "white liberals" or other dominant group politicians sympathethic to their cause has led minority groups to seek greater political influence by election or appointment of their own members to positions of political influence. Several studies have indicated the limited success of such efforts. Although a substantial proportion of the population of Chicago, blacks were only rarely found in major decision-making positions, especially in the private sector (e.g., on the boards of governors of the Chamber of Commerce, of private colleges and universities, etc.).[50] Those positions of political prominence that *were* held by blacks tended to be lower level positions, or to be those in which the constituency was almost exclusively black (e.g. a black labor leader in an all-black union, a black city councilman from a black ghetto ward). A study in Milwaukee found this exclusion of blacks from major power positions to be even more complete.[51] Among business leaders, for example, the study reports only one black among the 1,867 "key positions" in business that were studied.

[49]Jewel Bellush and Stephen David (eds.), *New York City: Five Studies in Policy-Making* (New York: Praeger, 1971).

[50]Harold M. Baron et al., "Black Powerlessness in Chicago," *Trans-action,* 6(November, 1968):27–33.

[51]Karl H. Flaming, J. John Palen, Grant Ringlien, and Corneff Taylor, "Black Powerlessness in Policy-Making Positions," *Sociological Quarterly,* 13(1972):126–133.

Similarly, a study in Toronto, a city with a notably high degree of ethnic heterogeneity (about 40 percent of the city's population in 1950 was foreign born), found a continued pattern of Anglo-Saxon domination of major power positions in the city.[52]

An ethnic group's prospects for political influence would seem to be considerably enhanced when the population of an area shows a majority or near-majority of members of that ethnic group. This would be especially true if, as recent analysis has suggested is true in the United States, there is a persisting "ethnic factor" in political behavior, with Catholics voting for Catholic political candidates, blacks for black candidates, etc.[53]

The possibility for political *dominance* of a minority group in a particular local situation has assumed special interest in the United States recently because of the increasing concentration of blacks in American cities. As blacks attain a majority or near-majority of population in a city, there is the prospect that they will elect political leaders who will presumably be able, once in office, to respond to the special political demands of black people. Richard Hatcher of Gary, Indiana, was, in 1967, the first black to be elected mayor of a major American city. Since then, cities that have had or now have black mayors include Newark, Los Angeles, Detroit, Cleveland, and Atlanta.

Whether black people in high political office will be able to effect changes desired by black people is another matter. Having "one's own kind" in political office may be no more a guarantee of complete domination than being a vital part of a coalition was a guarantee of favorable political decisions for New York blacks. An analysis of the experience of Mayor Hatcher in Gary illustrates some of the limitations on accomplishment of black mayors on behalf of black people.[54]

Hatcher's basic problem was to overcome the tradition of dominance in Gary by the main industry of the city, United States Steel, and the essentially white Catholic Democratic political machine that had ruled the city for years more or less in the interest of the steel company. Like most newly installed political heads, Hatcher "inherited" a bureaucracy of civil

[52]Merrijoy Kelner, "Ethnic Penetration Into Toronto's Elite Structure," *Canadian Review of Sociology and Anthropology,* 7(May, 1970):128–137.

[53]Mark R. Levy and Michael S. Kramer, *The Ethnic Factor: How America's Minorities Decide Elections* (New York: Simon and Schuster, 1973).

[54]Edward Greer, "The 'Liberation' of Gary, Indiana," *Trans-action,* 8(January, 1971):30–39.

servants who were in most cases white, who were more or less hostile to the Hatcher regime, but whose expertise was vital to his administration.[55] Thus the new mayor disappointed the expectations of many blacks who had assumed there would be a massive movement of blacks into public employment upon the advent of Hatcher's administration. To retain his black support (which Hatcher very successfully did), he had to shift his appeal from one of encouraging participation by blacks in government to one of demonstrating what his administration was doing for blacks in the way of improving their condition. On this matter, Hatcher was able to demonstrate a great deal. Since Gary was the first major city to elect a black mayor, the city was the focus of much black attention nationwide. At the time of Mayor Hatcher's election, the Johnson-Humphrey and the Robert Kennedy wings of the national Democratic Party were competing vigorously for black support. Hatcher found it quite easy, therefore, to get Model Cities and other federal money for Gary (to such an extent that a major "headache" in the early part of his administration was the almost total preoccupation of his staff with applications for federal aid). Other black political leaders must face many of the same problems that Hatcher faced, with the additional limitation that, unlike Mayor Hatcher, they lack the advantage of "novelty" or of being singled out as symbols of nondiscriminatory policy in the wider society.

Civil Rights of Ethnic Groups

Even *without* any direct influence on the agencies of government (and certainly without any power to maintain such agencies autonomously, apart from those of the wider society), members of an ethnic group may still assert certain "rights" as citizens because of the equalitarian ideology of the political institutions under which they live. Thus the constitution of a country may guarantee (as does the Fourteenth Amendment to the Constitution of the United States) the "equal protection of the laws" without regard to such matters as "race, creed, or color." Under such a constitution, the rights of citizenship may be extended to an ethnic group newly introduced to an area without regard for the political "clout" or influence of that group. That this "equal protection" of citizenship rights

---

[55]Greer compares the problem of Hatcher in this regard to that of the newly independent nations of black Africa, which are dependent on the technical expertise of the European colonizers of an earlier era. For a description of such problems in one African country, see Rothchild, "Kenya's Africanization Program."

may be based on political influence is not, of course, denied. The civil rights legislation of the 1960s in the United States (voting registration, use of public accommodations, etc.) was certainly influenced by the actuality of or threat of black political influence at all levels from the ballot box to the street riot. Many other ethnic groups (e.g., Chicanos) who were *not* influential participants in the process of making those decisions were nevertheless the recipients of the new "protection" so provided.

How, or indeed whether, a government chooses to enforce this "equal protection" guaranteed by the laws of the land is another matter. Lack of enforcement or unequal enforcement seems to be a feature of many social environments that are ethnically stratified. A frequent complaint of minority groups is that such agencies of law enforcement as the police and the courts are in fact discriminatory in their treatment of people from different ethnic groups. For this reason, it is often argued, the higher crime rates of some ethnic groups are actually the result of discriminatory practices in the administration of criminal justice. Blacks in the United States and Maori (aborigines) in New Zealand, for example, are found guilty of crimes at rates several times higher than those prevailing among the white populations of these two countries.[56] American blacks have felt that these differential crime rates reflect the oversensitivity of the police to delinquent acts committed by blacks. The "police brutality" about which blacks often complain is largely a matter of the humiliation blacks feel at being treated as suspicious persons simply because they are black. Thus, a major contribution to the racial tension that preceded the 1965 riot in the Watts section of Los Angeles was the police practice of stopping and frisking blacks found "loitering" on the streets in the area.[57]

The police, after all, can exercise a great deal of discretion in how they treat offenders or suspected offenders (arresting vs. a "stern warning," vigorous questioning vs. looking the other way, etc.). Indeed, one study of police treatment of juveniles suggests that this discretion is professionally expected, since juvenile officers are skeptical (probably with good reason) of the reformative value of arrest and possible incarceration on

---

[56]On black vs. white crime rates in the United States, see Marvin E. Wolfgang and Bernard Cohen, *Crime and Race* (New York: American Jewish Committee, 1970). On Maori crime rates in New Zealand, see Patrick O'Malley, "The Amplification of Maori Crime: Cultural and Economic Barriers to Equal Justice in New Zealand," *Race,* 15(July, 1973):47–57.

[57]Robert Blauner, "Whitewash Over Watts," *Trans-action,* 3(March–April, 1966):3–9.

young offenders.[58] Police officers are thus encouraged to make judgments about the suspect's "character." They tend to be most favorably influenced by suspects who are very deferential to or respectful of police authority, and by those who seem sincerely repentant. Black Americans who live in ghetto environments and view the police as "pigs," who are openly hostile to and alienated from the authority structure and legal norms of the society, may find it especially difficult to avoid having the police use their "discretion" against them in a negative way.

Once minority group members become embroiled in the formality of dealing with criminal charges in a court of law, they may find further evidences of "unequal" protection, such as the difficulty they experience in getting bail before trial, a suspended sentence if convicted, an early parole if sent to prison.[59] These discriminations may reflect some of the same determinants of "discretion" by judges, juries, and parole boards that were mentioned above in the case of police officers. For example, the constitution of New Zealand states that a defendant is "innocent until proven guilty." White New Zealanders, however, harbor certain "unfavorable stereotypes" about the typical behavior of the Maori with the result that, if a Maori is accused of a crime of a certain sort, white jurors will assume his guilt because they feel that "that's the way the Maoris are."[60]

Legal discrimination based on such stereotyping may produce a deprivation of civil rights of a more subtle nature as well. Dominant group stereotypes of minority group members as being "just that way" in relation to criminal behavior may lead to a condoning of acts of violence or petty theft. Since the victims of these acts are likely to be other members of the ethnic group, minority groups may find themselves without sufficient police and court protection against victimization by their fellow ethnics. Thus, in a traditional southern community the white stereotype of black sexual mores emphasizes the sexual promiscuity of blacks, especially women. It is very difficult, therefore, for a white judge or jury to believe that a black woman could be raped, since it is assumed that she is always

---

[58]Irving Piliavin and Scott Briar, "Police Encounters with Juveniles," *American Journal of Sociology,* 70(September, 1964):206–214.

[59]Austin T. Turk, *Criminality and the Legal Order* (Chicago: Rand McNally, 1969); Haywood Burns, "Can A Black Man Get a Fair Trial in This Country?" *New York Times Magazine,* July 12, 1970, p. 5+.

[60]O'Malley, "Amplification of Maori Crime."

willing to be "victimized" by any and all comers.[61] The complaint of women that it is difficult to prosecute a rapist because of the suspicion of the victim's own culpability is perhaps even more of a problem for blacks and other minorities who are made to suffer in this and other ways by the indifference of law-enforcement officials who operate on an "ethnics will be ethnics" basis.

SOCIAL STRATIFICATION

To discuss *social stratification*—that is, dominance and subordination in the area of social respectability—is virtually to deal with the whole range of social exclusions of ethnic minorities, since almost any such exclusion, occupational or otherwise, may be experienced as a humiliation or a degradation of a person's human worth. Thus, the weekly paycheck, if small, may not only fail to cover expenses for needed or desired consumer goods, but may be defined by its recipient as a "slap in the face," especially if the amount is less than that paid to one's colleagues who are seen as being no better than oneself. We have already noted how unemployment carries a connotation of negative respectability. Since the assignment of differential social worth is so complex and multifaceted, we cannot begin to cover the whole subject here. Instead, we shall concentrate on two major areas in which the "honor" of an ethnic people is involved, and in which discrimination is experienced as an assault on the dignity of members of minority groups.

Discriminatory Etiquette

Etiquette—the body of rules that determines "proper" behavior in social situations—is likely to be defined in terms of how people should behave toward members of other categories: a child should not talk back to an adult, a professor should try to learn the names of his students, a gentleman should open the door for a lady, etc. A small portion of such rules are codified in books of etiquette, but most are simply part of the way things are done in one's customary social milieu. Children learn these ways of doing things by observation and adult guidance and sometimes through social blunders as, for example, when a child asks an adult a very personal

---

[61]John Dollard, *Caste and Class in a Southern Town* (Garden City, N.Y.: Doubleday, 1957).

question only to be reminded by the adult's cool reaction that an implicit rule of etiquette has been violated.

As Goffman has noted, there is a general tendency for social norms to require that people treat one another in a way that protects the personal dignity or "face" of each individual.[62] While all people may have an equal "right" to respectful treatment by others, clearly some are more able than others to claim this right. Goffman illustrates this fact by noting that, in a hospital situation, there is an asymmetrical or nonreciprocal system of "touch rights"—doctors have the right to touch nurses or patients, nurses have the right to touch patients, but patients do not have the right to touch nurses or doctors, and nurses do not have the right to touch doctors.[63] Goffman is here drawing upon Simmel's insight that a person's "honor" is derived from that person's capacity to resist intrusion by others on his privacy, including familiar access to parts of his body.[64] Another familiar asymmetrical tendency in rules of etiquette is found in the fact that less honored persons, such as children, are forbidden to call more honored persons, such as their elders, by their first names, while the latter are free to call children by first names.

An additional dimension of discriminatory etiquette with potential for humiliating people in such situations is suggested by Goffman's study of *total institutions* such as hospitals, military camps, and prisons. In total institutions, the higher honor attributed to staff persons is symbolized by what Goffman calls an "echelon" relationship of authority of *any* staff member over *any* inmate.[65] Thus, any officer has the right to a salute from

---

[62]Erving Goffman, "On Face-Work: An Analysis of Ritual Elements in Social Interaction" *Psychiatry,* 18(1955):213–231. Also, on the fragility of a sense of self-respect and its dependence on a sustaining set of reactions by others, see Ernest Becker, *The Birth and Death of Meaning* (New York: Free Press of Glencoe, 1962).

[63]Erving Goffman, "The Nature of Deference and Demeanor," *American Anthropologist* 58(1956):473–502.

[64]Simmel, referring to an "ideal sphere" that surrounds each person, writes: "Although differing in size in various directions and differing according to the person with whom one entertains relations, this sphere cannot be penetrated, unless the personality value of the individual is thereby destroyed. A sphere of this sort is placed around man by his 'honor.' Language very poignantly designates an insult to one's honor as 'coming too close': the radius of this sphere marks, as it were, the distance whose trespassing by another person insults one's honor." Kurt Wolff (ed.), *The Sociology of Georg Simmel* (Glencoe, Ill.: Free Press, 1950), p. 321.

[65]Erving Goffman, *Asylums: Essays on the Social Situation of Mental Patients and Other Inmates* (Garden City, N.Y.: Doubleday-Anchor Books, 1961).

any enlisted man. In the same vein, any adult may take it upon himself to "correct" the behavior of any child, etc. If this thinking is extended to classes of persons—that is, if upper-echelon (higher-class) persons believe they have the right to receive shows of respect from lower-echelon (lower-class) persons—the psychological deprivation of belonging to a category of lesser social honor becomes obvious. This is particularly true when one thinks of the arrogance of some upper-echelon people who seem to enjoy making subordinate people uncomfortable.

Many ethnic group members have experienced such discriminatory assaults on their personal dignity. The matter of names will illustrate. White American southerners have long been accustomed to demand that *any* white person be addressed by *any* black person as Mr., Mrs. or Miss, while *any* white person can call *any* black person by a first name or, even more insultingly, by the generic terms *boy* or *girl* (no matter what the age of the black person). Some strain is put on this etiquette when whites of distinctively lower-class position must deal with blacks of distinctively higher ones. Johnson mentions one compromise in this situation. If the black person is obviously of too high a class to be called by a first name, the lower-class white might refer to him as "professor" (regardless of his occupation) without having to employ the more prestigious term *Mr.*[66]

Participation in Symbolically Significant Social Activities

One of the scarce privileges that people strive for—and that tend to be differentially distributed among people in different social categories—is the honor of participating in highly valued social activities. Thus it is considered an honor to carry the flag in the school parade, to fight for one's country in foreign wars, to represent one's country in international sports contests. To be excluded from an equal chance to enjoy such privileges may be defined as gross discrimination, and members of many ethnic groups have complained of just such exclusion.

Participation in organized sports can provide a case study in this kind of ethnic stratification. One version of the world of sports is that here is one area where ethnic discrimination does *not* tend to be practiced; that players, coaches, and fans of athletic teams want their team to win, and

---

[66]Charles S. Johnson, *Patterns of Negro Segregation* (New York: Harper, 1943).

it matters not the ethnic origins of the players on the team. It has also been argued that members of some ethnic groups become heavily involved in professional sports precisely because sports careers are open to them whereas other "legitimate" careers are closed by virtue of ethnic discrimination. Thus, Weinberg and Arond show that Irish, Jews, Italians, and blacks have successively dominated professional boxing in the United States, and that the period of dominance of each of these ethnic groups coincided with the period in which the masses of these people first entered the American urban social environment—the period when discrimination against their entering other occupations was at its height.[67]

Other studies of other sports suggest quite different conclusions, however. Baseball is often referred to as the "national sport" in the United States, and it is a well-known fact that no black American played in the major leagues until Jackie Robinson broke the color barrier in 1947. The chauvinism of Anglo-conformity may have served to keep professional baseball "pure" from contamination by "foreign" elements. The author has found that there was a significant shift in the years 1910–1930—the era of restrictive immigration legislation in reaction to the "rising tide of color" in the world—in the pattern of recruitment of professional baseball players.[68] Professional ball clubs of the nineteenth century recruited players mostly from northern urban areas; but with the turn of the century, players were increasingly recruited from the rural South. The suggested explanation is that the urban North came to be seen during the years 1910–1930 as harboring large numbers of "un-American" elements (i.e., the "new immigration") while the rural South, relatively free of these "contaminations," came to be seen as the more purely American region. This study also found almost no players in the early part of this century with Slavic or Jewish names, although there is some evidence that players from these ethnic origins Anglicized their names. Baltzell has observed the same tendency in a uniquely "American" institution, the motion picture industry.[69] A great many movie stars are of non-Anglo origin, but they adopt

---

[67]S. Kirson Weinberg and Henry Arond, "The Occupational Culture of the Boxer," *American Journal of Sociology,* 57(1952):460–469.

[68]Jerry D. Rose, "The Social Origins of American Baseball Players" (Paper read at the annual meeting of Upstate New York Sociological Association, 1969).

[69]E. Digby Baltzell, *The Protestant Establishment* (New York: Random House, 1964).

professional names that usually conceal their ethnic background and, of course, deprive their ethnic peers of the pride of having many famous people publicly identified as "our people."

Even when minority group members participate actively in sports—as black athletes obviously do in the United States in both amateur and professional sports—allegations and protests are sometimes made that the manner in which they are allowed to participate tends to minimize the honorific implications of the participation. Thus Edwards shows that the positions of center, quarterback, and defensive linebacker—the most visible, dramatic, or authoritative positions on a football team—are rarely held by blacks. In baseball, the outfield, which requires the least defensive action and is least visible to the spectators, is where black players tend to be "stacked."[70] The position of baseball pitcher, which *is* often held by blacks, seems to be an exception to the rule of excluding blacks from the centers of action. Edwards observes, however, that the pitcher, alone among the defensive players on a baseball team, has clear responsibility for winning or losing the game.[71] If winning is very important to professional sports teams and their fans, they may be willing to forego their tendency to "honor" the dominant ethnic member in favor of the best performer, without regard to race, creed, or color.[72]

A more subtle form of discrimination against blacks in sports participation has been noted in a study of playing patterns among college basketball teams. Yetman and Eitzen find that black players on college squads are heavily overrepresented among the starters and less represented among the substitutes or those who sit on the bench for most of the game.[73] The interpretation offered is that, to be selected for a team, a black has to be "twice as good" as a white. Thus, only those blacks of outstanding athletic

---

[70]Harry Edwards, *The Sociology of Sports* (Homewood, Ill.: Dorsey Press, 1973), p. 205.

[71]Jerry D. Rose, "The Attribution of Responsibility for Organizational Failure," *Sociology and Social Research,* 53(1969):323–332 shows that while players of other baseball positions tend to have their careers terminated during a team's "failing" season, pitchers are terminated independently of the success or failure of the teams for which they play.

[72]A former black professional basketball player, Bill Russell, has noted with some irony (and perhaps a touch of black chauvinism) the variability in the willingness of white fans to see "their" team represented by blacks. According to Russell, the formula is: play two blacks when playing at home, three on the road, and five if you get behind. Edwards, *Sociology of Sports,* p. 211.

[73]Norman R. Yetman and D. Stanley Eitzen, "Black Athletes on Intercollegiate Basketball Teams: An Empirical Test of Discrimination," in Norman R. Yetman and C. Hoy Steele (eds.), *Majority and Minority* (Boston: Allyn and Bacon, 1971), pp. 509–517.

ability make the team, whereas whites of only mediocre talent have the opportunity to travel with the team—primarily for the "honor" of the thing it seems, since they so seldom play. There may be some flaw in this interpretation. It could even be suggested that the predominance of blacks among first-string players may be a kind of discrimination in reverse, in which those relatively few black team members have a competitive advantage over whites in their chance to play if, for instance, the college or coach feels a need to demonstrate a nondiscriminatory policy. Several black athletes sitting on a bench while whites are playing may be too baldly suggestive of racial discrimination, so *some* blacks are played as a gesture to token integration. If there are only one or two black players on the squad, it may well be that a black player who is only "half as good" as a white bench sitter is played to satisfy integrationist demands.[74]

---

[74]The apparent fact of somewhat lesser representation of blacks on collegiate and professional football teams than on basketball teams would perhaps support this interpretation. A football team typically has twenty-two starters (eleven on an offensive unit and eleven on a defensive unit) while a basketball team has only five starters. Thus token racial integration may be achieved on a football team with a much smaller proportion of blacks as starters.

CHAPTER 6
ORIGIN AND MAINTENANCE OF ETHNIC STRATIFICATION

ORIGIN OF ETHNIC STRATIFICATION

Sociological analysis of the origins of any of the kinds of stratification discussed in the last chapter must begin with an unequivocal rejection of the view that these inequalities are based on any inherent inequalities between peoples of different racial stocks.[1] Rather, it is in the relative social situations of ethnic peoples in contact with one another that explanation must be sought.

A Three-Factor Theory

It will serve as a convenient starting point for our analysis to examine Noel's effort to formulate a theory of the origin of ethnic stratification.[2] Noel postulated that three factors are both necessary and sufficient to

---

[1] For a typical social scientific statement on the matter, see M. F. Ashley Montagu, *Man's Most Dangerous Myth,* 4th ed. (New York: World, 1964).

[2] Donald L. Noel, "A Theory of the Origin of Ethnic Stratification," *Social Problems,* 16(Fall, 1968):157–172.

explain why, when present, relationships of dominance and subordination emerge between ethnic peoples in contact, and why, when absent, more equalitarian relationships tend to prevail. The three factors are *ethnocentrism, competition,* and *differential power*. "Competition," according to Noel, "provides the motivation for stratification; ethnocentrism channels the competition along ethnic lines; and the power differential determines whether either group will be able to subordinate the other."[3] As a preliminary "test" of his theory, Noel examined the emergence of slavery in colonial America. There is a growing consensus among historians that prior to 1660, the condition of blacks was not too unlike that of white indentured servants. Over a period of several decades, however, blacks were increasingly subordinated into a condition of complete servitude while white indentured servants were increasingly able to gain their freedom from a slavelike condition. This stratification forms the basis for Noel's study.

Ethnocentrism.   Although, as we observed above, inherent inequalities of peoples are not part of the sociologist's arsenal of explanations, such ideas *are* often found in everyday life. Many people really feel that persons of alien custom are inferior by nature to persons in their own social groups, or, to use Sumner's definition, "one's own group is the center of everything, and all others are scaled and rated with reference to it."[4] Thus, the greater the difference between ingroup and outgroup, the greater the rejection of the outgroup by the ingroup. In applying this ethnocentric factor to the condition of servitude of blacks and whites in colonial America, Noel found that the initial element in determining black status was not so much color as religion. Europeans were especially prone to see blacks as heathens, that is, as non-Christian and, therefore, as basically inferior. The white European indentured servant was at least acknowledged to be Christian, however poor.

The factor of ethnocentrism is perhaps most clearly demonstrated in the differential social treatment in the United States of immigrants from different countries of origin. The acts excluding Orientals from immigration (Chinese in 1882, Japanese in 1924) reflected a feeling of the inferiority of "yellow" peoples, as well as a large element of perceived "unfair"

---

[3]Noel, "A Theory of the Origin of Ethnic Stratification," p. 157.
[4]William G. Sumner, *Folkways* (Boston: Ginn, 1940), p. 13.

competition from such people.[5] The quotas established by act of Congress in 1924 based the allowable immigration from a certain country on a percentage of the number of people from that country already in the United States, a formula designed to limit the immigration of people from eastern and southern Europe who came in large numbers only after 1890.[6] The latter immigrants were very likely to be Catholic or Jewish and to speak languages other than English. They experienced much greater discrimination of every sort than did immigrants from countries whose religion, language, and other social institutions were more familiar to people in an "Anglo-Saxon" country like the United States.

It could be argued that the factor of ethnocentrism is not absolutely *necessary* as a condition for the subordination of ethnic groups. We shall refer later to the possibility of discrimination "without prejudice," or discrimination simply by virtue of the fact that dominant groups gain significantly from the subordination of minorities and that the anticipation of such gain is sufficient to stimulate the effort to subordinate. From this viewpoint, the prejudices arising from ethnocentrism are at best a secondary phenomenon, an attempt by dominants to justify their domination, to exploit minorities with a clear conscience—in other words, to insure not only that the dominants will be able to sleep at night, but that they will be able to sleep without bad dreams.

Competition.   According to Noel, ethnic groups come into competition when they must strive against one another for the enjoyment of privileges or goals that are in limited supply, whether such goals be wealth, political power, or prestige. Sometimes two ethnic groups in contact are not in competition, since the groups are striving for different goals. Thus one group's accomplishment of its goals does not interfere with the other group's pursuit of its goals. A frequently cited example is the Tungus and Cossack peoples in Manchuria who are able to live in close contact in an essentially equalitarian relation with one another because the Cossacks, an agricultural people, do not compete with but rather benefit from their association with the Tungus, a nomadic hunting people who follow the

---

[5]William Petersen, *Japanese Americans* (New York: Random House, 1971), pp. 30–35.

[6]For a summary of the history of restrictive immigration legislation in the United States, see George E. Simpson and J. Milton Yinger, *Racial and Cultural Minorities,* 4th ed. (New York: Harper & Row, 1972), pp. 114–126.

reindeer.[7] The low level of anti-Semitic feeling among Italian-Americans provides another example. Since most Italian immigrants to the United States came from peasant backgrounds and tended to pursue blue-collar careers in America, whereas Jews, both in Italy and the United States, favored mercantile occupations, there has been little competition between the two groups either in Italy or the United States.[8]

More frequently, however, ethnic groups in contact *are* in competition, and competition has led to conflict over which group is to be dominant. As we noted in the last chapter, relations between black and Jewish Americans have been strained by the dominance of Jewish merchants in black ghettos and the feeling of many would-be black entrepreneurs that Jewish ownership of retail businesses deprives black people of such entrepreneurial opportunities.[9] Gans has given a similar interpretation to the struggle in the New York City schools during the late 1960s over the issue of community control, which became largely a conflict between blacks and Jews.[10] Blacks in New York City apparently expected that, as they established their numerical dominance in a given neighborhood, they would come to dominate neighborhood institutions as well. This would be in accord with the usual "succession" process in American cities whereby, as one ethnic group moves out, the newcomers take over. As we saw in Chapter 5, however, white retail merchants tended *not* to move out as an area turned black. Ghetto schools experienced a similar situation. The heavy concentration of Jews in the teaching profession resulted in many "black" schools having predominantly Jewish staffs. Many blacks felt that this situation deprived black teachers of employment opportunities, a discrimination they had hoped to reduce by community control of the hiring practices in the neighborhood schools.

---

[7]Ethel J. Lindgren, "An Example of Culture Contact Without Conflict: Reindeer Tungus and Cossacks of Northwestern Manchuria," *American Anthropologist,* 40(1938):605–621. For an analysis of this and other examples of noncompetitive or "symbiotic" relations between ethnic groups, see Michael Banton, *Race Relations* (New York: Basic Books, 1967), pp. 77–83.

[8]Joseph Lopreato, *Italian Americans* (New York: Random House, 1970), pp. 137, 139.

[9]That so-called black anti-Semitism is largely confined to negative stereotypes of Jews held by blacks in the area of *economic* behavior is indicated in Gertrude Selznick and Stephen Steinberg, *The Tenacity of Prejudice* (New York: Harper & Row, 1969).

[10]Herbert J. Gans, "Negro-Jewish Conflict in New York City: A Sociological Evaluation," in Donald E. Gelfan and Russell D. Lee (eds.), *Ethnic Conflicts and Power: A Cross-National Perspective* (New York: Wiley, 1973), pp. 218–230.

Irish-Americans and Italian-Americans have also been in competition, mainly over which ethnic group would come to control the Roman Catholic Church in the United States. In cities such as Boston, where neighborhoods have changed from Irish to Italian dominance, there has also been much competition, during the period of transition, for pieces of urban "turf."[11]

Again we may question whether one of Noel's factors—in this case, competition—is *necessary* for the emergence of ethnic stratification. Van den Berghe has argued that there are at least two forms of ethnic stratification systems.[12] One is based on *competition,* in which efforts are made by some groups to monopolize privilege at the expense of minorities who are seen as "dangerous." The other is based on *paternalism,* a relationship similar to that of parents to children, in which the parents carry the "burden" of protecting the children and the children in turn are expected to show respect to the parents. While parents and children are scarcely competitive with one another in most situations, neither is their relationship equalitarian. Likewise, minority groups are no less subordinated because the dominant group treats their inferiority with benign indulgence.

Noel's own interpretation fails to make clear the role of competition between blacks and whites in colonial America, or at least between black slaves and white slaveowners, whose attitudes and actions are emphasized by Noel. The usual interpretation is that the enslavement of blacks was in the economic interest (and Noel adds in the *status* interest) of the white aristocracy rather than in response to any demands by poor whites, who would be the only possible economic competitors of the blacks. Noel's interpretation shares this view, although he must stretch the meaning of *competition* to cover the situation in which there is a "utilitarian" interest in one group's subordinating another. (Thus, a rich man and a poor man may be "noncompetitive" in that they strive for different goals. The rich man strives perhaps for possession of a more commodious country estate while the poor man hopes to be able to furnish his house with a rug on the floor and a picture on the wall—to cite Lyndon Johnson's minimum aims for the antipoverty program. Still, the presence of that poor man,

---

[11]Lopreato, *Italian Americans,* pp. 110–113.

[12]Pierre L. van den Berghe, "Paternalistic versus Competitive Race Relations: An Ideal-Type Approach," in Bernard E. Segal (ed.), *Racial and Ethnic Relations: Selected Readings,* 2d ed. (New York: Thomas Y. Crowell, 1972), pp. 24–38.

willing or forced to work at minimum wages, may be one of the conditions for the luxurious life style of the rich man, who may require cheap labor to, for example, maintain the grounds of his estate.)

The explanation of why indigenous Indians in many parts of the Americas escaped the fate of enslaved blacks is made on similar grounds. Native Indians tended to adapt poorly as laborers in the mining and agricultural plantation operations favored by European colonizers, hence they could be viewed as a "nonutilitarian" labor supply. Blacks proved to be "better" slaves in these situations, much to their own worst interest.[13]

If such "utilitarian" perceptions of an ethnic minority can be equated with "competition," then Noel's competition factor covers the situation of slavery in the American colonies. Perhaps this stretches too far the sociological concept of competition, but there may be an additional factor here of considerable importance. Some such term as *exploitability* would perhaps more directly express the nature of this factor.

Differential power. For one group of people to dominate another, it is obviously necessary that the dominants have not only the *motivation* to establish their superiority (as is emphasized with the ethnocentrism and competition factors), but the power or "muscle" to do so as well. Which group becomes dominant often depends on which has the more destructive implements of warfare. The conquest of native peoples by the technologically more advanced Europeans is most obviously explained in this manner. Noel's analysis moves from truism to insight when he notes that white indentured servants in America, but not black slaves, had the advantage of an external source of power—the attitudes of their fellow countrymen toward the dominant Americans. Mistreatment of European servants was bound to be self-defeating for employers. If indentured servants were to get the word back to their countrymen—"For God's sake, don't come here!"—sources of additional domestic labor would dry up. Also, the home country governments could bring pressure to bear in support of their emigrants in America, an especially important factor, perhaps, for a young country striving for recognition among the nations of the world. The fact

---

[13]Part of the nonadaptability of Indians to the slave condition may have been abetted by the readiness of blacks but not of Indians to enter into servile relations with Europeans. Thus, as early as 1634, European travelers to South America were being advised to "take Negro servants with them as there were no Indians in Buenos Aires that could be used for that purpose." Frank Tannenbaum, *Slave and Citizen* (New York: Knopf, 1947), p. 9.

that black slaves were almost completely cut off from "back home" contacts and that there were no "African nations" to support their interests deprived them of these external power sources.

Such factors may remain operative in explaining the degree of subordination of ethnic groups in immigrant situations. The relatively high status of Japanese peoples in Latin American countries, to which there has been rather substantial immigration in recent years, is explained partly by: (1) the perceived desirability of such immigration to the host countries and their wish to encourage further Japanese immigration, and (2) the rather vigorous diplomatic interest that Japan takes in looking out for the welfare of the country's "overseas" people.[14]

A somewhat different influence of "external power" in ethnic stratification is indicated by Hannerz.[15] He attributes the success of Italian-Americans in dominating organized crime in the United States to their Italian ethnicity, which has furnished "extraterritorial resources" for the group. Italian contacts of Italian-Americans have provided such valuable criminal facilities as a network of contacts for the supply of narcotics and for recruitment of gang members, and a place of refuge from police action in the United States.

Further applications of the theory. Any theory should be testable by examining its power to explain situations other than the one for which it was originally developed. A recent study by McLemore attempts to do this with Noel's three-factor theory.[16] The situation McLemore chose for analysis was the relations between Mexican-Americans and Anglos in the state of Texas, an area over which Americans and Spaniards (later Mexicans) had long struggled for control. The factor most clearly illustrated is ethnocentrism. Texans of Anglo-Saxon origin have accepted the stereotype, which has become enshrined in American history books, of the sober, hard-working Anglo-American settler as opposed to the cruel, exploitive Spanish conquerors and their Mexican successors. Otherwise,

---

[14]See, for example, Mischa Titiev, "The Japanese Colony in Peru," *Far Eastern Quarterly,* 10(May, 1951):227–243; and J. F. Normano, "Japanese Emigration to Brazil," *Pacific Affairs,* 7(March, 1934):42–61.

[15]Ulz Hannerz, "Ethnicity and Opportunity in Urban America," in Abner Cohen (ed.), *Urban Ethnicity* (London: Tavistock, 1974), p. 51.

[16]Dale S. McLemore, "The Origins of Mexican American Subordination in Texas," *Social Science Quarterly,* 53(1973):656–670.

there is some doubt whether Noel's theory provides the "clear and parsimonious framework" for explaining Mexican-American subordination that McLemore believes it does. The element of competition between Anglo-Americans and Mexican-Americans seems especially dubious in light of McLemore's observation that most Mexicans in Texas were of lower-class origins while most Americans were of middle-class origins; hence, direct Anglo-Mexican competition must have been limited to the very few large Mexican landowners who undoubtedly resented the Anglo "land grab" in Texas. Whether or not Mexicans constituted a source of "utilitarian" interest to Anglos is left undefined.[17] Likewise there is little attention given to the external power sources of the Mexicans. Although McLemore observes that Mexico, after the loss of Texas in the Mexican War, "displayed great concern for the welfare of her citizens who were left within the territory of the United States,"[18] there is no evidence that this "concern" had any telling effect on the treatment of Mexicans living in the United States. Indeed, the relative national power of the two countries would lead one to doubt the practical impact of this concern.

MECHANISMS FOR THE MAINTENANCE OF ETHNIC STRATIFICATION

We have been discussing the question of how ethnic groups come to occupy a high or low place in a system of stratification—the question of origins. We turn now to a related, but nevertheless different, question: What are the forces that tend to maintain ethnic groups in a given position? In analyzing these mechanisms, a distinction will be made among those forces that arise from (1) dominant-group attitudes and actions, (2) minority-group attitudes and actions, and (3) structural or institutional arrangements that may not express the wishes of either dominant or minority groups.

Dominant Group Behavior

The degree to which a privileged ethnic group is determined to maintain its privileges at the expense of minorities is obviously a matter of great variability. While it is probably true, as Legum says, that "no privileged

---

[17]The heavy use by Anglo farm owners of immigrant Mexicans as farm laborers would suggest that, indeed, the subordination of Mexicans has been quite "utilitarian" to the Anglos.

[18]McLemore, "Origins of Mexican American Subordination," p. 667.

society—white or black or brown—has ever voluntarily surrendered its privileges at one fell swoop,"[19] some groups have moved farther in this direction than have others. This is apparent, for example, in the attitudes of colonial countries toward the political aspirations of the indigenous people of their colonies. The British have been far more favorable than have the French to the idea that someday, when the natives have "grown up" under British tutelage, they would gain full rights to self-government and the British would then withdraw.[20] Given such variability, then, we need to look for some lines of explanation of dominant-group insistence on maintaining the dominant position.

The expediency of ethnic stratification.   One source of variability depends on whether or not dominant groups really "gain" anything from the subordination of minorities. Dollard's analysis of black-white relations in a southern town suggests that whites do, indeed, gain from black subordination. Specifically, whites gain a supply of labor to do various kinds of dirty work; they gain a whole category of persons whom every white, no matter how lowly in social status, can look down on. In addition, white *men* gain sexual access to black women while ruthlessly denying any reciprocal sexual access of black men to white women.[21] In colonial situations, there can be little doubt that the natives were exploited in various ways, especially as a labor supply for the mining and agricultural enterprises of the colonists.

Some of the "equality revolutions" that we shall be discussing in the next chapter may reflect a loss of will of dominants to maintain their dominance. More specifically, in terms of the "gains" of subordination, it may increasingly be that the perceived "cost" of securing these gains has led some dominant groups to conclude that it "isn't worth it" to maintain their dominance. Some of this cost may be psychic in nature, referring to the possibility that dominants *do* have "bad dreams" or a bad conscience about their subordination practices. Myrdal's formulation of an American dilemma suggested, as has been suggested by many others, that the "black problem" in the United States is really a "white problem"—the problem

---

[19]Colin Legume, "Color and Power in the South African Situation," *Daedalus,* 96(Spring, 1967):483–495.

[20]Philip Mason, *Patterns of Dominance* (London: Oxford University Press, 1970), p. 84.

[21]John Dollard, *Caste and Class in a Southern Town* (Garden City, N.Y.: Doubleday, 1957).

of white Americans trying to reconcile continued racial discrimination with the "American creed" as reflected in the "all men are created equal" assertion of the Declaration of Independence, or with the constitutional guarantee of the rights of the minority and the ultimate constitutional definition of blacks as full-fledged citizens.[22]

Other "costs" of ethnic discrimination are more immediately practical in nature. Slavery was abolished in many places apparently not because slaveowners developed consciences, but because slavery became an inefficient mode of organizing human labor. Likewise, employment discrimination against blacks may be defined as costly to whites as well as to blacks because the whole economy suffers from the underutilization of the talents of a large part of the population.[23] The cost may also be measured in the loss of international influence or goodwill. For instance, peoples in the underdeveloped countries of the Third World are highly sensitive to racial discrimination in the United States. The United States, in competition with international communism, wants to exert its influence among these peoples. Consequently, many Americans have come to the conclusion that this cost of racial subordination is too high.

Finally, a perception of cost may arise from the determination and intransigence of minorities in demanding a reduction to discrimination. French colonial policy, as indicated above, did not envision the eventual independence of French colonies in Africa and Asia. However, the protracted native revolts in Indochina and Algeria led the French people ultimately to the conclusion that these wars could not go on. Similarly, British withdrawal from former colonies often took place before Britain herself determined that these colonies (e.g., Cyprus, India) were "grown up" enough for self-determination. However, the passive resistance of the Indian nationalist movement led by Gandhi wrenched the conscience of the British, thus hastening the decision of Great Britain to yield the advantages of empire under the spur of such costs.

One additional point should be made about the matter of gains and costs. The gainers and losers from a system of ethnic stratification may be

---

[22]Gunnar Myrdal, *An American Dilemma* (New York: Harper, 1944).

[23]Glenn does show, however, that there is a sense in which white people in America continue to "gain" from the presence of a large black population to do the dirty work. This gain is unequally distributed, however. Lower-class whites gain little, while some middle-class housewives gain the decided advantage of having a supply of relatively cheap household help. Norval D. Glenn, "White Gains from Negro Subordination," *Social Problems,* 14(Fall 1966):159–178.

different groups *within* a dominant ethnic group. Thus poor southern whites have relatively little to gain (and that mostly in terms of prestige, as Dollard noted) from black subordination and much to lose by not being willing to form coalitions along lines of economic self-interest, i.e., the poor of all races against the rich of all races. Employers, on the other hand, have much to gain from cheap labor (with, of course, some costs in the form of relative inefficiency of untrained labor). By the 1950s, few French people living in France had much to gain (except for some degree of "French pride") from continued suppression of the Algerian revolt, and de Gaulle was recalled from retirement with a mandate to end the war. French settlers in Algeria, however, correctly anticipated that their land holdings would be expropriated by a nativist government. Thus de Gaulle's problem in ending the war was as much a matter of "pacifying" the French settlers in Algeria as in dealing with leaders of the nativist revolt. Any analysis, then, of ethnic subordination based on the continued "interest" of dominant groups in maintaining the subordination must consider the *differentiated* interests of the various groups within the dominant group and the relative power of these groups to determine the direction of dominant group policy.

Ideological considerations: Domiant group prejudice.　We turn now to the question of whether dominant group members are able to justify their dominance in terms of any perceived inherent inferiorities of subordinated peoples. We shall consider here the element of "racism," or dominant group beliefs in the inferiority of subordinate races as these beliefs relate to the continued subordination of those races.[24] We shall be dealing, then, with the complex question of the relationship between dominant group *prejudice* and the degree of *discrimination* against minority ethnic groups.

So-called white racism in the United States will serve as an example for analysis. The black slavery that preceded the Civil War and the discrimina-

---

[24]In line with our practice throughout this book of treating race as one of three common bases for the definition of ethnic peoplehood—religion and national origin being the other two—it would be desirable if there were some term other than *racism* to reflect the beliefs of dominant ethnic groups in the inherent inferiority of subordinate ones. Rather than coin a word like "ethnicism," the term *racism* will be used to cover any dominant ethnic group prejudice so that, for example, the tendency of some Caucasian Americans to think of other Caucasians as "dumb Polacks" or "pushy Jews" would be covered by the concept of white racism.

tory Jim Crow laws that developed in the aftermath of Reconstruction were justified by whites in the belief that blacks were essentially nonhuman or subhuman. The three-fifths compromise at the Constitutional Convention of 1787, whereby a state's representation in Congress would be determined by counting a free person as one and a black slave as three-fifths of a person, was, of course, arrived at by political negotiation between those states with many and those with few black slaves. However, the fraction does serve as a symbol for the degree of humanity imputed to the black. Even this modicum of humanity was seemingly reduced to nothing by 1857 in the Supreme Court's Dred Scott decision, in which Justice Taney pronounced the ultimate in black subordination by asserting that blacks "had no rights which the white man was bound to respect."[25] The racism embodied in this mode of thought eventually found its way into an emotionalized rejection of people who are racially Caucasian but are thought to be of inferior stock. In a study of evolving American attitudes toward the "new immigration" from southern and eastern Europe at the turn of this century, Higham shows how the "romantic" nativism traditional to the country—a kind of smug Anglo-Saxon superiority that expected all aliens to assimilate to an Anglo-Saxon mold—was able, with the aid of a new "science" of racial biology, to develop the idea that the new immigrants were of inferior racial stock and a threat to the "integrity" of the traditional Anglo-Saxon stock.[26]

Recent studies of white racism in the United States have suggested changes in the form if not the substance of racist justifications for ethnic discrimination. One of these changes—discussed later—refers to an "institutional" form of racism without explicit ideological justification. Another change can be found in white responses to such questions as, Are blacks as intelligent as whites? Public opinion surveys show that American whites overwhelmingly affirm the equality of native abilities of blacks and whites,

---

[25]The background of official attitudes toward blacks that led to the Dred Scott decision is described in Leon Litwack, "The Federal Government and the Free Negro, 1790–1860," *Journal of Negro History,* 43(October, 1958):261–278.

[26]John Higham, *Strangers in the Land: Patterns of American Nativism,* 1860–1925 (New Brunswick, N.J.: Rutgers University Press, 1955). For a description of similar ideas of native Britons toward Jews with the influx of Jewish immigration at the beginning of the twentieth century and toward coloured people during the more recent heavy immigration of Commonwealth immigrants to England, see John A. Garrard, "Parallels of Protest: English Reactions to Jewish and Commonwealth Immigration," *Race,* 9(July, 1967):47–66.

a marked change from attitudes expressed thirty or forty years ago.[27] At the same time, however, whites tend to blame blacks for the blacks' continued subordinate position, believing that blacks lack the *will* to better themselves. Many American "white ethnics" make comparisons between the passiveness or "bitching" of contemporary blacks and their perception of the actions of their own immigrant ancestors, who "got up off their asses" and made something of themselves. In terms of Schuman's analysis, most whites do not accept the "deterministic" view of social science that the condition of a person or group of persons is "caused" by the social environment.[28] The popular view is that a person can make anything of himself that he "wills," and the failure to achieve is ascribed to a failure of will.

To complete this discussion of dominant group prejudice as related to ethnic stratification, we should examine the relative importance of official or authoritative attitudes and actions as they reflect the customary morality of a people. Sometimes the official (e.g., governmental) policy itself is one of explicit discrimination against ethnic minorities. The intensely discriminatory racial policy of *apartheid* in South Africa has been justified by an outpouring of authoritative "explanations" by government officials and leading intellectuals, explanations that embody, more or less, an ethnocentric assertion that the native is inferior and poses a threat to the superior white position if there is any racial intermingling.[29]

In other societal contexts, the official policy may be one of nondiscrimination, although the rank-and-file dominant group members who must implement the policy may harbor many prejudicial feelings. The question, then, is whether official policy can be effective in the face of popular resistance. One viewpoint is that "you can't legislate morality," cannot force people against their wills to practice nondiscrimination. There is some evidence in support of this viewpoint. The "massive resistance" undertaken by southern American whites against enforced racial integration has had some success, but also a considerable degree of ultimate failure. To cite a less familiar case, Communist Czechoslovakia has an

---

[27]Mildred A. Schwartz, *Trends in White Attitudes Toward Negroes* (Chicago: National Opinion Research Center, 1967).

[28]Howard Schuman, "Free Will and Determinism in Public Beliefs About Race," in Norman R. Yetman and C. Hoy Steele (eds.), *Majority and Minority: The Dynamics of Racial and Ethnic Relations* (Boston: Allyn and Bacon, 1971), pp. 382–390.

[29]Pierre L. van den Berghe, *South Africa: A Study in Conflict* (Middletown, Conn.: Wesleyan University Press, 1965).

official policy of nondiscrimination against ethnic minorities. However, the gypsies, who represent a sizable ethnic minority in this country, find in fact a great deal of popular prejudice and discrimination against them.[30] This discrimination is actually *supported* in a somewhat indirect way by governmental policy. In a Communist state, the expectation is that minority peoples, while retaining the form of their traditional life styles, will learn to practice this style with a socialist content. Those who, like the gypsies, are seen as being especially recalcitrant toward adopting the socialist content *do* suffer official discrimination. Also, Party officials at the local level *do* reflect local prejudices in their actions. Local administrative officials—so-called People's Committees—are responsible for such decisions as the allocation of housing space among applicants. In a situation of severe housing scarcity, they tend to yield to local demands that dominant group members be favored over gypsy applicants. Accordingly, although Party officials in the capital exhort local officials to implement the nondiscriminatory policy, local officials complain that "you people in Prague" just don't know the gypsies like we do and, of course, do not have to deal with the pressures exerted by one's immediate neighbors. This is reminiscent of the complaint of local officials in the United States who had to implement civil rights legislation that "you people in Washington" (e.g., those bureaucrats at HEW who write guidelines for racial integration) do not, in the language of the traveling salesman, "know the territory." It seems that the more closely political officials must deal with "the territory," as defined by local prejudices, the more difficulty they have in implementing official policy.[31]

---

[30]Otto Ulc, "Communist National Minority Policy: The Case of the Gypsies in Czechoslovakia," *Soviet Studies,* 20(April, 1969):421–433.

[31]A parallel to this situation is furnished in the action of Protestant ministers in Little Rock, Arkansas, during that city's school integration crisis. Although the denominational hierarchies of most of the Protestant churches had made pronouncements in favor of racial integration, few ministers (and primarily only those younger ministers not planning to stay in the area) gave any active support to the integrationist side of the controversy. The necessary sensitivity of local ministers to the attitudes of their white parishioners was an obvious factor. The "success"—and therefore future career prospects—of Protestant ministers is determined by their ability to keep a local congregation "happy" as reflected, for example, in growing membership rolls and increased financial support for the church. A minister who alienated his local constituency by taking a liberal stance, even though in strict accord with the official position of his denomination, stood to lose this local support and to be judged *by the hierarchy itself* as a failure as a minister. Ernest Q. Campbell and Thomas F. Pettigrew, "Racial and Moral Crisis: The Role of Little Rock Ministers," *American Journal of Sociology,* 64 (March, 1959):509–516.

This view that "you can't legislate morality," especially at the local level, can be countered with much evidence to the contrary. Personally prejudiced persons—whether officials or ordinary citizens—become what Merton calls prejudiced nondiscriminators or "fairweather illiberals" under certain circumstances.[32] The general rule seems to be that, if a minority group member asserts a right in a direct confrontation with a prejudiced dominant group member, and the minority group member has the backing of the law, then that right will be granted. The intransigence of a Lester Maddox, who handed out ax handles to his white customers at his Atlanta restaurant to prevent racial integration, is rare indeed.

The directness of the confrontation is apparently a matter of some importance. To demonstrate this effect, LaPiere traveled across the United States with a Chinese couple and was never refused hotel accommodations in this "mixed" situation; however, when he *wrote* to a sample of hotels and asked whether accommodations would be available under such circumstances, most replies were negative.[33] It is a commonplace that it is easier to reject someone in a "Dear John" letter than in a face-to-face confrontation.

The importance of statutory backing has also been demonstrated. In a study by Kohn and Williams, blacks who were collaborating in the research entered restaurants to which blacks had never before been admitted, while white collaborators observed the ensuing reactions.[34] The observers reported that the restaurant managers, aware *both* of the public accommodations laws against discrimination and of the negative attitudes of their white customers toward racial integration, vacillated considerably. Although managers sometimes ejected blacks when white customers indicated disapproval, the management of one restaurant did back down when a civil rights "case" was made with the support of the local NAACP.

It appears, then, that nondiscrimination can be achieved in the face of local opposition, but perhaps only under special conditions, such as direct confrontation and statutory backing, conditions that, because of fear, timidity, ignorance of legal rights, or lack of funds to pursue litigation, may be rather difficult conditions to realize. The fundamental question for any

---

[32]Robert K. Merton, "Discrimination and the American Creed," in Robert M. MacIver (ed.), *Discrimination and National Welfare* (New York: Harper, 1949), pp. 99–126.

[33]Richard A. LaPiere, "Attitudes vs. Actions," *Social Forces,* 13(1934):230–237.

[34]Melvin L. Kohn and Robin M. Williams, "Situational Patterning in Intergroup Relations," *American Sociological Review,* 21(April, 1956):164–174.

permanent implementation of a nondiscriminatory policy would seem to be, Will more or less forced nondiscrimination lead to a reduction in popular "massive resistance"? Two lines of analysis suggest this as a possibility.

First, as we noted in Chapter 4, when people are placed against or without regard to their wills in equal-status contacts with members of other groups—as would be the case if black workers were hired for the first time to work alongside whites on an assembly line—this contact may lead to reduced social distance by reducing unrealistic stereotypes.

Second, and this analysis involves a more subtle psychological process, the "cognitive dissonance" associated with forced action may lead to prejudice reduction.[35] Most experiments in cognitive dissonance place subjects in situations in which they must do something that is contrary to what they would like to be doing or feel they should be doing (as when people who hate spinach are told—and sometimes paid—to eat it). Postulating a tendency toward dissonance reduction in human psychology, cognitive dissonance theorists note that a person can bring these disharmonious self-perceptions into balance *either* by ceasing the objectionable activity, *or* by ceasing to view the activity as objectionable—in other words, by making a virtue of necessity. The "fairweather illiberal" who is being forced to practice nondiscrimination might, at the first opportunity, restore cognitive balance by resuming the discrimination. If, however, the forces arrayed against discrimination are too powerful for him to disregard—as when a really tough equal opportunity enforcement official threatens to cancel a government contract—he may have to restore cognitive balance by changing his prejudicial attitudes. From a "fairweather illiberal" he may become a self-regulating ethnic liberal. Although it is admittedly difficult to enforce nondiscrimination if it runs contrary to the deep-seated prejudices of a people, there is at least sociological warrant to suggest that it *is* possible. While coercion may initially be necessary, the degree of this coercion can eventually be greatly reduced for the two reasons just discussed.

Minority Group Attitudes Toward Subordination

Attention now shifts to an examination of the characteristics of minority group members as explanations of their own continued subordination. Without in any respect subscribing to the new form of white racism that

---

[35] Leon Festinger, *A Theory of Cognitive Dissonance* (Evanston, Ill.: Row, Peterson, 1957).

would blame minorities for their own condition,[36] it is still possible to see ways in which minorities self-enforce a weakened power position in some social situations.

1. Internalization of dominant group prejudices.   A well-known principle in social psychology is that human beings tend to take the attitude toward themselves that they find expressed in the attitudes of others toward them.[37] If the attitudes of dominant group members imply that minority group members are inferior people, then these minority members may easily develop some of the attitudes of self-hatred described in Chapter 3. There are many subtle ways in which minority group members are given the message of their inferior social worth. A frequent target of ethnic militants is the allegedly prejudicial treatment of ethnic groups in literary materials, especially in books written for school children. American Indians are treated as savages with few admirable human qualities. Blacks are depicted in stereotyped submissive social roles, or slavery is described as a rather idyllic time for blacks, implying that a slave condition is really most compatible with the black's "nature."[38] Such prejudicial depictions of ethnic character are indirectly harmful because they influence dominant group members who, in turn, convey these negative attitudes to the minority group members with whom they deal. Such depictions are directly harmful because they deprive minority group children of any pride in a valued heritage. Only very recently have school book publishers begun to consciously eradicate such harmful stereotypes from their products.

---

[36]The author is, frankly, about as hardnosed a determinist in explaining human behavior as one may wish to find. From this viewpoint, behavior is always caused ultimately by external or situational factors, and our tendency to blame someone whose "free will" generated the behavior is really an admission of failure to understand the complex situational forces operative in a given instance of human behavior. It might be added, for the reader's relief, that the author is also something of a functionalist or pragmatist who would admit that, for purposes of "correction" of unwanted forms of behavior, it may be necessary to assume that a person or group of persons is "responsible" for that kind of behavior and to make someone responsive to social control, to hold some persons responsible for the "sins of their fathers" lest the perpetuation of those sins become the sins of the fathers of the next generation.

[37]George Herbert Mead, *Mind, Self and Society* (Chicago: University of Chicago Press, 1934).

[38]For some examples of such stereotypical treatments of Indians and blacks, as well as of Chicano, Jewish, and Oriental Americans, see Lewis H. Carlson and George A. Colburn, *In Their Place: White America Defines Her Minorities, 1850–1950* (New York: Wiley, 1972).

2. Accommodative reactions to subordination. Minority behavior that appears to the outsider to reflect self-hatred may, in fact, be simply a tactic for survival in a situation of unequal power relationships. Just because minority group members neither "wince nor cry aloud" when humiliated by dominant group members does not mean that they feel no pain; it means, rather, that they have learned not to express their pain because to express it would only worsen the suppression. In other words, minority ethnics are not only required to take it, they are expected to give the appearance of liking it. This appearance of "liking it" has been construed as self-hatred by some.

Poussaint, a black psychiatrist, denies that black people's accepting reaction to their humiliation by whites is a matter of black self-hatred.[39] He described an incident of personal humiliation in which a white man rudely ordered him to "come here, boy." His sense of shame at acquiescing was heightened, he said, by the fact that he was in the company of a black woman. (Black men, Poussaint noted, have always had a difficult time establishing their credentials of masculinity in the face of all the affronts to their personal dignity they suffer in their social environment.) On reflecting on the above incident, Poussaint realized that he had been in a truly dangerous situation in which he might have been badly beaten or even killed had he not acquiesced. Thus, he concluded, subservience to the white man is a survival tactic practiced by blacks forced to live in a white world.[40]

Dollard's study of blacks in a southern town emphasizes similar behaviors, which he calls the "accommodation attitudes" of blacks.[41] In the presence of whites, blacks adopt a "white folks manner" in which they act out the white stereotype of the black as a happy-go-lucky, rather slow, bumbling, inefficient individual. That such attitudes are not entirely *inter-*

---

[39]Alvin F. Poussaint, "A Negro Psychiatrist Explains the Negro Psyche," *New York Times Magazine,* August 29, 1967. Reprinted in Yetman and Steele, *Majority and Minority,* pp. 348–356.

[40]Italian-Americans are another ethnic group whose members have been noted for their outward acceptance of a lowered social position. Mario Puzo, author of the controversial novel *The Godfather,* asserts that Italian-Americans never push into where they know they aren't wanted (adding the comment that one place they know they are not wanted is Italy). He epitomizes the attitude of many Italian-Americans by comparing them with a character in a Carl Sandburg poem about whom it was said, "He et what was set before him." Mario Puzo, "Italians, American Style," *New York Times Magazine,* August 6, 1967.

[41]Dollard, *Caste and Class in a Southern Town.*

nalized but are "put on" as a way of manipulating the situation to the black's advantage is indicated by the fact that blacks express among themselves a great deal of derision of white people and tell stories of how they or fellow blacks have gotten the better of a white in some interactive situation. Of course, blacks must refrain from explicit violation of the discriminatory system of etiquette, lest severe sanctions be brought to bear. A black woman explains how she deals with whites who abuse her:

> You know there is a way of being so polite to white people that it is almost impolite. I say polite things, but I look at them hard and I don't smile, and while what I am saying is polite, the way in which I say it isn't.[42]

Notably absent in Dollard's Southerntown, then, was any open expression of protest or defiance of the discriminatory racial system. Aggression against the system that could not be resolved in subterranean expressions of anger against whites tended to be channeled into aggressive attacks against "safe" targets, that is, against other blacks. This accounts partially for the high level of verbal and physical violence expressed by blacks in dealing with one another.[43] This pattern of deflected verbal aggression has been observed in a game called "playing the dozens," which consists in trying to outdo one's opponent in trading insults.[44] Rainwater's study of black residents in St. Louis contains a graphic transcript of a "dozens" session in which there are endless variations on the insulting theme "I fucked your mother. . . ."[45]

The interracial atmosphere in the urban North has, of course, been for many years quite different from that in Dollard's Southerntown. As early as 1943, Johnson was reporting the results of interviews in which northern blacks were telling whites in no uncertain terms that they were no longer willing to "take it" in terms of traditional humiliations.[46] Nevertheless,

---

[42]Charles S. Johnson, *Patterns of Negro Segregation* (New York: Harper & Row, 1943). In another stratification situation, an army enlisted man informs a buddy (in the play *No Time for Sergeants*) that "if you call an officer 'sir,' you can tell him anything."

[43]We commented in the last chapter on an additional possible reason for black violence against blacks: the reluctance of police and courts to treat these as "serious" crimes.

[44]Roger P. Abrahams, "Playing the Dozens," *Journal of American Folklore,* 75(July, 1962): 209–220.

[45]Lee Rainwater, *Behind Ghetto Walls* (Chicago: Aldine, 1972), pp. 346–355.

[46]Johnson, *Patterns of Negro Segregation.*

there has developed a "cool," hedonistic life style among blacks, both North and South, that might be seen as an alternative to protest against racial subordination. Living life for its kicks,[47] being unable or unwilling to structure one's life according to any long-range plan of "improvement"[48] suggests accommodative tendencies among blacks aimed at lessening concern for their low position in the system of ethnic stratification.[49]

3. Traditional ethnic values. Whether members of minority groups remain in socially subordinated positions or improve their power position over a period of time depends partly on the emphasis placed on achievement or "success" in their traditional ethnic life styles. Japanese-Americans and American Jews have been notably successful at improving their social positions, at least economically. In the case of Japanese-Americans, it has been noted that there were basic values of traditional Japanese culture—thrift, orderliness, etc.—that facilitated Japanese advancement in an American society dominated by the Protestant ethic.[50]

A comparative study of Jews and Italian-Americans in New Haven suggests several reasons for the greater success of the Jews in attaining high social status in the United States. For one thing, Jewish (but not Italian) families placed great emphasis on schooling and intellectual activity. For another, Jews tended to exhibit a future-oriented concern for the advancement of themselves and their children (as opposed to the present-oriented tendency among Italians).[51] It might be added, in light of Zborowski's study of "pain behavior" among patients in a Veterans Administration hospital, that this future-oriented tendency of Jews takes the *pessimistic* form of worrying about the future (rather than the optimistic future orienta-

---

[47]Harold Finestone, "Cats, Kicks and Color," *Social Problems,* 5(1957):3–13.

[48]John Horton, "Time and Cool People," *Trans-action,* 4(April, 1967):5–12.

[49]In a similar way, Sykes has noted that prisoners tend to disapprove the activity of the recalcitrant protestor, the "ball buster," in favor of the prisoner whose manner suggests to all observers that he can "take it" without being "taken in" by the rehabilitation ideology of his captors. The honor accorded this "cool" type prisoner is indicated by a frequent characterization of such prisoners as "real men." Gresham Sykes, *The Society of Captives* (Princeton, N.J.: Princeton University Press, 1971).

[50]William Caudill and George De Vos, "Achievement, Culture and Personality: The Case of the Japanese Americans," *American Anthropologist,* 58(1956):1102–1126.

[51]Fred L. Strodtbeck, "Family Interaction, Values and Achievement," in Marshall Sklare (ed.), *The Jews: Social Patterns of an American Group* (Glencoe, Ill.: Free Press, 1958), pp. 147–164.

tion of the "old Americans"). This tendency to worry may retard Jewish success where success is based on a willingness to take risks with confidence in a favorable future outcome.[52]

American Indians and Spanish-speaking Americans are two other ethnic groups that have been described as having a present-oriented outlook on life that supposedly retards social advancement.[53] Oscar Lewis, a student of the social attitudes of the poor, has suggested that we ought not to give an ethnic interpretation to such values. Lewis postulated the existence of a "culture of poverty" in the United States (and other parts of the world) that is marked by, among other things, a fatalistic acceptance of things as they are, with no expectation of improvement in the future; furthermore, Lewis believed this culture embraces the poor of all ethnic origins.[54] One study of poor families in California attempted to test the culture-of-poverty thesis by comparing equally poor blacks, Anglos, and Spanish-speaking people. The authors found that the "poverty" attitudes described by Lewis are far more typical of the Spanish-speaking than of the other groups.[55] Had Lewis not based his generalization on studies of Spanish-speaking (Mexican and Puerto Rican) groups only, the authors concluded, he might not have asserted the noninfluence of an ethnic factor in this regard.

4. Persistence of dependency relations. It sometimes happens that minority group members are reluctant to take advantage of an opportunity for more equalitarian relations if they have developed a "habit of dependence,"[56] which they find difficult to break. This "habit" may be the result of previous experiences of the minority group with a particular ethnic group. Although many American Indians complained bitterly of the gov-

---

[52]Mark Zborowski, *People in Pain* (San Francisco: Jossey-Bass, 1969).

[53]Florence R. Kluckhohn and Fred L. Strodtbeck, *Variations in Value Orientations* (Evanston, Ill.: Row, Peterson, 1961).

[54]Oscar Lewis, "The Culture of Poverty," *Scientific American,* 215(October, 1966):19–25.

[55]Lola M. Irelan, Oliver C. Moles, and Robert M. O'Shea, "Ethnicity, Poverty, and Selected Attitudes: A Test of the Culture of Poverty Hypothesis," *Social Forces,* 47(June, 1969): 405–413. Likewise it was shown that, when the variable of metropolitan or nonmetropolitan residence was controlled for, the poor and the nonpoor among Spanish-speaking groups displayed about the same degree of "culture of poverty" values, suggesting the priority of an ethnic over a class influence for this group. Nancy G. Kutner, "The Poor vs. the Non-Poor: An Ethnic and Metropolitan-Nonmetropolitan Comparison," *Sociological Quarterly,* 16(Spring, 1975):250–268.

[56]Mason, *Patterns of Dominance,* p. 26.

ernment's paternalistic treatment of them in the past, they apparently feel even more bitter about the recent "termination" of governmental guardianship of their interests. The frequent stories of freed black slaves who refused to leave the service of their masters after emancipation are undoubtedly embellished by southern sentimentality, but they probably have some basis in historical fact. Native people who have lived in highly stratified societies in which the masses of people were dependent on dominant traditional rulers, somewhat like the feudal societies of Europe, were not particularly disoriented by contact with conquering migrants. Conquest simply meant exchanging one set of masters for another. It is reported, for example, that natives of Madagascar attempted to establish relations of total dependence with Europeans, a relationship that most Europeans were inclined to reject.[57] European employers may expect contacts with native employees to be narrowly circumscribed by the specialized employer-employee relation, while the native tends to expect a more diffuse commitment by both sides. Thus Europeans may see natives as fawning or demanding, while the natives see the Europeans as aloof and unresponsive to their efforts to involve themselves in the "private" lives of the Europeans, and the Europeans in their own lives.

Institutional Discrimination
The social forces that deprive ethnic groups of the opportunity to improve their power position may emanate not from the attitudes of either dominant or minority groups but from discriminations built into the system.[58] The basic formula for explaining this structural or institutional discrimination is that social arrangements that reflect a previous state of will or dominant position of certain groups of people tend to persist even after the will to maintain that position has vanished.

To illustrate, let us consider the continued discrimination against black Americans in the area of employment. Even though equal opportunity employment policies have become the standard in many areas, blacks continue to be underemployed in the better jobs. Since such discrimination

---

[57]O. Mannoni, *Prospero and Caliban* (London: Methuen, 1956).

[58]For a study that similarly defines institutional discrimination as outside the willful actions of either dominant or minority group but that presents an analysis of the dimensions of this discrimination that differs from the analysis to follow, see Robert Friedman, "Institutional Racism: How to Discriminate Without Really Trying," in Thomas F. Pettigrew (ed.), *Racial Discrimination in the United States* (New York: Harper & Row, 1975), pp. 384–407.

is part of the basic experience of black Americans, and of many other ethnic groups in the United States and elsewhere, we shall discuss several "institutional" reasons for this situation.

One problem is that most highly paid employment requires extensive education or training, and these educational opportunities have not been available to blacks. This unavailability reflects, at least recently, not discriminatory college admissions policies *per se* but the fact that blacks have had inferior educational preparation for college or other advanced training, and therefore are not able to compete with whites for these opportunities.[59] Thus, even though many trade unions, for example, have ended their discriminatory practice of excluding blacks from opportunities to obtain apprenticeship training in skilled labor, relatively few blacks have been able or willing to take advantage of such opportunities.[60]

Another institutionalized source of discrimination, at least at the higher levels of economic opportunity (e.g., the management of large corporations, the world of the junior executive), is the "particularistic" atmosphere that blacks—and women—must face in their places of employment.[61] In such places it is often necessary to be "one of the boys" to advance in the bureaucratic hierarchy and if, for any reason—sexual, ethnic, or otherwise—a category of people does not fit into the "clubhouse" atmosphere of the workplace, then the career prospects of such people are obviously limited. This may explain why blacks and women prefer civil service employment with public agencies to employment in private corporations,

---

[59]Lieberson and Fuguitt are thus able to show that the concentration of blacks in lower-level employment would persist in the United States for some sixty to eighty years simply on the basis of past disadvantage of blacks in terms of education and occupation. Stanley Lieberson and Glenn V. Fuguitt, "Negro-White Occupational Differences in the Absence of Discrimination," *American Journal of Sociology,* 73(September, 1967):188–200.

[60]James S. Coleman, *Resources for Social Change: Race in the United States* (New York: Wiley, 1971), pp. 82, 83.

[61]Cynthia F. Epstein, "Encountering the Male Establishment: Sex-Status Limits on Women's Careers in the Professions," *American Journal of Sociology,* 75(May, 1970):965–982. Cohen suggests that the informal organization of business leaders in the City of London is made necessary by the tremendous volume of transactions between businesses, often conducted on an informal verbal basis. This way of conducting business requires much mutual trust between leaders. "Such a high degree of trust can arise only among men who know one another, whose values are similar, who speak the same language in the same accent, respect the same norms, and are involved in a network of primary relationships that are governed by the same values and the same patterns of symbolic behavior." Cohen, *Urban Ethnicity,* pp. xix–xx.

since in public service the "white male establishment" is less a determining factor in career advancement.[62]

Finally, it may be argued that continued racial segregation, even of the de facto, or institutional, variety, operates to exclude blacks from employment opportunities. For example, people typically locate jobs through a network of personal acquaintances.[63] The fact that blacks, because of segregated housing patterns, have little opportunity to become acquainted with whites[64] deprives blacks of sources of information about employers —most of whom will necessarily be white—with jobs to offer. Crane tried to show that those blacks who are most successful in obtaining jobs have attended integrated schools and can therefore include whites in their acquaintance networks.[65] Of course formal desegregation is no guarantee that blacks and whites will become acquainted, since it is entirely possible for blacks and whites to separate themselves into mutually exclusive groups of acquaintances even *within* an integrated school.

An attempt to combat structural or institutional discrimination lies behind recent efforts in the United States to equalize opportunities. "Forced" school integration through busing, the establishment of quotas to require schools to include a certain proportion of minorities or employers to hire a given proportion of minority group members are major elements in the assault on institutional discrimination. As we shall see in the next chapter, such efforts are especially likely to meet opposition from dominant group members, who may brand such programs as instances of "discrimination in reverse."

---

[62]It has been shown, however, that even in government employment there are several kinds of pervasive discrimination against racial minorities. U.S. Commission on Civil Rights, "Employment Discrimination on the Government Job." Reprinted in Pettigrew, *Racial Discrimination in the United States,* pp. 159–167.

[63]Mark S. Granovetter, "The Strength of Weak Ties," *American Journal of Sociology,* 78 (May, 1973):1360–1380.

[64]Charles Korte and Stanley Milgram, "Acquaintance Networks Between Racial Groups," *Journal of Personality and Social Psychology,* 15(1970):101–108.

[65]Robert L. Crain, "School Integration and Occupational Achievement," *American Journal of Sociology,* 75(January, 1970):593–606.

CHAPTER 7
ETHNIC DYNAMICS

INTRODUCTION

As we have noted in this book, sociological interest in ethnicity tends to focus especially on the fact of *variation* in the influence of the ethnic factor under different conditions of human existence. This interest has been reflected, in most of the analysis so far, in comparisons of ethnic relations in different countries or regions: for example, racial segregation in northern and southern parts of the United States. Another dimension of this variation is discussed in this chapter: variation over a period of time in the nature of ethnic relations in a given community, region, or country. The relationships between whites and blacks in some communities in the American South have changed drastically in the last thirty years, whether this change is measured in lessened segregation of the races in some areas of social interaction or in new opportunities for blacks to enjoy economic, political, and social privileges that had previously been denied them. In this chapter we examine some lines of explanation of these and similar changes in ethnic relations.

Three general kinds of forces for change will be examined here. First, changes in ethnic relations may be one of the several consequences of very general social changes that are occurring in a given country, community, or region. The introduction, for example, of a new, large industry into a small town is likely to affect many aspects of the social existence of the town's residents, including the possibility of a change in ethnic relations if, say, there are many workers of an alien ethnicity who are imported as workers in that industry. We refer to such changes as *spontaneous* changes, not because they just spring up without any human planning or expectation, but because they are by-products that were not specifically planned by those responsible for the changes.

Second, the status of ethnic relations in an area may become defined as a social problem by people in positions of authority, who may use that authority to attempt to institute changes. They may, for example, pass laws. forbidding the continuation of given kinds of ethnic discrimination; or they may undertake massive programs of assistance to underprivileged ethnic groups to try to help them improve their collective social positions. We refer to such efforts as *planned* change, since they reflect direct attempts to design a newer and better model of ethnic relations in an area.

Third, individuals or groups outside positions of authority may see those in authority as lacking in appropriate concern or capacity to solve a given problematic state of ethnic relations. These concerned outsiders may place pressures on decision makers to pass antidiscrimination laws, to institute assistance programs, etc. We shall refer to such efforts as *social movements,* and we shall examine several of the pressure tactics used by these movements to push for changes in various aspects of ethnic relations.

SPONTANEOUS CHANGES

In the history of a given country, region, or community, certain events are likely to occur that will have a profound influence on ethnic relations as on all other aspects of social relationship in that area. International wars, the discovery of new natural resources, and demographic changes involving altered fertility, mortality, or migration rates may have such consequences. To illustrate the effects on ethnic relations of such changes, we shall in this chapter focus on a single area of broad social change: a type of change called *modernization,* a very general term for a set of related processes that have been occurring in many parts of the world. Some more specific elements of modernization include the processes of *urbanization* (the movement of people from country to city); *industrialization* (the mass production of goods and services by the modern factory); and *technological development* (the adoption of more efficient tools that will allow fewer laborers to produce more goods and services). Urbanization, industrialization, and technological development are widely defined as social problems. Among the problematic effects of such modernizing changes are their consequences for ethnic relations where such changes occur.

Urbanization

According to a prevailing school of sociological thought, urbanization has resulted in the development of a modern, urban cosmopolitanism to replace the provincialism of regional or tribal loyalty in traditional societies.[1] On the assumption that traditional ethnic identities are fast disappearing, anthropologists have been urged to move quickly to study the few remaining primitive peoples, since rural or traditional societies will soon be things of the past.

This view of the "de-ethnicized" urban person has come under devastating attack as studies of modernizing peoples have accumulated. It has been said, for example, about African migrants to cities that, not only are they not "de-tribalized," they tend to be "supertribalized" by the urbanization experience.[2] Cohen thus shows how the ethnic consciousness of Hausa tribesmen, nourished by a British colonial policy that kept them from being overwhelmed by the more numerous Yoruba, was sustained and indeed intensified in the period following the independence of Nigeria.[3]

There have been at least two major lines of explanation for the persistence of ethnic identity in urbanizing countries. Little's work on urbanization in West Africa illustrates one kind of explanation.[4] He sees the proliferating ethnic unions or tribal associations among urban migrants as prominent among those voluntary associations that make social life in the city possible. Migrant tribesmen find among their tribal peers in the city

---

[1]Daniel Lerner, *The Passing of Traditional Society: Modernizing the Middle East* (Glencoe, Ill,: Free Press, 1958); S. N. Eisenstadt, *Modernization: Protest and Change* (Englewood Cliffs, N.J.: Prentice-Hall, 1966).

[2]William J. Hanna and Judith L. Hanna, *Urban Dynamics in Black Africa* (Chicago: Aldine-Atherton, 1971), p. 107.

[3]Abner Cohen, *Custom and Politics in Urban Africa: A Study of Hausa Migrants in Yoruba Towns* (Berkeley: University of California Press, 1969).

[4]Kenneth L. Little, *West African Urbanization: A Study of Voluntary Associations in Social Change* (New York: Cambridge University Press, 1965). For further analysis in this vein, see Philip Mayer, *Townsmen or Tribesmen: Conservatism and the Process of Urbanization in a South African City,* 2d ed. (New York: Oxford University Press, 1971).

a network of people ready to help them with problems of adjustment to urban living—getting a job, finding housing, etc.[5] Such associations provide migrants with a sense of continuity between their older and their newer social existence. Most important, perhaps, tribal associations in the city act as agents of resocialization from traditional to modern ways of life:

> On the one hand, they emphasize tribal duties and obligations; on the other, they urge the adoption of a modern outlook and they establish new social practices. . . . They build for the migrant a cultural bridge and in so doing they convey him from one kind of social universe to another.[6]

This line of analysis clearly implies that persisting ethnic consciousness is only a stage in development of the modern person, providing a bridge that, once crossed, will allow people to leave behind them their traditional ethnic affiliations.

Another line of analysis seems to come to grips more fully with the "supertribalization" feature of urbanizing societies. This is the view that ethnic divisiveness is emphasized as a means for organizing people into interest groups to contend for the scarce privileges available in a modern society.[7] These privileges may be (to use Weber's terms again) either economic or political or "social" in nature.

Following this perspective, the recent intensification of ethnic organization and rivalry in African countries (the bitter Yoruba-Ibo warfare in Nigeria being an extreme example) may be attributed not only to the urbanization of these countries, which brought together people of many tribal origins in the same urban economy, but to the various national independence movements as well. As European dominance of positions of wealth, political power, and social prestige lessened, native Africans had more prizes to contend for. These remained *scarce* privileges, however,

---

[5]J. Clyde Mitchell (ed.), *Social Networks in Urban Situations* (Manchester: Manchester University Press, 1969).

[6]Little, *West African Urbanization,* p. 87.

[7]See Abner Cohen (ed.). *Urban Ethnicity* (London: Tavistock, 1974), pp. ix–xxiv; Robert H. Bates, "Ethnic Competition and Modernization in Contemporary Africa," *Comparative Political Studies,* 6(June, 1974):457–484; George Bennett, "Tribalism in Politics," in P. H. Gulliver (ed.), *Tradition and Transition in East Africa* (Berkeley: University of California Press, 1969), pp. 59–88; Claude S. Fischer, "Toward a Subcultural Theory of Urbanism," *American Journal of Sociology,* 80(May, 1975):1319–1341.

and competition for dominance in these various areas became intense. Interethnic contention is based on "a widespread fear that power in the hands of members of another ethnic group will lead to the deprivation of one's own group."[8] The "new men of power" in postcolonial Africa were accordingly motivated to play on these fears of being outdone by ethnic rivals to create an ethnic constituency for themselves from among their tribal peers.[9]

These two versions of persisting or heightened ethnicity in urbanizing countries do not have to be seen as mutually exclusive. This point is illustrated in Schildkrout's study of Mossi migrants from Upper Volta in the city of Kumasi in Ghana.[10] For first-generation migrants, Mossi tribalism serves most of the functions of adaptation to the urban situation suggested by Little. The ethnic group tends, for example, to provide tribal "kinsmen" to replace real family members from back home. In the second generation, real kinsmen are in the city, and this function of the ethnic group becomes superfluous. Mossi association persists, however, in more formalized ways because the Mossi, like all ethnic groups in Ghana, "must find ways of gaining economic and political power, and for many individuals (though by no means all) identification with the ethnic group is one possible way of increasing the likelihood of success."[11]

Industrialization

Consideration of the industrializing aspect of modernization will reveal, as in the case of urbanization, an older and a more recent emphasis on different types of effects on ethnic relations. Industrialization, according to the earlier view, discourages social organization on the basis of ethnic affiliation.[12] Modern industry requires a highly *rationalized* system of employing whatever techniques will maximize productivity. Ethnic discrimination—for example, the discriminatory wage policy that pays Eu-

---

[8]Hanna and Hanna, *Urban Dynamics in Black Africa,* p. 107.

[9]See Richard L. Sklar, "Political Science and National Integration—A Radical Approach," *Journal of Modern African Studies,* 5(1967):1–11; and P. C. Lloyd, *Africa in Social Change* (New York: Praeger, 1968), p. 302.

[10]Enid Schildkrout, "Ethnicity and Generational Differences Among Urban Immigrants in Ghana," in Cohen, *Urban Ethnicity,* pp. 187–222.

[11]Schildkrout, "Ethnicity and Generational Differences," p. 215.

[12]For a summary of such viewpoints, see Harold Wolpe, "Industrialism and Race in South Africa," in Sami Zubaida (ed.), *Race and Racialism* (London: Tavistock, 1970), pp. 151–154.

ropeans more than native workers for the same work (as discussed in Chapter 5)—is seen as inconsistent with industrialization because it is wasteful of native talent and also because, by depriving natives of adequate income, it deprives manufacturers of a domestic market for their products. On this basis it had been predicted that the great emphasis on industrialization in South Africa would undermine the sharp racial discrimination in employment in that country.[13] Another "de-ethnicizing" effect of industrialization has been suggested. As industry develops, "classes" (in the Marxian sense of the distinction between owners and wage workers) will develop among all ethnic groups, and these class differences *within* ethnic groups will tend to reduce ethnic solidarity and the clear-cut subordination of one ethnic group by another.[14]

Recent studies of modernization, especially in Africa, suggest that the development of industry does not always have the asserted effect of reducing the importance of ethnic affiliation. Wolpe shows, for example, that industrialization in South Africa has not resulted in the elimination of racially discriminatory wage policies on the indicated grounds of industrial "rationality."[15] Given the extreme opposition of white workers to an equalization of pay between themselves and black workers, employers may find it entirely rational to continue the discriminatory policy; failure to do so could lead to strikes by white workers. The cost in wasted talent of discriminatory racial employment may also be a fallacious argument. As Wolpe points out, the racially repressive society of South Africa has been able to train and employ native workers in highly skilled and responsible occupational positions, even while grossly underpaying them for this work. The adaptability of a racist society to industrial conditions is thus well illustrated in the case of South Africa.

The idea that class will replace ethnicity as a basis of social organization in industrialized society has also been challenged, again primarily using African examples. Industrialization will have this effect only if the new occupational division of labor leads to association of people from various

---

[13]Sheila van der Horst, "The Effects of Industrialization on Race Relations in South Africa," in Guy Hunter (ed.), *Industrialization and Race Relations* (London: Oxford University Press, 1965), p. 101.

[14]For a critical review of several formulations of this sort, see Leo Kuper, "Theories of Revolution and Race Relations," *Comparative Studies in Society and History,* 13(January, 1971):87–107.

[15]Wolpe, "Industrialism and Race in South Africa."

ethnic groups in the same occupation. Actually, the experience in Dakar, Senegal, and elsewhere is that there tends to be a sharp differentiation of occupational roles between the various native tribal groups.[16] In South Africa, working class solidarity between black and white workers was effectively eliminated in the 1920s, when protests by natives against discriminatory employment practices resulted in an alliance between white workers and owners of industry. The owners bought the white workers' loyalty to the white supremacy system by yielding to their demands for a continuation of favorable treatment for themselves and their all-white labor unions.[17]

PLANNED CHANGES

We turn now to those changes in ethnic relations that are the result—or the intended result—of efforts of persons in positions of formal authority to bring about change. We noted earlier two different dimensions along which human relationships could be analyzed: social *distance* and differential *power*. It would be possible, therefore, to focus on planned efforts to alter social distance between ethnic groups either by decreasing social distance through planned integration or increasing social distance by such efforts as the apartheid system of racial separation in South Africa or the reduction of contact with "aliens" through restrictive immigration legislation. Also, there are or have been efforts made to apply systematic plans to subjugate an ethnic people by reducing the privileges they have previously enjoyed. We shall not, for lack of space, deal here with such programs of change. Rather, we shall focus on an area of great practical interest today: the effort made in many countries, regions, and communities to reduce the inequality between ethnic peoples, to make less stringent the various systems of ethnic stratification. It seems clear that such equalizing efforts are the wave of the present if not of the future. Governmental bodies of various sorts are hard at work attempting to devise ways of implementing in social practice the rather idealistic assertion that "all men are created equal." Some kinds of effort in that direction—and some of the persistent difficulties in the way of the "best laid plans"—will now be examined.

---

[16]Hanna and Hanna, *Urban Dynamics in Black Africa,* pp. 131–132.

[17]Michael Banton, *Race Relations* (New York: Basic Books, 1967), pp. 173, 174.

Equality by Statute

Ethnic equality may be established as a matter of policy in a given political jurisdiction through the enactment of laws or regulations making discrimination unlawful or through the articulation of such policies by administrative agencies of government. We shall be examining something of the experience of anti-discrimination policy in the United States and Great Britain to illustrate some of the persisting problems of enforcement in this area.

In the United States, as elsewhere, official action to end discriminatory treatment of minorities has involved a series of piecemeal efforts in different directions and under different jurisdictions. The executive branch of the federal government has often moved considerably ahead of the legislative in its willingness to pursue official attacks on discrimination. The current era of civil rights action began with an executive order of President Franklin D. Roosevelt in 1941 (apparently in response to the threat of a massive demonstration by blacks) in which he articulated "the policy of the United States that there shall be no discrimination in the employment of workers in defense industries or government because of race, creed, color, or national origin."[18] Executive departments granting defense contracts were instructed to write nondiscrimination clauses into the contracts, and a Fair Employment Practices Committee (FEPC) was established, which had at first only a vague mandate to "redress grievances" and advise the president. In 1943, however, the duties of the committee were more closely defined to enable it to hear grievances and to negotiate agreements with offending companies to end racial discrimination in employment. These actions—pressure through the purse-strings power of government to withhold federal aid from discriminating agencies, and the use of conciliation, the negotiated settlement of grievances by persuading discriminators to agree to change their practice—are two elements of federal policy that have been continued. These techniques have generally not been effective in achieving their aim, but the fact that they could be introduced by the executive branch in the 1940s is probably significant. President Truman tried unsuccessfully for two years to have Congress establish FEPC by statute; finally, he established a revised version

[18]George E. Simpson and J. Milton Yinger, *Racial and Cultural Minorities: An Analysis of Prejudice and Discrimination,* 4th ed. (New York: Harper & Row, 1972), p. 424.

of the program himself by executive order in 1948.[19] These events illustrate, perhaps, that the executive branch may be more responsive than the legislative to the need for protection of minority rights. Congressmen represent individual constituencies and tend to reflect prejudices of local majorities.[20] Presidents represent more directly the "national interest," whether that interest is defined, for example, as maximizing war production (a major concern in 1941) or as enabling the country to have a credible posture in international relations (a consideration in 1948).

Congress finally did, in 1957, enact legislation that created a Commission on Civil Rights with the responsibility to investigate alleged areas of discrimination, and provided the Justice Department, through its Civil Rights Division, with the power to prosecute on behalf of complainant blacks any denial of voting rights.[21] While the Civil Rights Commission has performed valuable service by its thorough and critical examinations of ethnic discrimination in American life, the Civil Rights Division of the Justice Department was hampered for a number of years by its lack of coercive authority to force local voting registrars in the South to release registration rolls. In effect, the Justice Department had to prove a "pattern and practice" of racial discrimination without any way to establish the existence of such a pattern.

The momentous Civil Rights Acts of 1964 and 1965 corrected some of the deficiencies in effective enforcement of nondiscrimination while continuing some other deficiencies. Title VII of the 1964 act dealt with employment discrimination and established an Equal Employment Opportunity Commission (EEOC) to enforce rights in this area.[22] The EEOC can receive complaints from anyone who feels that because of ethnicity or sex he or she is being discriminated against in employment, in membership in labor unions, or in treatment by employment agencies (with some exceptions, since certain types of employers, unions, and employment agencies are not covered by the act). If the commission finds evidence of discrimination, it so informs the offending agency and then tries to reach

---

[19]Simpson and Yinger, *Racial and Cultural Minorities,* p. 426.

[20]Southern representatives in Congress were extremely resistant to the passage of FEPC laws. Simpson and Yinger, *Racial and Cultural Minorities,* p. 425.

[21]Frederick M. Wirt, *Politics of Southern Equality* (Chicago: Aldine, 1970), p. 67.

[22]Simpson and Yinger, *Racial and Cultural Minorities,* p. 429.

a "conciliation" that is satisfactory to both parties.[23] Failing conciliation, the commission can turn the case over to the Justice Department for possible legal prosecution. Very similar procedures are typical of most of the commissions on fair employment practice that have been established by most states and many cities.

In an evaluation of the operation of these commissions at both the local and national levels, Witherspoon observes that "perhaps the most significant factor contributing to the typical ability of a human-relations commission to dispose through the techniques of conciliation of almost all violations brought to its attention is its possession of ultimate authority to enforce compliance with the law if conciliation fails."[24] Although the EEOC has this power in the roundabout way of taking the case through the Justice Department, in practice it has not often operated this way partly, perhaps, because of the complications arising when two different governmental agencies get involved in the enforcement act. A description by Blumrosen of a "brief shining moment" in the history of EEOC illustrates this point in a negative way.[25] The case described was that of a shipbuilding company in Newport News, Virginia, that was found in violation of federal policy by virtue of racially discriminatory hiring practices. Blumrosen was at the time an official of the EEOC, and he insisted that there be a clear understanding between his agency and the Civil Rights Division of the Justice Department that failure to cooperate with the commission's conciliation efforts (which had been the company's first inclination) would certainly lead to prosecution. This understanding was reached in a rare feat of bureaucratic cooperation, and a substantial reduction of employment discrimination by the company was achieved. However, there was vigorous public criticism of the settlement and this, in addition to the resumption of "business as usual" rivalry between governmental agencies, seemed to

---

[23]The difficulty of reaching such conciliations is suggested by a plaque that hung on the wall of Burke Marshall, first head of the Civil Rights Division of the Justice Department, which read: "Blessed are the peacemakers—for they shall catch hell from both sides." Wirt, *Politics of Southern Equality*, p. ix.

[24]Joseph P. Witherspoon, *Administrative Implementation of Civil Rights* (Austin: University of Texas Press, 1968), p. 115.

[25]Alfred W. Blumrosen, "The Newport News Agreement—One Brief Shining Moment in the Enforcement of Equal Employment Opportunity," in John H. McCord (ed.), *With All Deliberate Speed: Civil Rights Theory and Practice* (Urbana: University of Illinois Press, 1969), pp. 97–158.

insure that this "brief shining moment" would be the only one enjoyed by EEOC.[26]

A complicating factor in the enforcement of civil rights laws is the tremendous expansion of coverage of these laws, especially at the local level. "Equal opportunity" laws and regulations have increasingly focused on demands to eliminate discrimination against women. Further, as Martin shows in a survey of state and city laws, there have been many other extensions of coverage. There are laws forbidding discrimination against recipients of public assistance, people of deviant "sexual orientation," the aged, the physically handicapped. In Pennsylvania, there is even a law "prohibiting discrimination against a hospital employee who refused to participate in performing an abortion."[27] These extensions of coverage have resulted, Martin suggests, in a new form of "racism." With greatly expanded work loads and, often as not, with diminished budgets to provide mandated services, enforcement agencies are simply not able to perform as well their original job of enforcing laws against ethnic discrimination.

The 1965 Civil Rights Act, and its subsequent enforcement, demonstrates the possibility of more positive results in planned nondiscrimination. As noted above, the Justice Department had been frustrated in intervening in southern states to insure black voting rights by its inability to prove discrimination as a justification for the intervention. The 1965 act made it possible to determine simply by "administrative oversight" that intervention was necessary.[28] According to the act, a prima facie case of racial discrimination in voting registration exists in any county where less than half of the nonwhites of voting age are actually registered to vote. In such counties, the Civil Rights Division of the Justice Department could and did

---

[26]For an essentially negative evaluation of the impact of EEOC actions on the reduction of discrimination in employment, see Arvil V. Adams, *"Toward Fair Employment and the EEOC: A Study of Compliance Under Title VII of the Civil Rights Act of 1964"* (Washington, D.C.: U.S. Equal Employment Opportunity Commission, 1972). For evaluations emphasizing the operation of fair employment commissions on the state and local levels, see Frances R. Cousens, *Public Civil Rights Agencies and Fair Employment* (New York: Praeger, 1969), and Morroe Berger, *Equality by Statute,* rev. ed. (Garden City, N.Y.: Doubleday, 1967), chap. 4.

[27]Galen Martin, "New Civil Rights Coverages—Progress or Racism?" *Journal of Intergroup Relations,* 4(April, 1975):14–37. Quotation on p. 19.

[28]Wirt, *Politics of Southern Equality,* p. 70.

send in federal registrars to insure the opening of the voting rolls to non-whites. Under its cool but determined directors, Burke Marshall and John Doar (later to gain national recognition as majority counsel for the House Judiciary Committee during hearings on the impeachment of President Nixon), and with a staff of enforcement officers of similar determination, the Civil Rights Division was able to produce such "drastic results" as a rise in the percentage of eligible blacks actually registered from 14 percent in 1960 to 61 percent in 1969 in Alabama, and from 5 percent in 1960 to 67 percent in 1969 in Mississippi.[29]

Title VI of the 1964 act has generated another highly controversial approach to enforced nondiscrimination. The act makes it illegal for any agency receiving federal assistance to practice ethnic or sexual discrimination. President Johnson, by executive order in 1965 (which was amended in 1967 to cover the employment of women) gave impetus to the implementation of this title by requiring all federal departments to take "affirmative action" to insure that discrimination is not practiced among agencies —e.g., hospitals, schools, housing authorities—receiving federal assistance.[30] The Department of Health, Education, and Welfare has interpreted its mandate as requiring that financially assisted agencies, such as universities, must either: (1) demonstrate that minorities and women are employed in numbers proportional to their number in the employment market, or (2) show why they have not been able to achieve this practice, or (3) face the possible loss of federal assistance.

This so-called quota approach to the enforcement of nondiscrimination has been severely criticized, even by some "liberal" individuals and organizations who have actively promoted civil rights.[31] The American Jewish Committee has, for example, vigorously opposed such quotas largely, it seems, because Jewish participation in certain intellectual occupations has given Jews an advantage in a situation of open competition without regard to ethnic origins. The pages of *Commentary,* published by the committee, have been filled with articles highly critical of "affirmative action" based

---

[29]Wirt, *Politics of Southern Equality,* p. 89.

[30]For the text of the 1965 order, see *Race Relations Law Reporter,* 10(1965):1833–1839.

[31]Judith Caditz, "Ambivalence Toward Integration: The Sequence of Response to Six Interracial Situations," *Sociological Quarterly,* 16(Winter, 1975):16–32.

on the application of quotas for the participation of minorities.[32] In one such article, Abrams asserts that EEOC actually violates Article VI of the Civil Rights Act of 1964, which specifically forbids the establishment of minority quotas.[33] According to Seabury, American universities have been harassed by "affirmative action" programs into relaxing standards to employ minority group members of lesser qualification. These practices violate the oft-cited statement by Justice Harlan (in a dissent to the 1896 Supreme Court decision in *Plessy* v. *Ferguson,* which established the constitutional basis for racially "separate but equal" school systems until 1954) that "our Constitution is color-blind." Universities, influenced by this color-blind concept, have been reluctant even to classify their employees ethnically, as they would have to do to prove their compliance with affirmative action.[34]

The development of antidiscrimination legislation in Great Britain shows some similarities to and differences from the American experience.[35] After World War II, Britain had a considerable influx of Commonwealth immigrants, especially from former British colonies in India, Pakistan, and the West Indies. Native Britons tend to lump these people together and classify them as "coloured." Although such immigrants have never constituted more than 2 or 3 percent of the English population, their concentration in urban industrial centers has made them highly visible and put them in competition with working-class people in these areas. The Labour Party in Britain has maintained an ambivalent position with reference to the plight of these immigrants. On the one hand, as the political party formally affiliated with the trade union movement, the Labour Party must necessarily associate itself with the feelings of white working-class people of the country. On the other hand, the generally liberal and internationalist ideo-

---

[32]Stephen Steinberg, "How Jewish Quotas Began," *Commentary,* 52(September, 1971): 67–76; Martin Mayer, "Higher Education For All?—The Case of Open Admissions," *Commentary,* 57(February, 1973):37–47; Elliott Abrams, "The Quota Commission," *Commentary,* 54(October, 1972):54–58; Paul Seabury, "HEW and the Universities," *Commentary,* 53(February, 1972):38–44.

[33]Abrams, "The Quota Commission."

[34]Seabury, "HEW and the Universities."

[35]The following discussion is based on E. J. B. Rose, *Colour and Citizenship: A Report on British Race Relations* (London: Oxford University Press, 1969); Simon Abbott (ed.), *The Prevention of Racial Discrimination in Britain* (London: Oxford University Press, 1971); and Sheila Patterson, *Immigration and Race Relations in Britain, 1960–1967* (London: Oxford University Press, 1969).

logical position of the Labour Party has demanded a degree of sympathy with minorities in the country.[36] Accordingly, the Labour Party acquiesced in the movement for immigration restriction that began in 1962, and expressed its "other face" by sponsoring an antidiscriminatory Race Relations Act in 1965 and in 1968.

The nature of this legislation and its implementation illustrates a partial exception to the generalization, suggested above, that legislation tends to develop as a "correction" of past mistakes in the attempt to regulate an area of social life. One critic of this legislation, Kushnick, comments on the fact that British legislators had at their disposal much information about the experience of civil rights legislation in the United States, but seemed nevertheless to repeat some of the American mistakes.[37] This observation leads Kushnick to the assertion that "there is no immutable law which requires every country to make the same mistakes as others."[38]

The basic "mistakes" of the 1965 act were: (1) it limited coverage to cases of alleged discrimination in "places of public resort"—hotels, beaches, etc.—leaving uncovered the more vexatious problem of discrimination in housing and employment, and (2) it provided a very weak enforcement mechanism, similar to but even weaker than that granted the EEOC in the United States. The Race Relations Board (a rough counterpart to the EEOC) created by the act had the power to seek conciliation where there was alleged discrimination (but only through the operation of appointed local committees), with the additional power to refer unconciliated cases to the attorney general for possible prosecution in the county courts. These local committees were not even provided with subpoena powers to compel attendance at their hearings. This restricted coverage and these restricted methods led the Race Relations Board itself to become a major critic of the act under which it operated. The board kept records of all those complaints that it could *not* process and cited these and other

---

[36]The comment above about the influence of local constituencies in inhibiting American Congressmen from taking a "national" viewpoint is probably somewhat less operative for a British member of Parliament, who finds that his loyalty to the official party line may be more important to his political career than the attitudes of the constituency that elected him. The national party can always find a "safe" constituency for a loyal party member, making it possible for M.P.'s to display "profiles of courage" in taking stands not popular in their home districts.

[37]Louis Kushnick, "British Anti-Discrimination Legislation," in Abbott, *Prevention of Racial Discrimination in Britain,* pp. 233–268.

[38]Kushnick, "British Anti-Discrimination Legislation," p. 266.

limitations in its annual reports.[39] This activity, abetted by a widely publicized survey of the continued discrimination against Commonwealth immigrants,[40] led to a successful movement in 1968 to extend the coverage of the Race Relations Board to deal with housing and employment discrimination. The enforcement weaknesses of the 1965 act were left very largely intact, however.[41] The classic practice in British politics of "muddling through" had produced a rather weak start in the direction of civil rights legislation.[42]

Development Strategies

Planners of greater ethnic equality in the United States apparently failed to reckon with the limitations of "equal opportunity" approaches to produce a lessening of ethnic stratification. The urban street riots of the 1960s dramatized the fact that the masses of black Americans were hardly affected by antidiscrimination legislation, and probably would not have been even *if* the legislation had been effectively enforced. Ghetto blacks seemed to suffer not so much from lack of the right to compete with whites for social privileges, but from a lack of resources—financial, educational, personal—with which to compete *successfully*. As a product of the past "separate and unequal" educational system, for example, the typical black could not hope to hold his own in school or work against the better educated white. It became increasingly apparent to planners at this time that a new approach to the problem of minorities was needed: one that

---

[39]Brian Cohen and Marna Glyn, "The Race Relations Board," in Abbott, *Prevention of Racial Discrimination in Britain,* pp. 267–285.

[40]W. W. Daniel, *Racial Discrimination in England* (Harmondsworth, England: Penguin Books, 1968).

[41]Much of the weakness of the 1968 act may be attributable to the influence of a famous speech by a Conservative member of Parliament, Enoch Powell, on April 20, 1968. Powell at this time was able to "speak the unspeakable," to give voice to white British fears that, as Powell put it, "in this country in fifteen or twenty years' time the black man will have a whip hand over the white man." For a description of some of the political impact of this speech, see Dilip Hiro, *Black British, White British,* rev. ed. (New York: Monthly Review Press, 1973), pp. 241–253.

[42]One novelty of the 1965 act (compared with American legislation) was that it included a provision against "incitement" to racial violence. The background of this provision was a recent rather vociferous anti-Semitism in the country in which, among other slogans, it was being urged to "Free Britain From Jewish Control." Kushnick, "British Anti-Discrimination Legislation," pp. 241, 242.

would emphasize not so much civil rights as the opportunity to develop the resources of those minorities. President Johnson's "war on poverty," as administered through the Office of Economic Opportunity (OEO), was the most dramatic and visible manifestation of this approach.

Two aspects of such "development" strategies will be discussed here. One approach takes the *individual* minority group member as the target for greater resource development. The American Indian relocation program of the Bureau of Indian Affairs would illustrate this approach. According to the philosophy behind relocation, the individual Indian will never be able to develop his personal resources when he is bound by the limited economic resources available on the Indian reservation, perhaps the most extreme area of hard-core poverty in American life. The relocation program flies in the face, of course, of the Indian revitalization movement that we discussed earlier. By most calculations, relocation is essentially a failure in terms of its own aims, since the Indian faces various discriminations in the city without the cushioning effect of the moral support of his tribesmen. As a result, the Indian either "remains Indian" by association with fellow ethnics who, like himself, undervalue material acquisition and social mobility,[43] or he reacts to the anomie of the urban situation with excessive drinking or some other social pathology.[44]

Another example of planned development of individual resources can be found in the area often referred to as "compensatory education" for minorities. For instance, the federal government provides funds to school districts in impoverished areas under Title I of the Elementary and Secondary Education Act of 1965. Evaluations of the program have suggested that Title I funds have been used in ways that are of doubtful benefit to their intended recipients. Apparently, the Office of Education, in administering the funds, has not insisted on carefully drawn plans for efficient use of the money.[45] More visible programs are provided through such schemes as Head Start, which provides preschool preparation for disadvantaged youngsters, and Upward Bound programs, which admit limited numbers

---

[43]Joan Ablon, "Relocated American Indians in the San Francisco Bay Area: Social Interaction and Indian Identity," *Human Organization,* 23(Winter, 1964):296–304.

[44]Theodore D. Graves, "The Personal Adjustment of Navajo Indian Migrants to Denver, Colorado," *American Anthropologist,* 72(February, 1970):35–54.

[45]Howard A. Glickstein, "Federal Educational Programs and Minority Groups," *Journal of Negro Education,* 38(Summer, 1969):303–314.

of minority group students to colleges without the usual requisite high school records. Such programs are limited by: (1) the opposition of the Archie Bunker-like "forgotten American" taxpayers, who see their tax money being spent on expensive welfare programs for minorities while they can barely make ends meet; (2) such nonminority students as Marco DeFunis, who instituted a "discrimination in reverse" lawsuit against the University of Washington for passing over his law school application in favor of less-qualified minority applicants;[46] (3) the indifference or hostility of some minorities themselves toward such programs. It is observed, for example, that many reservation Indians resent Head Start and other youth-oriented programs that concentrate attention on children rather than on what they see as the *real* need of Indians: the development of on-reservation job opportunities.[47]

With the advent of the "new ethnicity," with its emphasis on development of the ethnic community, such individual-oriented approaches to the development of minority resources have understandably come under vigorous attack. Public policy takes account of these feelings in an alternative approach that emphasizes *community* development. The Equal Opportunity Act of 1964 authorized the Office of Economic Opportunity to administer Community Action Programs in which the poor themselves plan and run programs of community self-improvement.

A natural area for the development of community action programs was the Indian reservation, which typically qualifies with no difficulty on the criterion of poverty and which has in existence some sort of tribal council to provide an organizational base for program planning and administration. There were, accordingly, sixty-eight such funded Community Action Programs on Indian reservations in 1971.[48] Unfortunately for the success of such programs, they were engrafted on a structure of community decision making that many Indians defined as highly paternalistic. Reservation Indians had been subjected for years to procedures whereby the Bureau of Indian Affairs provided various services *for* the Indian. A modicum of

---

[46]Nina Totenberg, "Discriminating to End Discrimination," *New York Times Magazine,* April 14, 1974, pp. 8–9.

[47]Murray L. Wax and Rosalie H. Wax, "The Enemies of the People," in Howard S. Becker, Blanche Geer, David Riesman, and Robert S. Weiss (eds.), *Institutions and the Person* (Chicago: Aldine, 1968), pp. 101–118.

[48]George P. Castile, "Federal Indian Policy and the Sustained Enclave: An Anthropological Perspective," *Human Organization,* 33(Fall, 1974):219–228.

Indian participation was provided by the tribal councils, which were largely creatures of federal Indian administration rather than a continuation of tribal Indian tradition.[49] Even the "enlightened" administration of John Collier, who was Commissioner of Indian Affairs from 1933 to 1945, with its ostensible policy of Indian self-determination, violated this policy when it was seen to be for the Indians' "own good." Collier himself describes his practice of extending benefits by "administrative action" to those tribes that had voted against receiving such benefits,[50] thereby depriving the Indians of the "right to make mistakes."[51]

Because of these past practices, Indian reservations have been described as "administered communities" in the sense defined by Weingrod as a community "whose social, cultural, economic and political development is directed by outside agencies."[52] In an analysis of recent developments in OEO-sponsored programs, Castile argues that there is some hope that reservations may become "sustained enclaves" rather than administered communities.[53] He means by this that reservations will require outside support for an indefinite period but that such programs will be acceptable to Indians if: (1) the current tendency to leave planning and operation of those programs to the Indians is continued—the sustained enclave is based on "a program of economically supported but fundamentally nondirected change"[54]—and (2) the Indians can be assured by resolution of Congress or otherwise that *termination* of federal support for Indians is not in the offing, so they may be assured of the continuation of such support. Some doubt about Castile's optimistic assessment may be in order. Leaving Indian programs to "the Indians" may not change fundamentally the fact that political power on the reservation may rest in a tribal council structure that is more responsive to "the government" than to "the people."

---

[49]This separation between tribal councils and "the people" is shown to exist for Sioux Indians in Gordon Macgregor, *Warriors Without Weapons* (Chicago: University of Chicago Press, 1946); and in Robert K. Thomas, "Powerless Politics," *New University Thought,* 4(1966): 44–53. For a similar observation among the Navaho, see Tom T. Sasaki, *Fruitland, New Mexico: A Navajo Community in Transition* (Ithaca, N.Y.: Cornell University Press, 1960).

[50]John Collier, *From Every Zenith* (Denver: Sage Books, 1963), p. 177.

[51]Sol Tax, "The Freedom to Make Mistakes," *America Indigena,* 16(1956):171–177.

[52]Alex Weingrod, *Reluctant Pioneers: Village Development in Israel* (Ithaca, N.Y.: Cornell University Press, 1966), p. viii.

[53]Castile, "Federal Indian Policy and the Sustained Enclave."

[54]Castile, "Federal Indian Policy and the Sustained Enclave," p. 219.

A further limitation of Community Action Programs may result from the notorious corruption and misuse of funds that have been uncovered in several instances. Another potential if not actual abuse of such programs is indicated in the operation of the "minority responsiveness program" of the Nixon re-election campaign of 1972, a set of practices that caught the interest of the Senate Select Committee on Presidential Campaign Activities, which was established to investigate Watergate.[55] Campaign planners, according to some evidence, intended to use the threat of withdrawal of poverty program funds to coerce campaign support from those involved in development programs. Such practices seem to illustrate the limitations —or at least the problems—of trying to assist minorities to improve their condition through the administration of funded programs of support.

ETHNIC MOVEMENTS

Ethnic groups that occupy minority positions in a system of ethnic stratification or whose members experience social distance toward themselves by dominant group members may not feel inclined to wait for their situation to be improved either spontaneously or through the benevolent actions of political officials. They may act in some way to protest their position, expecting that such protests will lead to an alteration of their situation. Such collective protests are commonly referred to as *social movements,* and the field of ethnic relations is certainly an area in which social movements are likely to be an important part of the social scene.

Social movements can and have been studied from a wide variety of perspectives. Sociological interest may focus on such questions as: (1) How do social movements begin? (What conditions generated the Black Power movements among Negroes, the Red Power movements among Indians, the Brown Power movements among Chicanos?) (2) From what segments of a total population does a social movement draw its support? (What social classes of blacks have been attracted to the Black Muslim movement?) (3) How do changes occur in the aims and tactics of a movement? (Why did the black civil rights movement come to adopt the "direct action" or civil disobedience tactics of Martin Luther King, Jr.?)

None of these important questions about ethnic movements will be directly dealt with here. Rather, we shall keep attention focused on the subject of this chapter: an analysis of those forces that tend to produce

---

[55]Tony Castro, "Nixon's Minority Responsiveness Program," *Race Relations Reporter,* 5(July, 1974):25–29.

change in a system of ethnic relations. As in our discussion of spontaneous and planned changes, we are concerned with the *effects* of ethnic movements: the degree to which they act as contributory factors in the change process. There is one perspective on recent protest activity in the United States and elsewhere that insists that collective protest—ethnic or otherwise—is an extremely fertile source of social change. This is a major conclusion of a study conducted in 1969 by the social science staff of the National Commission on the Causes and Prevention of Violence.[56] Black militancy, antiwar protest, and student demonstrations are all described as having a strong political design and effect, with major influences on such official actions as civil rights legislation, the ending of the Vietnam war, and the introduction of reforms in college and university administration. Lowi accounts for some of the success of social movements in the United States by arguing that the checks and balances built into the structure of American government make the system ideal for the preservation of a status quo but not as amenable to change except when the power structure is "pushed" by social movements.[57]

Our major problem for analysis is thus the question of what conditions make it relatively easy or difficult for ethnic movements to push in the direction of desired changes in prevailing ethnic relations. A basis for this analysis is provided in the *conflict* perspective on human society that asserts the ubiquity and importance of struggles between social groups in determining any current state of social order. Much of the impetus for this approach derives, of course, from the Marxian insistence on the importance of the class struggle and with the continuing efforts of Marxist theoreticians to explain or to explain away the actual history of class relations in modern industrial countries. Although our interest here is in ethnic rather than class relations, many insights on our problem can be borrowed from the longstanding effort to reach an intellectual understanding of the course of this class struggle.

Ralf Dahrendorf is one contemporary "conflict theorist" who writes from a perspective of primary interest in class relations but who also articulates a general model of social conflict that will be useful for our analytic purposes.[58] Instead of beginning, as do the functional theorists,

---

[56]Jerome Skolnick, *Politics of Protest* (New York: Simon and Schuster, 1969).

[57]Theodore J. Lowi, *The Politics of Disorder* (New York: Basic Books, 1971).

[58]Ralf Dahrendorf, "Toward a Theory of Social Conflict," *Journal of Conflict Resolution,* 2(1958):170–183.

with an assumption of equilibrium—that is, the notion that social systems have an inherent tendency to sustain the status quo and that social changes arise from uncontrolled deviations from this tendency—Dahrendorf proposes starting from an opposite set of assumptions. Thus Dahrendorf would have us assume that in every social group with "imperative coordination" (with rulers and ruled), subordinate members of the group have an inherent tendency to revolt against the system in which they are disadvantaged. Any variation from this tendency—any situation of stability or minimization of struggle between the advantaged and the disadvantaged —is explained by the *constraints* on this revolutionary tendency that can be brought to bear against potential revolutionaries.

The idea of constraint as a factor in inhibiting the success of ethnic movements will be useful to us in the analysis that follows. It will serve to focus attention on a very important consideration in determining the effects of an ethnic movement: the reactions of persons in positions of authority to those movements or even their anticipations of such movements. Because of the constraining potential and inclination of those who hold the reins of power, it is by no means obvious that the conflict perspective on social change is, as Dahrendorf asserts, much better suited to the explanation of social change than is the functionalist perspective. It may well be, ironically, that a systematic consideration of constraint on revolutionary movements would lead to some skepticism about the possibility— as opposed to the desirability—of radical social change through the influence of social movements.

In analyzing ethnic movements in relation to constraints on them, we shall be guided by Dahrendorf's suggestion that there are three sorts of "conditions" that must be favorable if revolutionary action is to succeed in realizing its "inherent" potentialities. Dahrendorf calls these conditions of organization, conflict, and change.

Conditions of Organization

Before any movement on behalf of any ethnic minority can hope for any success, ways must be found to get together enough people with enough power and unity of action to bring effective pressure to bear for the production of change. The mere fact of "common victimization" is, as we noted in Chapter 3, not always sufficient to generate unity among an ethnic people. If each victimized individual acts *as* an individual, without the discipline of a group-determined course of action, there might be much protest against subordinate positions, but no preponderance of force in the direction of a given change in the status quo of ethnic relations.

Problems of factional division. One prominent organizational problem is the prevalence of *factionalism* among minorities. Such factionalism often arises because effective action may require coalitions of several minorities. The following examples will illustrate some of these factional problems.

In Britain in 1964 there was launched a Campaign Against Racial Discrimination (C.A.R.D.) aimed at protesting continued discrimination against Commonwealth immigrants (primarily West Indian, Pakistani, and Indian).[59] C.A.R.D. was designed to be an "organization of organizations," coordinating the efforts of the many organizations formed by specific coloured groups (e.g., the Standing Conference of West Indian Organizations, the Indian Workers Association, Great Britain).[60] In fact C.A.R.D. soon found itself unable to cope with the factionalism of these separate organizations. The West Indian organization soon withdrew because the West Indian leaders thought C.A.R.D. was "white-dominated" and because the West Indian group apparently felt its independence of action threatened by the necessity of coordinating its activities with those of the "organization of organizations." The difficulty of a unified Commonwealth immigrant social movement in Britain may also reflect a more pervasive divisiveness among the masses of immigrants from different parts of the Commonwealth. It is suggested, for example, that there is a kind of "Pak v. Black" rivalry in Britain that reflects a general tendency for all other immigrant groups to practice social distance toward Pakistani immigrants.[61] Partly because of this factionalism, perhaps, it has been observed that, as contrasted with civil rights legislation in the United States, the protest activity of minority ethnic groups in Britain played very little part in the passage of the Race Relations Acts of 1965 and 1968.[62]

A second instance of factionalism in an ethnic movement is furnished by the passive resistance movement in South Africa, especially an episode in 1952 called the Campaign for the Defiance of Unjust Laws.[63] As we

---

[59]Benjamin W. Heineman, Jr., *The Politics of the Powerless: A Study of the Campaign Against Racial Discrimination* (London: Oxford University Press, 1972).

[60]"The brute fact of discrimination, thought the founder of C.A.R.D., would bring Indians, Pakistanis, and West Indians together to form such an organization." Heineman, *Politics of the Powerless,* p. 1.

[61]David White, "Black v. Pak?" in Donald E. Gelfand and Russell D. Lee (eds.), *Ethnic Conflicts and Power: A Cross-National Perspective* (New York: Wiley, 1973), pp. 109–113.

[62]Patterson, *Immigration and Race Relations in Britain,* p. 412.

[63]Leo Kuper, *Passive Resistance in South Africa* (New Haven: Yale University Press, 1957).

noted in Chapter 1, South African *apartheid* policies have increasingly reduced to the same level of extreme deprivation of rights the three major nonwhite groups in the country: native blacks, Indians, and the coloured people of mixed racial ancestry. By 1952 the separate organizations of those groups came together in a campaign of civil disobedience. The plan was to violate the various *apartheid* rules in the country, using the passive resistance techniques developed by Gandhi in leading Indian protests in South Africa before he moved on to leadership of the anti-British movement in India. While the campaign failed for other reasons mentioned below, it failed partly because the different discriminatory features of *apartheid* worked on these three groups in different ways, so that it was difficult to agree on an appropriate set of targets for the protests. The black leadership ultimately moved away from the tripartite Congress of South African minorities toward an affiliation with a Pan-African organization of blacks from various countries of Africa. As in Britain, cooperation was also hampered by feelings of social distance. The coloured population gave minimal support to the movement, partly because they did not wish to be associated with groups (blacks and Indians) that they had traditionally considered inferior.

Quite apart from such difficulties of federation or coalition, the very nature of protesting social movements may engender a sort of factionalist tendency. The C.A.R.D. experience in Great Britain again serves as an example. The organization was almost immediately torn by a dispute over aims and tactics: specifically, over the issue of whether C.A.R.D. should demand repeal of the Commonwealth Immigration Act of 1962, or whether it should concentrate efforts to strengthen the impending antidiscriminatory legislation in the Race Relations Act of 1965.[64] The Black Power movement in the United States similarly has been subject to such factional disputes. Each separate black organization (even each local branch of a given organization) is likely to reflect in aims and tactics the idiosyncracies of its particular members.[65] Such tendencies are perhaps understandable if one reflects that it takes the mentality of a zealot to be highly involved in a movement. If movement participants are people of conviction, they may not always be willing to compromise their convictions to accommodate the different convictions of other participants. This

---

[64]Heineman, *Politics of the Powerless,* pp. 39–44.
[65]Luther P. Gerlach and Virginia H. Hine, *People, Power, Change: Movements of Social Transformation* (Indianapolis: Bobbs-Merrill, 1970), pp. 34–55.

being the case, it may be, as Weber suggests, that a crucial factor in a successful revolutionary movement is the presence of a *charismatic* leader (such as Martin Luther King or Cesar Chavez) who can hold together people of diverse commitment simply on the basis of that leader's *personal* appeal.[66]

Problems of leadership. Concerted action in a social movement requires leadership that has not only charisma but also the skill and experience to deal with the complex problems of leading a mass of people. Some movements have failed largely because of the lack of such leadership. Kuper noted that in the 1952 passive resistance campaign in South Africa, most of the campaign's leaders were found guilty of violating laws against opposition to *apartheid* (some of these laws were enacted during the campaign itself) and given lengthy jail sentences that were suspended on condition that the rebellious acts not be repeated. "This had the effect of removing these leaders from active roles in the resistance movement."[67] From a perspective of twenty years distance from these events, Kuper offers the suggestion that the campaign may, after all, have been ill-advised. The leaders of the campaign knew full well that the masses of South African nonwhites were not ready to risk great personal danger in the defiance campaign, and Kuper asks, with obvious skepticism: "Was it expedient to surrender the militant cadres to the prisons of the land?"[68]

Conditions of Conflict

Even assuming organized action of an ethnic movement in the direction of some desired change, the revolution may still become stalled at some point far short of the aims of the movement's leaders. The sociological concept of *accommodation* may be brought to bear at this point. As Simmel emphasizes, extreme conflict between parties (e.g., a war between two countries) tends to generate forces to bring that conflict to an end.[69]

---

[66]The charisma of Martin Luther King apparently exercised a prominent role in the initiation of the C.A.R.D. movement in Britain. It was shortly after Dr. King visited London and urged such a course of action for the "coloured" people of Britain that the campaign was launched. Heineman, *Politics of the Powerless,* pp. 16–19.

[67]Kuper, *Passive Resistance in South Africa,* p. 192.

[68]Leo Kuper, "Nonviolence Revisited," in Robert I. Rotberg and Ali A. Mazrui (eds.), *Protest and Power in Black Africa* (New York: Oxford University Press, 1970), p. 794.

[69]Georg Simmel, *Conflict,* trans. by Kurt H. Wolff [and] *The Web of Group-Affiliations,* trans. by Reinhard Bendix (Glencoe, Ill.: Free Press, 1955).

Although some conflicts terminate in the unconditional surrender of one party to another, it more often happens that before this point is reached, the contending parties will both define continuation of the conflict as too costly and will search for some compromise by which both parties will settle for "half a loaf" (or some other fraction thereof).

This compromising tendency sometimes has been attributed especially to the *leaders* of social movements. Myrdal thus defines a pattern of "accommodative leadership" among American blacks in which, it is suggested, these leaders develop a vested interest in stalling a revolution at some point short of total achievement of aims.[70] Such leaders enjoy the "advantages of the disadvantages" as their vanity is catered to by powerful persons who bring them into the councils of the mighty, with the implicit understanding that they will act as a "moderating" influence on their own followers. Perhaps the most insightful sociological analysis of this process (written, however, in a tone of high moral indignation) is Sorel's analysis of the behavior of "parliamentary socialists" who play the difficult game of appearing militant to their proletarian followers but moderating to the bourgeois rulers.[71] The other side of this game, also stressed by Sorel, is the tendency of rulers to be cowardly or fearful of the masses and to practice a policy of "social peace" whereby they make minor concessions to proletarian demands to seduce workers into abandoning their more extreme aims.

The recent situation of the stalled revolution of nonwhites in South Africa seems to highlight this "social peace" stage of the relationship between whites and nonwhites. According to Adam's analysis, the Afrikaner political rulers of South Africa have abandoned their more extreme racist positions. White supremacy ideologies are no longer articulated and, while the *apartheid* system continues, it is based on a softened *racialism,* which emphasizes "separate development" for nonwhites, rather than on a strident *racism.* As an indication of this mellowed official attitude, Afrikaner politicians can now "shake hands and organize civil receptions for foreign African dignitaries."[72] Nonwhites, on their side, appear to have been seduced by the lure of separate development as reflected, for exam-

---

[70]Gunnar Myrdal, *An American Dilemma* (New York: Harper, 1944).

[71]Georges Sorel, *Reflections on Violence* (New York: Macmillan, 1961).

[72]Heribert Adam, *Modernizing Racial Domination: South Africa's Political Dynamics* (Berkeley: University of California Press, 1971), p. 72.

ple, in plans for self-governing Bantustans, or native reserves. Although earlier writers had accurately commented on the niggardly resources being offered nonwhites for these separate developments, Adam feels that the idea of tribally based "black homelands" has an appeal that allows many blacks to throw themselves enthusiastically into these schemes. As of the summer of 1975, there were eight such homelands in various stages of progress toward self-government; one—the Transkei, one of the homelands of the Xhosa people—had petitioned for self-governing status.[73]

Although some observers who have noted such accommodative tendencies in social movements have come to despair of their ultimate success, Sorel's analysis suggests another possibility: accommodation may be only a temporary stage on the way to more profound social changes.[74] Sorel predicts, with obvious relish, the day when the proletarian masses will repay with "black ingratitude" the benevolences of their so-called leaders by a violent mass action that lays bare the ephemeral nature of this accommodative stage. At this point, rulers will understand the futility of tinkering with "social peace" and will go back to their accustomed practice of exploiting the masses. Thus the movement for change will continue toward the ultimate revolution of an aroused mass against a suppressive leadership. It is tempting, certainly, to apply the Sorel schema to the development and course of the Black Power movement in the United States. The urban street riots of 1962–1968 were certainly interpreted by many whites as evidence of "black ingratitude," a resort to violence just when blacks were beginning to make significant gains by nonviolent means. The white backlash that supports, for example, the political aspirations of George Wallace reflects the possibility of a greater polarization of the conflict between the races in the United States.[75] The frequency with which American blacks defined the riots as in some respects a "good thing" contrasts sharply with the perceptions of white Americans, who saw the riots as counterproductive of good race relations in the country.[76]

---

[73] *South Africa Digest,* June 13, 1975, p. 1.

[74] Sorel, *Reflections on Violence.*

[75] Seymour M. Lipset and Earl Raab, "The Wallace White Lash," *Trans-action,* 7(December, 1969):23–25.

[76] Hazel Erskine, "The Polls: Demonstrations and Race Riots," *Public Opinion Quarterly,* 31(Winter, 1967–68):655–677.

Conditions of Change

We have just examined conditions that might lead ethnic minorities to take a more moderate view of desired changes. Even if this accommodative tendency is circumvented, however, it is by no means obvious that a movement will succeed in its more radical aims. Much depends on the capacity of dominant groups to maintain their power in the face of minority assaults on that dominance. Since dominant groups, by definition, possess most of the power in the current social order, it would seem that some failure of will to use that power would be a necessary condition for any radical change in the ethnic status quo. The question for our consideration is: Under what conditions do dominant groups lose their will to dominate?

One possibility is that, over a long period of evolutionary development, there may come a dawning realization by dominant group members that there are inequities of social practice that must be remedied. According to E. J. B. Rose, borrowing a phrase from the late Adlai Stevenson, there often comes to be in a country a "liberal hour." "This is the moment when public men of all shades of opinion, from radical to conservative, accept the necessity of a movement in policy on a social problem issue, in the liberal direction."[77] Rose felt that the liberal hour for race relations in Britain was from about 1966 to 1968, ending, perhaps, with the Enoch Powell speech. The zenith of the liberal hour in the United States must surely have been reached in 1964, when Senator Everett Dirksen, not known for his political liberality, gave his support to the 1964 Civil Rights Act by indicating that, once an idea's time has come, nothing can stop it.

The description of this liberal consensus as a moment in history suggests that most social movements most of the time will have to operate in a situation of less generous disposition of will on the part of dominant powers. We must ask, then, how dominant groups, even *against* their wills, can be forced to make radical concessions to the demands of ethnic movements.

A very useful idea in this regard is Lipsky's suggestion that a protest movement will succeed to the extent that it is able to mobilize the sympathy or support of *third parties* to the direct confrontation between dominant and subordinate groups.[78] As long as the civil rights movement in the United States was simply a struggle of southern blacks against the white

---

[77]Rose, *Colour and Citizenship*, p. 10.

[78]Michael Lipsky, "Protest as a Political Resource," *American Political Science Review*, 62(December, 1968):1144–1158.

power structure of the South, there was no question of any success of the movement. When non-Southerners like Senator Dirksen decided the time for civil rights legislation had come, it was surely because the highly publicized nonviolent sit-ins and Freedom Rides of southern blacks (abetted by a number of concerned northern and southern whites) had jostled the consciousness and the conscience of Americans outside the South. Similarly, perhaps the only real hope nonwhite South Africans have ever had that their protests against *apartheid* would be successful was the possibility of attracting sympathetic support from other black nations in Africa, of having sanctions imposed against South Africa by the United Nations, or of persuading one of the major world powers to intervene directly on behalf of their protests. The failure, as described by Legum, of any of these third party supports to materialize helps explain, along with some other reasons discussed above, the recently stalled state of the nonwhite protest in South Africa.[79]

One key, then, to a successful ethnic movement, is the capacity of the movement to capture the attention and the sympathy of wide audiences. Movement leaders require a *dramatic* flair for those actions that will gain favorable publicity to their cause. Some of the recent activities of proponents of the American Indian movement are notable in this connection. Indian protest activity has made good copy for news reporters: the seizure of the island of Alcatraz, the land claims suits demanding compensation for confiscated Indian lands, the "fish-ins" along the Pacific coast, some of the personalized protest actions of Mad Bear Anderson.[80] It is not so easy to assess the impact of these actions on general public support for Indian demands. American Indians have certainly made these demands visible. Whether they cast the Indian in the public mind in the *heroic* role of the long-sufferer or in the *fool's* role of a perpetrator of "antics" is an open question.[81]

---

[79]Colin Legum, "Color and Power in the South African Situation," *Daedalus,* 96(Spring, 1967):483–495.

[80]For a detailed description of the activities of Mad Bear Anderson, see Roy Bongartz, "The New Indian," in Howard M. Bahr, Bruce A. Chadwick, and Robert C. Day (eds.), *Native Americans Today* (New York: Harper & Row, 1972), pp. 490–498; for a more general discussion of Indian protest activities, especially the "fish-ins," see Robert C. Day, "The Emergence of Activism as a Social Movement," in Bahr, Chadwick, and Day, *Native Americans Today,* pp. 506–532.

[81]The distinction between the hero and fool types in public images is developed in Orrin E. Klapp, *Heroes, Villains, and Fools: The Changing American Character* (Englewood Cliffs, N.J.: Prentice-Hall, 1962).

Exposing such alleged injustices to wider audiences does not always produce markedly greater pressure on dominant groups to change their practices. In the case of South Africa, it has been shown, the condemnation of *apartheid* by most of the rest of the world has not noticeably shaken the faith of whites in the rightness of their practice. The South Africa government has successfully assured its own citizens that the world's "adverse criticism springs from sheer ignorance. Clearly, outside observers cannot have so intimate a knowledge of the nonwhites as people who have spent their lives among them. The only experts on white-black relations are white South African adults."[82] Similarly, southern white Americans have claimed that northern criticism is based on lack of familiarity with the black. Many southern whites undoubtedly appreciated the "humor" of the practice of White Citizens Councils of sponsoring in 1962 "reverse freedom rides" in which indigent blacks or those with criminal records were given "free rides" to northern cities. Council members observed that "we want to see if northern politicians really love the Negro or whether they love his vote."[83]

Whether or not third parties are appealed to, it would seem that the ultimate success of a movement depends on some ability to play successfully on the consciences of the power holders. Except for that "moment" of the liberal hour, this may be a very difficult thing to do. Mahatma Gandhi's successful use of *Satyagraha*—conversion through suffering— was based on just such a conversion of the powerful through pangs of conscience upon witnessing the extreme suffering of Gandhi's followers on behalf of his cause. Martin Luther King—and through his influence, the Congress of Racial Equality (C.O.R.E.)—adapted the Gandhi technique with considerable success.[84] As Kuper points out, the same technique largely failed when attempted in the South African defiance campaign of 1952. Demonstrators were not prepared for their minor transgressions of *apartheid* laws to be met with such an intense official response. But officials saw these small offenses as symbolic of an intolerable tendency to defy all established "law and order," and reacted accordingly. Kuper

---

[82]Kuper, *Passive Resistance in South Africa,* p. 167.

[83]Neil R. McMillen, *The Citizens Council: Organized Resistance to the Second Reconstruction, 1954–64* (Urbana: University of Illinois Press, 1971), p. 231.

[84]Inge Powell Bell, *CORE and the Strategy of Nonviolence* (New York: Random House, 1968).

notes, "The resisters were told that all they needed to do was to submit to imprisonment for a period of three to six weeks; they were prepared only for a limited amount of suffering, and not for continuous suffering, to death if necessary, as Mahatma Gandhi required from Satyagrahis."[85]

We might come finally to the reluctant conclusion that ethnic movements depend for their ultimate success on either those rare persons of conscience in high places, such as Adlai Stevenson; or upon those rare charismatic individuals, such as Gandhi or Martin Luther King, who are prepared to undertake a "suffering to death." Given the rarity of these conditions, it is understandable that all the sound and fury of social movements so frequently terminate in less than spectacular changes.

[85]Kuper, *Passive Resistance in South Africa,* p. 86.

AUTHOR INDEX

SUBJECT INDEX

Printed in U.S.A.